CAPTAIN BABYFACE™

Look for these other Age of Aces Books

The Red Falcon:
The Dare-Devil Aces Years (Vol. 1)
BY ROBERT J. HOGAN

The Adventures of
The Three Mosquitoes:
The Wizard Ace
BY RALPH OPPENHEIM

The Red Falcon:
The Dare-Devil Aces Years (Vol. 2)
BY ROBERT J. HOGAN

Chinese Brady:
The Complete Adventures
BY C.M. MILLER

The Red Falcon:
The Dare-Devil Aces Years (Vol. 3)
BY ROBERT J. HOGAN

COMING SOON!

From the tattered pages of
DARE-DEVIL ACES

CAPTAIN BABYFACE™
THE COMPLETE ADVENTURES

by **STEVE FISHER**

ILLUSTRATED BY
FREDERICK BLAKESLEE

AGE OF ACES BOOKS · ORCHARD PARK · NY

Captain Babyface: The Complete Adventures reprint edition © 2007 by Bill Mann

CAPTAIN BABYFACE stories were first published in the following issues
of DARE-DEVIL ACES magazine:
  "Captain Babyface," January 1936
  "The Squadron From Hell," February 1936
  "The Dark Angel," March 1936
  "Death Laughs Last," April 1936
  "Death Rides Alone," May 1936
  "Death in the Dawn," June 1936
  "The Brand of Death," July 1936
  "Death's Screaming Wings," August 1936
  "Death, Guts and Glory," September 1936
  "Death in the Fleet," November 1936

About the Author © 2007 by Bill Mann

The original illustrations in this volume have been digitally edited to better fit the layout.

Edited by Bill Mann
Designed by Chris Kalb
Printed on demand by BookSurge Publishing
Second printing March 2008

The Editor gratefully wishes to acknowledge the contributions of Joel Frieman,
David Kalb and Click, the hell-hound, in the preparation of this volume.

ISBN: 978-0-9794092-0-2

TABLE of CONTENTS

Captain Babyface

When the metal Albatross laid its eggs of death, neither Vickers lead nor the Yank batteries below could blast it from the sky. This would be a man's job—and hardly show-off bait for a bragging kid. Yet Captain Babyface and Click, the hell-hound, meant to bring it back—alive!

Captain Babyface

JED GARRETT'S babyish face was grim. His trim Spad was droning closer and closer into the darkening embraces of night. He stared over-the side of his cockpit and down at the reeling brown blanket of No-Man's-Land. Gradually, the trenches, winding roads, shell torn towns, and clumps of trees were blending together so that all was blackness.

All save the blinding light of the shrapnel and the bursting of multi-colored bombs in the air. Once in a while the American pilot could see a gleaming searchlight streak out, and popping orange dots which were rifle and machine gun fire would follow it.

Most Spads were single seaters, but not so Jed Garrett's plane, for he didn't travel alone. He had an unusual flying companion with him. Turning in the cockpit he reached back now to the enclosure which accommodated his passenger.

"Won't be long now, Click," he shouted.

The huge German police dog blinked from beneath the specially designed helmet and goggles that had been made for him. He barked once, but the sound was lost in the roar of the wind and the throb of the Spad's motor.

Jed Garrett faced forward again, his lips a tight line. His eyes searched constantly ahead. In spite of his leather jacket he shivered a little. The night was cold; and from the looks of the trenches below, and the flashing fire across No-Man's-Land, it wasn't very peaceful.

He'd be glad to land at the American Unit 4 air field. He had a duty to perform and the quicker he reported in and got to doing it, the better it would be. His service on the Front as Captain Jed Garrett of the Special Detached Special Agent's Corps, was in demand only when the most peculiar and baffling cases came up. At such times he did what he was ordered to do and got it over with quickly.

His whirling propeller pulling him through the air lines, he rode a few more minutes, like a silent night comet. Then he spotted the lights of the field. He cut off the motor; began circling for a landing.

He glided swiftly out of the sky and rolled across the smooth dirt of the hangar.

Mechanics rushed out to take the plane. Jed Garrett hopped from the cockpit. He released a strap and the German police dog jumped to the ground beside him.

A huge lieutenant came striding across to the plane. He stopped short in front of Garrett, staring at him. The huge officer's eyes were a somber brown. He had a large nose and a cruel looking mouth.

"What are you—another kid reporting in?"

Garrett took off his helmet. Short clipped blonde hair was revealed. He had hard blue eyes, and a pointed jaw. Save for this, however, he didn't look to be over seventeen years of age. He had matured to his true age of twenty five in every other way—physically and mentally—but his face hadn't changed since he'd been in high school.

"I, er—" Jed Garrett began.

"Damn it!" the lieutenant snorted, eyeing him, "I don't know why they always send us babies. I don't—"

"I'd like to see the Commanding Officer," Jed said.

"What's your rank?"

Jed hesitated. Sometimes the commanding officers who suspected a spy in their midst didn't want him to reveal his identity as a special agent. He decided he'd take a chance of lying to this lieutenant and explain his true status later if it were necessary.

"Second Lieutenant," he said meekly.

"Just as I thought. My name's Burns," the larger man replied. "I'm always in charge of the rookies who land here." He extended his hand, but did it grudgingly. His dark brows were knitted together. "I wish you luck," he said, "but I doubt if you'll have it. I haven't seen one of you babies yet that hasn't crashed in the first or second dog fight he gets into."

"Well, thanks."

"Don't thank me," Burns grumbled, "the C. O. insists I wish you guys good luck when you land, that's all."

"Could I see him now?"

"Sure," Burns said. He rubbed his hawk-like nose. Then he eyed 'Click.' "What d'ye call this?" he asked.

"My mascot," Jed told him. He took Click's helmet off and stuck it in his pocket.

"Can't have him around here," Burns snapped. "He'll have to be shot."

Jed's face dropped a little, but his eyes were sparkling with amusement. "Well, at least we can ask the Commanding Officer about it," he said.

"It won't do any good though," Burns replied. "Not a bit of good."

Suddenly a wailing siren screamed out. Almost immediately the hangar doors slid back. Planes were wheeled out. Clanging bells began sounding.

Jed Garrett ran toward his plane, with Click on his heels. A mechanic slammed down the hood.

"Calling out special planes," he shouted. "It's that damned gray mystery ship. Comes over every night at this time."

Garrett climbed into his machine. The mechanic spun the propeller and the ship hummed. Click leapt to his place. Hurriedly, Jed Garrett put the dog's helmet on him, and strapped him in.

As he climbed rapidly for altitude, his Spad kicking and sputtering with the sudden action and not sufficient warming, his eyes took in the dark figures of several other American ships taking off.

Then before Babyface Garrett could realize what had happened, a huge gray Albatross was almost on him. He kicked his ship down. Jerked the stick; swung back up. His wings screamed, the canvas flapping, as he banked against the wind.

His propeller whirled with twice the ordinary speed. Doggedly, he leveled his ship, at the same time, climbing back to his position. He saw the Albatross just ahead of him; throttled toward it, his motor wide open.

When he was within fifty yards he cut loose with the machine gun.

Babyface Garrett drove his Spad on. His experienced hand guided the stick; another hand ripped the fire through the cracking machine gun.

All around were spurts of orange in the air. Several American Spads were attacking the slower moving German ship with all the fire possible. Jed Garrett was sure that some of his shots had made marks in a vital part of the ship. Yet, nothing seemed to happen.

Tac tac tac tac tac

Tracer after tracer of machine-gun fire, and without avail. It was sickening. Garrett failed to understand. He drew the stick back and raised the ship to a higher position. He sailed over the Albatross, his hot motor throbbing.

Then suddenly bombs began bursting on the ground. Giant torpedo bombs released by the Albatross. The ship's cockpits were entirely covered. But the men inside of them were sending their bombs of death down on the air field and the trenches beyond the field.

The pursuit of the Yank planes was without success. They wasted bullets, yet the Albatross's great wings never trembled, nor did the big ship swerve one inch from its course.

Garrett looked around at his dog. "What the hell do you think of that, Click?" he shouted. Then smiling grimly, he zoomed his ship skyward. He was banking to his starboard to make a turnabout for the airfield, when something caught his attention in the sky above. It was a blue flash and it seemed to be very far away.

Jed nosed up toward it. He climbed, climbed. The blue flash disappeared, yet the American pilot continued his course upward. He arrived to find nothing. His spotlight searched the air lanes. Nothing was in sight. The Albatross below had also disappeared. The Western front was quiet, at least for the moment.

As he nosed toward earth, Jed Garrett realized that this time his job was going to be a tough one. This was the invincible German Albatross he had been sent to down. The American and British reports were that the ship could not be shot out of the sky. Each night it unloaded death dealing bombs on the American ground forces, and neither anti-aircraft guns nor the tracer bullets of the Spads could stop it.

He had just talked to the commanding officer, and now Jed was going to the barracks, an ironical grin playing about his thin lips. His hard blue eyes were sharp with amusement. They had no particular spy worries at the hangar, but the C. O. had thought it wise for Jed to play "dumb" and keep his mission a secret. He had bunked him in the same tent with Lieutenant Burns.

Burns was sitting on his bunk reading a letter when Jed entered. The huge lieutenant looked up and scowled. When he saw the large police dog follow Jed in, however, his face became darker; then livid with rage.

"Listen, Babyface, what did I tell you about that pooch?"

Jed Garrett produced a half sheet of paper. "The Old Man seemed to think it was a good idea to keep Click around," he said. "Even gave me permission to have him sleep under my bunk."

Click's ears were pointed straight up. He hesitated at the entrance of the door, and then came forward.

"By God I won't sleep in the same tent then," Burns roared. "You damned kids come here with your paper dolls and your pet dogs—"

Jed laughed inwardly. He muttered something low. Click raced forward, put his paws up on Burns' lap and licked Burns' big nose.

The lieutenant leapt to his feet howling. He kicked at Click. The dog bared his teeth.

"Better just try and get along with him," Jed said.

Lieutenant Burns glared at the youthful special agent, then a cunning look came into his dark eyes. "We've got little treatments for you wise rookies," he said. He walked to the door, turned about. "An eighteen year old kid and you think you're smart because you're a second lieutenant— a shave tail in this man's army—" Grunting, he left the tent.

Captain Jed Garrett laughed aloud. He reached down and petted his dog. Click returned the affection with a low, happy growl.

Jed took off his tunic and his shirt. He pulled the top blanket of his bunk back. And then he heard the noise of many voices outside the tent. Burns entered, two or three other flyers behind him.

"Come out and meet the gang," he said. He was smiling, but his shifty eyes were watching Click, whose fur had bristled at his entrance.

Jed went to the tent's entrance. Several pairs of arms reached for him. Strong hands grasped him tight. The group of aviators began swinging him bodily, in their arms.

Burns was at the door of the tent. "That's Babyface Garrett," he shouted, "and he's the youngest, and freshest we've gotten out here so far. He needs a little of the old initiation boys!"

It was damned uncomfortable, being swung by a bunch of American pilots, but Jed was still amused. Back in college he remembered his fraternity brothers acting something like this; and occasionally the football squad went wild after a big game. Jed had been a quarterback, and he'd made All-American twice in succession. When he left school he had taken up the infant profession of stunt piloting and since it was so new, he had made lots of money. The war coming along had been a natural for his air ability. They'd sent him to West Point for army training, and after a few weeks had shipped him to the Front as first lieutenant in the special agents. Since then he had been made captain.

So he had missed out on rookie "dubbings," and this was his first dose of it. He heard Click at the door of the tent, barking. But the dog was intelligent enough to understand that it was all in fun. Had Jed wanted him to attack, a short whistle of a mere word of command would have turned the beautiful brown animal into a devil of fury.

They swung off down the tarmac, carrying Jed; all singing. The Captain in the Special Agent division wondered just where they were taking him. Once, as they swung him, he saw Click galloping along in the rear, and just behind him, Lieutenant Burns, glowering satanically.

The procession passed the plane hangar, and proceeded on through a short thicket of trees. There was so much noise, jeers, call and yells, that Jed only managed to hear the continual shouts: "You like us, babyface,"; "This is what you need to make you a real flyer, babyface," and, "Maybe you'll look more like you're grown up when we're through."

The ultimate end was a whirling through the air as they threw him, and then the splash, and the cold dip into a mud puddle that they seemed to have saved for such an occasion. Before Jed could climb out the shouting, laughing men had disappeared.

Jed Garrett's young looking face was twisted in amusement as he shook out his wet clothing. It was dark, and he couldn't see far; but besides that, he could no longer hear the voices of his tormentors. And then sudden realization came. Click was gone!

Jed whistled long and shrilly. From somewhere he heard the howl of a dog. And that was all. He whistled again and again, but the only answer he got was that of his own echo; his echo and the dull, far-off sounds of the guns on the Western front.

He had brought his bag and some of his clothing, so that he was already changed to a dry outfit when Lieutenant Burns showed up at the tent. The brown-eyed officer's face was tranquil, but somewhere — perhaps it was in the little lines about his cruel mouth—Jed saw traces of a sneer.

Babyface Garrett stepped to the lieutenant. He put his hand on his shoulder and spun him about.

"Where's Click?" he snapped. "He's outside somewhere," Burns answered. "Whistle for him."

Jed did that. There was a padding of feet. Presently Click stuck his head inside the tent. Jed gasped. The company of pilots had given the dog a society—or circus-lion hair cut. They had trimmed his tail, all except a clump of hair on the very end; had shaved his collar in the same manner. Click, having seen his master submit to the fun, had evidently not become vicious.

Jed turned about. His face was scarlet. Lieutenant Burns could hold back no longer. He burst into a fit of laughter. "Funny, eh?" Jed snapped. "Aw, what's the matter with you? All those Boche dogs ought to be shaved that way. All of 'em, see? Trouble with you, babyface, you can't take it, that's all. You're just a kid."

"I didn't care what you did with me,"Jed snapped, but—"

"Shut up," Burns rasped, "or I'll push your infant face in!"

Captain Jed Garrett stepped close to the lieutenant who towered a full head over him.

"You're pretty tough, aren't you? You know a helluva lot, don't you, Burns? Well, here's something for you off the record!"

With that Jed smacked his fist to the lieutenant's jaw. There was the power of steel, and the strength of incensed fury behind the blow. Burns toppled back over his bunk. He sat on the floor, looking up. Slowly, his hand reached out for a cot stick.

Jed turned about to his bunk. Burns lifted the stick. But suddenly it was out of his hand.

Click trotted to the door of the tent and dropped the cot stick out on the ground. Click didn't look much like a lion with his new hair cut, but he did look very funny.

The shrill notes of the bugle blasted up and down the line.

Tat ta ta.

Click crawled out from under the bunk. He had been with Jed Garrett since his birth. That had been back during Jed's stunt pilot days; while learning stunts to do in the air Jed had taught Click all of the tricks to do on the ground. Jed and Click were an inseparable pair. And now, as the master showed signs of not awakening with the first sounds of the bugle, Click scratched his paw over his chest.

Jed tumbled from his bunk; he rubbed his eyes. It was still dark outside. He heard the surly voices of the awakened pilots of other tents. Across from him, Lieutenant Burns slept on, unperturbed. Jed arose, then started across to wake the lieutenant. Then decided "To hell with him, let him be late." With that he slipped into his trousers, boots and shirt before he shook the slumbering officer.

Burns' brown eyes popped open. He looked up glaringly. "What in the name of Cripes do you think you're doing?"

"Dawn patrol," Jed said, "come on, lieutenant, pile out."

"You lousy rookie," Burns snorted, "you insignificant, half-baked, babyfaced piece of tripe you, I'm not on the dawn patrol!"

"Why not?" Jed demanded.

"None of your lousy business. The Doc took me off the list because of trouble I have in my muscles when I go out early in the morning."

For a moment Jed couldn't remember that he was a rookie. He jerked the covers from Burns and pulled him out of the bed.

"So you're the big gazook that tells the kids who arrive here how to go up and get killed, are you? I know all about sore muscles during the morning flying— particularly during dangerous dawn patrols. You're a stinking gold brick, that's what! And you were telling me—" A sergeant stuck his head in the tent. "Come on, babyface, into your kite!"

Jed turned slowly. As he did so Burns gave him a kick that sent him headlong out of the tent. Click leapt forward and nipped the lieutenant's foot.

Burns howled, and the dog jumped from the tent out beside his master who was picking himself up. Burns' livid face appeared at the tent door.

"I hope you and your lousy dog get shot down!" he screamed.

When the patrol had returned and Jed had his breakfast, he reported to the Commanding Officer to discuss some possible capture of the big Albatross which seemingly could not be shot down.

The gray-haired CO. leaned back in his chair. "They never use machine guns," he said. "Just drop bombs. I don't know—"

"I think I've got a plan, and also have the thing doped out," Jed said. "Last night I saw something flying high above the Albatross. Blue sparks of some kind were coming from it. Now, if that means—"

It was dark. Click was already seated in the Spad and Jed was standing near the wing smoking a cigarette. They were all awaiting the usual arrival of the Albatross. Burns came along, going to his plane.

"Night air doesn't harm your muscles?" Jed called to him.

Burns strode over to the smaller pilot. "Don't get wise, babyface. I'm considered an ace around here; when you get ace wings—"

"Don't tell me," Jed interrupted, "let me guess. When I get ace wings I'll have sore muscles if I fly in the morning, and when I go out at night I can hide in some peaceful place without being seen, while the other boys do the dirty work."

"You dirty rat. You babyfaced little—"

"Save it," Jed told him quietly, "what I called you over here for was to tell you that I might not be home tonight until late. I'm following the Boche plane behind the lines."

"What?"

"Yeah, the CO. wants me to try and destroy it. Of course he'd like it a lot better if I could bring it back and let the Americans inspect it and see what makes it tick."

Burns began laughing. "You—you catch that plane!" He laughed louder. Two or three other officers gathered around. Burns' face was blue. "The kid here," he gasped, "is going to catch the Albatross and bring it back as a trophy."

They all joined in the laughter. Click, in spite of his flying helmet, leaned over the side of the plane and barked at them furiously.

"Yeah, bring it back, babyface," Burns screeched, "and land it right in our front yard!"

Captain Jed Garrett winged his way after the ominous, death-dealing Albatross. He saved his tracer fire this time for he knew it would be useless. His Spad was humming along at an even gait. The Boche mystery ship had dropped all its bombs and was going home. The tiny American Spad that contained Babyface Garrett, was going with it!

As they approached the Hun lines Jed nosed for altitude. His slip stream flew back in the wind; the canvas rigging began to flap again, but the powerful little motor bore the ship high into the sky.

Adjusting his goggles, Jed peered through the darkness for the blue sparks he had seen the night before. For fifteen minutes there were none. But when he did sight them, he lowered his ship and dropped a flare which searched through the heavens for the Albatross. He saw the big ship swerve and begin circling. They were some twenty miles behind the lines.

A Boche air drome was just below, but Jed realized it too late. German spot lights were already sweeping the sky in search of him. His only satisfaction was that he had been right in his deductions about the Albatross.

He would have to land, but he had to escape the searchlight first. Zooming like a rocket, he climbed straight upward; began zig zagging.

Tac tac tac tac tac.

Tracer bullets screamed through the night; livid orange sparks cut the darkness. Jed ducked. He reached his hand back and shoved Click down in the seat. The dog was trained for such action; he crouched low.

Jed pulled back the handles and opened fire with his own gun.

Tac tac tac tac tac.

Screeching, twirling, speeding little demons of death. Babyface was grim. His thin lips were tight. His goggles tight, he leaned forward in the cockpit. Sweat drenched his forehead. His muscles were like tempered steel.

Tac tac tac tac tac.

Around him, ripping through the wings, eating on his tail assembly, were the Fokkers. His guy wires were loose and threatened to crack at any moment. The canvas around the plane was cut loose. Flying in a skeleton crate that kicked, and missed, and tore frantically in the wind, Babyface Jed Garrett drove on.

Again—as his thin lips trickled blood from the biting pressure put on them— Jed saw a Boche plane explode in the air and go sailing to earth like the flaming coffin it was. He clung desperately to his cockpit. His gun belts were finished, empty. The propeller was wrecked. And yet he was gliding, gliding.

To the north, lights pin-pricked the dark carpet of earth. He smiled thinly—at least he wasn't coming down smack on the German drome. If a searching party had not already been sent out to apprehend him, he might have a chance to escape!

The earth came up suddenly, and his wheels touched. Luck—and the skilled and expert handling of Babyface Jed Garrett—made a perfect landing. The next moment there was a sickening lurch. The plane rolled forward; pitched on its nose. It had struck a shell hole.

Almost before the ship had turned over and begun flaming, Jed had leapt from it, releasing Click's strap as he did so. He didn't know whether or not Click had survived until he saw the dog jump to the ground beside him.

"Come on, boy," he called hoarsely, "come on!"

They began running, stumbling across the field. The lights of the air drome were just beyond, combing the field. Jed swerved away and headed toward a clump of bushes where a searchlight caught him. He fell on his stomach in time to escape the roar of machine-gun bullets that followed from a hidden nest.

Click crouched beside him. But the position couldn't last. It wasn't possible. He was only one man—a man and a dog. They had to act fast. Had to do something!

Grimly, breathlessly, Babyface and Click crawled forward. The field seemed to be pitted with shell holes. They tumbled into another one as machine-gun fire swept over them.

And there, in the muddy hole, they waited, shivering, as the giant spot lights combed the empty field. Once Jed saw figures grouped about his burning plane. Later he heard voices.

He pulled out his automatic; grabbed Click's collar and jerked the dog back. He waited there one minute; two minutes. How slowly time crept by!

Steps crunched toward them. There were low, guttural voices. His face grim, Jed leaned close to the dog.

"We've been in tough spots before," he whispered, "but just in case we don't—"

Click licked Jed's hand. The next second a light flashed down on them. There was a lightning-like movement as Click leaped, snarling. He knocked over the nearest Boche. Bared teeth sank into the writhing man's throat.

Jed Garrett was on his feet. His automatic pumped bullets. The Germans, attacked by surprise, were easy to conquer. There were only three. Click accounted for one; Jed shot the other two down.

There was silence after that, and the very stillness was ghastly.

Babyface leaned forward. He studied the corpse of one of the Germans. Somehow he had to get onto the Boche field and examine the mysterious Albatross. He was sure now that he knew its secret, but there was a chance that he was wrong. He had to see the ship. Besides, with his plane wrecked, he was stranded in Germany unless he could do something.

Click hovered nearby, his alert eyes constantly on watch. Suddenly Jed began taking the clothes from the dead Boche. The spotlights had ceased. Concealed in darkness, Babyface made a complete change of uniform.

How many hours he lay there in the tall grass bordering the German air drome, Jed didn't know, but he did know that it was miserably damp and uncomfortable.

Click hadn't once closed his eyes. Although the police dog was well hidden, his sharp ears were standing straight up. His muscles quivered and tightened when the bugle blasted out in the dark morning air.

"We've been waiting for it, old boy," Jed whispered, "they're going to send out their morning patrol, and after that—"

In a few more minutes the Boche pilots began coming out of the barracks. The hangar doors were pushed open. Trim Fokkers were brought out. Flood lights illuminated the field. Soon the planes began taking off. The roaring motors were deafening as some of the ships passed only a few yards above Jed's head.

When the dawn patrol was out the mechanics returned to the barracks, and Jed guessed that like American mechanics, they'd snatch another two hours' sleep before morning chow. Everything was as quiet now as it had been before the bugle blasted.

Slowly, his muscles stiff from lying inert so long, Babyface Garrett rose to his feet. His cheeks were covered with mud. He snapped his finger and Click also got up.

A small feeling of panic gripped Jed as he brushed over the German he had learned in college, and the little they had taught him since he had been in France. But he felt that few words would be sufficient.

A few streaks of early morning light showed in the East. Just ahead was a Boche sentry standing guard on the drome's outpost.

The man crossed his gun and challenged him.

"Was ist da?"

"I'm a special messenger," the American captain snapped. "My car got wrecked on the way. It is important that I inspect the bullet-proof Albatross immediately. Which hangar is it in?" He hoped that he had gotten all the phrases in correct form.

The sentry stared at the blood on the Boche tunic, at Jed's mud smeared face, and his grimy Hun boots. Then he eyed the police dog.

He turned and pointed. "The Albatross is in there," he said quickly, but another thought seemed to seize him as he said it. He turned back. "You can not see it until I have informed the officer of the watch. I will bring him here."

"It's important that I get to the hangar at once," Jed replied. "Tell herr offizier to hurry."

The sentry seemed undecided, then he turned and started for the barracks. Jed Garrett streaked across to the indicated hangar. Click was at his heels.

Another guard blocked their entrance. He was a tall man who had short clipped hair.

"I must get in," Jed told him.

"Have you permission?"

"Sure—" Jed snapped his finger and uttered something low. Click leapt for the man's neck. As he did so Jed stepped forward. He wrenched the rifle from the falling German, twisted it, and smashed the butt on his head.

He was into the hangar before the unconscious Boche hit the ground. He knew that time would be short because when the other sentry returned with the officer of the watch, there'd be hell to pay.

The hangar was a fairly large one. One window shafted the first morning light through it, but all else was dark. The big Albatross faced outward. Jed went over and tapped on it.

"Just as I thought," he murmured. It was made of light sturdy metal. That was why bullets hadn't been able to pierce it. Crawling beneath the ship, Jed saw the place where the bombs were released. There was no door or cockpit in the metal plane for a pilot.

The observation took only a moment, and Jed knew that he had only that much to spare. Parked alongside the Albatross was a strange looking Fokker. It appeared as though it had been remodeled.

"Good old blue sparks," Jed said, eyeing it. Quickly he raced over and leapt up, peering into the cockpit. He saw an ebony panel near the control. Strange little lights and levers.

The Americans had been working on a similar invention for their squadron. Special agents were always present during lectures on the newest air developments. Jed had heard enough about this one to know what it was all about. And—he hoped—to be able to handle it.

A grim smile creased his lips. "Hop in, old fellow," he called to Click.

But just then there were excited voices outside the hangar. Click backed, snarling. Jed went for the automatic he had retrieved from his American uniform. He glanced at Click. The light from the window shadowed down on the dog so that with the "lion" haircut he looked like an actual jungle beast. Particularly now that his hair was standing on end, bristling.

An idea flashing in his mind, Jed stepped back behind the small Fokker. A group of Germans rushed in, passed the large Albatross. Then one of them spotted Click.

He shrieked. The police dog lunged forward; as he did so the rising sun glinted through the window and made him look yellow.

"A lion!"

Stunned, the German officers and guards were taken off their feet. Two of the privates turned and fled. Others began shooting. Click was in and among them. Bullets clattered along the tin walls of the hangar.

Stepping forward, Jed Garrett opened fire. Three men went down. The fourth backed, leveling a revolver on Jed. Click bound forward and wrenched the weapon from the man's hand.

One of the men, whose natural panic and surprise at seeing what he thought was a lion had caused him to flee, returned. He aimed a rifle at Click and pressed the trigger. The dog leapt in the air howling.

Mercilessly, Babyface pressed the trigger of his automatic. The last bullet he had in the gun went squarely through the Boche's forehead. Jed picked Click up and put him in the cockpit of the Fokker. Click's eyes were open, and they were shining. The American was glad when he saw that Click's pointed ears were standing straight up. He was still all right!

A moment of eternity—to get out before more Germans entered the hangar. Already, the alarm was ringing out. A shrill emergency siren was screaming. Jed reached inside the Fokker and fixed the ignition, turned the levers necessary on the dash board, and then he went around and spun the propeller. Next he squeezed in beside Click and raced his motors to warm the Fokker.

Ahead of him he saw scores of Boches rushing from the barracks. Quickly, Jed taxied forward. He caught a last glimpse of the metal Albatross as he passed it. He sent the Fokker forward faster; swept into the midst of a mob of Germans who scattered before his wings.

He was down the field and ready to take off before the anti-aircraft guns started popping. The bullets ripped through the canvas. Jed pressed the stick forward, then he jerked it back. The Fokker rose quickly. Bullets ripped about the lower wings.

The surging joy of victory sprang into Jed's throat as the Fokker lifted higher and higher. Turning and twisting, with the wind screaming in his ears, and the Fokker's motor purring evenly, he turned grimly to the black panel of controls in the cockpit.

Babyface worked those little levers anxiously, and then from his high roost in the heavens, he almost laughed with the completely insane laughter of a madman when he saw the metal Albatross taxi out of its hangar below and—despite what the Huns and their weapons could do—race across the field and lift into the sky.

In one moment a man is sure of victory, and in the next, doubtful. No sooner had the Albatross lifted to a good altitude when Jed saw black specks on the distant, reeling horizon. A Boche dawn patrol was winging toward him.

He patted the wounded dog, then nosed his Fokker higher. It would be a fight to the finish now. He'd do one thing, though—no matter what happened afterward. He would turn the Germans' diabolical death machine down on them!

His fingers worked on the controls. Quickly, efficiently he worked, while the dawn patrol drew closer and closer. Jed stared over the side of the cockpit and down at the Albatross. His thin lips drew back in a ghastly smile as he saw the torpedo bombs dropping from the belly of the metal ship. They were dropping on the German air drome!

One, two, three—all of them perfectly aimed! Babyface Garrett saw the drome blown to bits; saw the barracks smashed in two; the ground around sent flying!

He began winging forward then, and the Albatross, at a lower altitude did the same. Jed stepped the Fokker up to full speed. There was a slight chance that he could pass through the dawn squadron of Boches unharmed.

He spotted the ace who was leading. The helmeted German lifted a gloved hand and waved a greeting. The Fokkers flew serenely past. Jed was speeding alone and safe into the Western skies when instinct prompted him to turn.

The German patrol had wheeled around in hot pursuit! Jed's Fokker would travel no faster. The Huns had evidently spotted the wrecked drome. Perhaps ground signals had flashed out the news to them. But their planes could travel no faster than the Fokker that Jed drove. In that he was safe at least for the moment.

Minute piled on minute. Tracer bullets kept screaming past his wings. Jed's Fokker raced across the trenches. The German patrol was a thousand yards behind. Below, still at a low altitude, the Albatross flew at the same speed as Jed's plane.

American anti-aircraft guns raked the skies. They bathed the black-crossed wings in snarling fire. But the pursuing Fokkers behind kept stubbornly on. The metal Albatross must be landed on Allied territory unharmed!

Tac tac tac tac tac.

The closest Fokker was in range now, for Jed had slowed, looking for a landing spot. Tracers whined around his ears. Click raised his head and howled. Jed patted him. Grimly his eyes searched the ground beneath.

There were no guns in his specially made-over Fokker. He couldn't return the fire!

Then his mouth widened in a grin. Just below tiny specks which were American planes were taking off from a mist shrouded drome. The planes were Spads and the drome was that of the 29th! Jed shifted the levers on the black panel in his cockpit.

The metal Albatross circled and made a landing. Jed followed it. He tried to do it quickly before the Americans, mistaking him, could shoot him down. As his wheels touched he hurled himself from the ship, with Click—in spite of his wound —right behind him.

He lifted his hands, then glanced upward. The Boche planes were already retreating before the on-rushing Yanks.

The Commanding Officer was smiling. Lieutenant Burns and others were standing around the Albatross, mouths open.

"Men," the CO. said, "I want you to meet Captain Garrett of G-2. He gets what he goes after!"

A groan broke loose from the lips of the officers who had thrown Jed in the water the night before. Some began immediate apologies. Lieutenant Burns' face was scarlet. His eyes couldn't meet Jed's.

"The set-up with the Albatross was quite good," Jed explained, to relieve the tension. "It is mechanical and is run entirely by radio."

"But—" the C.O. began.

"That Fokker I flew in," Jed went on, "is equipped with the radio. The Albatross was controlled from the Fokker, just as I controlled it."

The Commanding Officer was still amazed. "And you landed the Albatross right here for us—doesn't that beat all hell, though?"

"Oh well," Babyface Jed Garrett said quickly, "I had to do that, Lieutenant Burns wanted me to. Didn't you, Burns?"

"Why I—"

Click pricked up his ears. He growled at the huge lieutenant. The officers roared with laughter. Burns gulped, his face went white.

"By the way," Babyface continued, "if its all right with the CO., since your muscles are bad, Burns, we have some German police dogs that we captured, behind the lines now. You suggested that all police dogs should have a lion hair cut. These dogs are pretty vicious, but I think you'd be the ideal man to give them these haircuts. What do you think, Major?"

The Commanding Officer nodded grimly. "You may consider it an order, Lieutenant Burns."

"Oh Lord," the officer with the hawk-nose gasped, staring at Babyface Jed Garrett, "oh Lord—"

But that was all he could say.

Squadron From Hell

Jed Garrett knew that Death was riding the skies—saw Vickers lead matched feebly against the wrath of phantom flame—writing the awful truth in blood-red letters "The Allied Cause is doomed." —But not even this could halt the grim purpose of this Ace who flew heedlessly into the jaws of Hell.

Squadron
From Hell

BABYFACE JED GARRETT climbed from the cockpit of his Spad. Turning, he released a strap and a huge German police dog hopped out of the ship and landed on the ground beside him. Babyface took off his helmet and goggles and looked down at the dog.

"Well, Click, this is the 27th. What d'ye think of the outfit?"

The dog's sharp ears were standing straight up. His answer was a long gaze at his master. As a sergeant-mechanic took his ship off the tarmac and wheeled it into the hangar, Babyface saw a young second lieutenant loitering near the edge of the drome.

"Which way to the C.O.'s office?" Garrett asked.

"That way, sir," the boy replied, pointing.

Garrett headed in the direction that had been pointed out, Click following on his heels. Babyface was by no means a baby —it was only that he had a face which might have been that of a sixteen year old. He was one of those men who just didn't grow old. He belonged to G-2 and ranked as captain. When not on an assignment from G.H.Q. he held the rank on a roving commission. His reputation as an excellent pilot and a ruthless Boche killer was known along every Allied line. Equally as famous was the fact that wherever Babyface went, his dog Click went also. The too were practically inseparable.

He reached the C.O.'s office, climbed the steps and entered. A tall lieutenant adjutant was typing some flight orders.

"Tell Major Lewis that Captain Garrett is here," Babyface said. Then looking up, he saw the major framed in the doorway beyond.

The Commanding Officer of the 27th had a face that was lined with worry and there was a half empty bottle of liquor in his right hand.

"G-2, eh" he asked. "Come on in, Garrett."

Babyface went in past the adjutant and took a chair that Major Lewis indicated. Click lay down at Garrett's feet. The CO. sat down behind his desk, poured Babyface a drink and pushed it over to him.

The young secret agent tossed it off, lit a cigarette, then his eye brows raised questioningly in invitation for the major to speak.

"A squadron from hell," the CO. said in a husky voice. He rubbed his unshaven jaw, looked up slowly. "It sounds screwy. I know it does. Two days before we start our 'Big Push' we get the Old Nick plastered out of us by a lot of Fokkers that spit fire." He poured another drink hastily, leaning over the desk.

"But it isn't funny, Garrett. It's serious. Yesterday morning I sent the dawn patrol of seven ships out—y'know we've been keeping a pretty good record—and only two planes returned!"

"G.H.Q. sent me over to investigate," Garrett said. "The story was that your patrol met with Fokkers that shot streams of fire at the Spads; that they couldn't fight because they caught on fire right away.

Major Lewis nodded. "One Fokker blew up during the combat, but that was their only loss. Our two ships that got away did it only by skillful flying. I don't know what the hell's wrong, but I knows we can't fight it, that's all."

The babyish face of Captain Garrett tightened. "We'll have to fight it," he said in a brittle tone. "The biggest Allied push of the war, so far, starts in two days. The 27th has to be in that, major!"

Lewis took another drink. Click eyed him woefully as he did so. "Sure we've got to," the major barked. "But with what? I have only a few crates left, and a dusk patrol has been ordered out for tonight I've got about four old pilots and the rest are a bunch of replacements—school kids. Little babies in canvas coffins and I'm supposed to send 'em out to meet a bloody squadron from hell!"

"G.H.Q. told me you didn't want to send out the dusk patrol."

"Of course I don't want to. It's suicide! Can't you officers in the headquarters staff understand that we can't fight fire with Vickers. My kids are scared to death. They're in the bar drinking themselves sick. And why not? With a dusk patrol, their time on earth is cut down to minutes. They haven't got a chance."

"The orders are for the dusk patrol to go out," Babyface said, "and it'll have to go, major. I'll lead the flight myself."

Lewis' black eyes turned to Garrett. "You'll lead it?"

Babyface nodded.

Lewis handed him a list.

"All right, here are the names of the men for the flight." He looked at his wrist watch. "It takes off in an hour." He tossed off another drink. "Hell, I feel like I'm running a slaughterhouse for boys. Damn such a war!"

The seven Spads were lined up, wing to wing, mechanics racing the motors and getting them warmed. Captain Babyface put Click in a special compartment in the cockpit, then turned about and eyed the six pilots he was to command for the flight.

None of them seemed to be over twenty-three, and four were even younger than this. In their teens, as Major Lewis had said. Garrett noticed a man who was unusually, short; his helmet was already on his head.

"Your name?"

"Collins, sir."

Babyface looked sharply. The man's countenance was vaguely familiar. There wasn't time for asking questions now though, for the planes' motors were making too much noise.

Babyface climbed into his plane. The mechanics pulled the chocks and he glided slowly down the long tarmac. Presently he lifted gently into the air, his leader's pennant flying in the wind.

One after another, the six remaining planes taxied across the tarmac, took off behind him and glided into the sky, shifting into squadron position on either side of him.

With his prop spinning merrily, and his Vickers grimly in place, he stared down over the side of the Spad. Far below his right wing tip he could make out the ragged, twisting scar that was the American infantry line.

White puffballs appeared intermittently, and in places the ground was hidden beneath a wispy cloud of smoke. Instinctively he drew his stick back, nosing into the heavens at a steep altitude. They were drawing near "No-Man's-Land" now, and he had no desire to get the squadron picked off by Archies or high artillery fire.

Glancing back, he patted Click's head. The dog, used to flying and wearing a specially made helmet to protect him from the wind, nosed up tenderly. They had been together since Garrett's days as a stunt flyer before the war. Special permission from G.H.Q. allowed him to carry Click wherever he went; the police dog came in handy more often than might be expected.

Grimly, Captain Babyface watched the darkening horizon ahead of him for a fleeting speck, which would be a lone fighting plane, or for the dark cloud which would be a complete Fokker squadron equipped with the newest terror of the sky—flame guns!

He hated the thought that he was leading the young Yank pilots into suicide, yet the ghastly business had to be investigated and stopped.

Suddenly there was a roar over his head and Click stood up and began barking. Babyface stared! A huge squadron of German ships, which had been flying a thousand feet higher, was swooping down on them.

Babyface jerked back on his Vickers handles. His thin lips were set tight. Click was crouched in his place, ready for the action.

The Vickers roared their flaming challenge.

Orange flames spurted from the American tracers and bullets zoomed through the sky. The Spad behind Babyface opened fire. A stream of steel tore into the attacking Fokkers.

Two Boche planes burst into flames. Whirling dizzily, they started down, struts screaming as they fell. Dusk had already covered the sky like a dark blanket, and the yellow flames of the falling Fokkers made a hideous glow in the night.

Madly, Babyface Garrett swung his Spad at the nearest Fokker. He jerked back on his Vickers again.

Tac tac tac.

Suddenly, a red flame spurted from the Fokker, streamed like a streak of lightning across the sky and touched the wing-tip of Babyface's Spad. Only the iron hand of Garrett's flying skill saved the ship. He dove into a headlong loop and whirled toward the earth. Then jerking his stick back, he brought the plane up and out of it. Quickly, he banked into the wind, turning over and over, crazely, insanely. Wind on the wing!

The flame was out and Babyface nosed his ship up toward the Fokkers again. Then he stared as if he had been struck dumb. The whole squadron of Boche ships were firing those ugly red flames at the American Spads!

One—two—three—Spads dropped out of the sky, whirling coffins of red hell. One Spad had dropped out of the fight, tailing it back for the American lines.

Babyface guided his ship back up into the fray. He saw a Yank pilot fighting doggedly, pitting his experience against the pilots of Satan who flew the Fokkers.

A Boche, spotting Babyface, zoomed toward him. Jed Garrett yanked his stick to the left. He rolled out of position, then pulling the stick the other way, swung back again, climbing straight up beneath the Fokker.

The German flew his ship out of the way to avoid collision. As he did so, Babyface followed him across the flame-streaked heavens and jerked on the Vickers' handle.

Tac tac tac tac.

Quickly, Babyface looped his ship out of the way as the Fokker burst into flames and began falling. He rose again, the expert hands which had guided stunt ships long before the war, tight on the stick. He saw the American ace above him, still fighting doggedly with two Fokkers.

Babyface came up under the German planes and thumbed the trips again.

Tac tac tac.

His blue eyes, narrowed to slits under the heavy goggles, watched as the Boche planes blew up. Again Babyface flew out of the way of the falling debris of Fokker flames.

There were still six Fokkers left, and only three Spads. Three had fallen in flames, and the fourth had headed home. Grimly, Babyface wondered who it was that had fled.

But as he wondered he held his stick down. He reached another

Fokker and a burst of tracer spat angrily out through the prop field. The ship opened in explosion and began falling.

This very daredevil, reckless style of fighting had won Babyface Garrett his roving commission and a reputation for fearlessness in the Yankee air corps. Yet he realized that an element of sheer luck was bringing him through this encounter.

He banked his ship into the wind and rolling right, he came up under another Fokker.

Tac tac tac.

The American ace above had done in two of the ships that had been attacking him, and only two Fokkers were left. Babyface began heading for one of them but just then he saw the red stream dart out again. A Spad burst into flames and went screaming down the sky.

Babyface drove up under the Fokker and saw the pilot leap before his Vickers ripped the ship to pieces. The remaining Spad and Babyface attacked the last Fokker, but it turned and sped away.

Major Lewis had shaved, and now sat at his desk with a fresh bottle of whiskey. A broad grin was spread across his face.

"Geez," he said, "you sure cleaned up the Squadron from hell, from what G.H.Q. reports over the field phones. But tell me, don't you think they will have more of them next time? Our boys can't go up and do for themselves what you did tonight. They haven't the experience."

Babyface Garrett patted the sleek head of his German police dog. "I know it— there'll be more Fokkers shooting streams of fire. It's up to me to do something about it and I think I have an idea. Who was the pilot that arrived back about ten minutes before we did?"

"Collins. He said you fellows didn't have a chance. I guess he was surprised to see you and Logan pull in."

"Have Collins sent here," Garrett ordered. Then he added: "Logan, eh? He fought like almighty hell. Have him sent here, too"

Logan was a tall, rangy lieutenant who had a high cheek boned face and narrow gray eyes. He looked like an ex-cowboy and spoke with a Texas drawl.

"Just did my best, that's all, Captain."

Babyface turned to Lewis.

Tell G.H.Q. that I've recommended Logan for commendation; also that I've appointed him acting captain and highly recommend a commission of that rank for him. He can handle a flight for you, can't he, major?" The CO. nodded, smiling. "That's all, Logan. You may go." The cowboy pilot grinned. "Thanks." Hoisting his trousers, he left the office.

Babyface Garrett and Major Lewis both turned and stared at the remaining man. He was the short, blonde-haired Lieutenant Collins who had fled the squadron during the fight. Words were not necessary, for every man knew what the penalty was for deserting a combat. But Babyface had other ideas.

"Where'd you come from, Collins?"

The pilot smiled, "New York."

Babyface leaped to his feet, pointed, and shouted, in perfect German, "That's a lie—you came from Berlin!"

"I did not!" Collins replied. Then his face turned crimson. In the excitement that Babyface had caused, he had answered in German!

Major Lewis had his automatic gripped in his right hand, and Babyface moved toward the lieutenant. He grabbed him by his leather jacket.

"Spy, eh? You're going to do some talking, Collins! You told your lines that we were starting the big push day after tomorrow, didn't you? No wonder you didn't get killed in the fight today!"

"You can't make me say a word," Collins snarled.

Babyface turned to Lewis. "Get your adjutant to hold the gun on him, Major, then send for that fellow who was trying to produce a show here at the drome; that make-up expert. We haven't got a helluva lot of time, y'know. I've got a lot to do before your dawn patrol of schoolboys in canvas coffins goes out!"

Even the dog Click knew his master only by smell. Captain Babyface Garret had completely transformed his countenance. The Boche spy was tied up in a corner of the C.O.'s office and an ex-actor was putting the finishing touches to the American G-2 ace. Garrett's hair had been bleached. His skin was pulled taut; lines were drawn skillfully about his eyes, so that even close inspection would not reveal them to be false.

They had slapped, punched and grilled Collins for the pass word that would permit his spy-Spad passage over into Boche lines. But Collins kept his lips tight, and there was a sneer on his face.

"It won't work. They'll catch up with you when you try to make a report."

"Oh, so you have to make a report as soon as you get back?" Babyface snapped. "Thanks. I might not have known that. You can bet your boots, Collins, that the report I make will be the screwiest one the Kaiser's lads ever heard!"

"They'll get you in the end," Collins lipped.

"Maybe—maybe not," Babyface said. "But I'll bet that I wreck the little factory you must have over there for making those fancy liquid fire guns and the stuff they shoot!"

Babyface straightened up. He had the papers they had found in Collins' effects, and he stuffed them into an inside pocket. He stared straight at the man whom he now resembled so closely.

"Adios, my unhappy twin, don't let the boys choke you before I get back!"

With that he swung out of the office, and Major Lewis accompanied him to the tarmac where a mechanic had a Spad already warmed up. Click came running along in time to be jammed into his usual place.

"Don't you think you'd better leave the dog home?"

Babyface grinned. "Not on your life, Major. If I left him I wouldn't even get past the first Archie. He's my charm against sudden death."

He climbed into the plane, adjusting his helmet and goggles as he did so. With a wave of his gloved hand, he rolled the ship across the worn earth, and lifted into the black midnight sky.

With the guidance of his compass and a small map which he held on his knee, he was able to find the German airdrome which was indicated in Collins' papers. He circled and made a landing before the Archies—following the powerful Boche searchlights—could cut him to pieces.

He leaped from the cockpit and helped Click out. The dog stood on the ground beside him as Germans surrounded them. A captain stepped forward.

"Herr Oberleutnant Collins reporting back from special duty in American 27th Squadron, sir!" Babyface snapped, speaking in German.

The captain's tense face relaxed. "Welcome back, Herr Oberleutnant! You have valuable information for the Commanding Officer, have you not?"

"Yes, sir," Babyface replied. He stared at the sea of Hun faces around him. They were staring at his American uniform and at the dog, Click.

"Where'd you get him?" the captain asked, pointing to the police dog.

"It is a dog from our lines," Babyface reported, "I found him—the Americans had captured him. I brought him back with me."

The captain's eyes narrowed. He had a square chin; short clipped black hair. "There is a United States G-2 officer who carries a dog in his plane with him."

Jed Garrett's heart tripled its speed. The blood rushed up into his face; he was glad that it was dark. "Yes," he answered, "I have heard much about him. He was wounded, they say. They put him in a French hospital."

The German officer, convinced, rubbed his hands together. "That is good—very good! Come, Oberleutnant, we will see the Commanding Officer."

They walked across the tarmac, Click following faithfully. Babyface glanced back to see the Hun mechanics rolling the Spad into a hangar. He was careful to note just where they put it in case he needed to make a quick getaway.

Reaching the office of the Commanding Officer, the captain went ahead and explained the situation. The door was opened, and a short, stocky German with bright blue eyes came rushing out.

"Collins! You come back early. Come in, tell me what you have found."

"You recognize him?" the captain asked.

"Of course," the C.O. said huskily. "He was sent from headquarters; reported to me before he left for the American lines. He is one of our finest spies, Herr Captain!"

One of the finest spies—that was why Collins had looked familiar to Babyface. Garrett had been up against the man before. He was ushered into the office and seated at a table. Before he was allowed to talk, the short C.O. told an orderly to bring in a batch of official papers. The officer pulled on his wiry mustache and seated himself. Though small, he reminded Babyface of a small terrier; a human machine. The skin of his face was very white and his blue eyes were hard, glittering marbles without real emotion. The Hun appeared to be a cold, ruthless killer.

"Now, Herr Oberleutnant," he said sternly, "we can talk. Is my new invention of fire guns going to be successful in blocking the push? Are the Americans afraid of the guns?"

He shot crisp questions at Babyface one after another. Garrett noted with a singular grimness that he was Herr Ritcher, inventor of the liquid fire guns, and he was not surprised, for Collins' papers had indicated that the inventor was attached to this drome. When the C.O. finally let up with his barrage of questions, Babyface began to speak.

While the grim little Commanding Officer was busy reporting a score of hideously untrue fables to the German H.Q.—fables that Captain Jed Garrett had created—Babyface took the opportunity to visit the Boche canteen.

As he walked across the ground of the drome with Click at his heels, Jed took in the territory with keen interest. He heard a burst of sound in the distance— the canteen!

Though it was after two in the morning, and many of the Huns present were going out on the four o'clock dawn patrol, the young pilots were standing at a bar, singing folks songs at the tops of their lungs, and slopping beer across the floor as their mugs beat in rhythm.

They were steeling themselves for the hell they'd have to face in the morning. Kids, Boche kids, drinking to restore courage—the kind of courage that would make them go out and face death with a grin. The Yanks did it, too. Everybody did it. No one knew, when the sun came up, that they were going to see it go down again. They were living life at its highest while it lasted!

Babyface ordered Click to lay down in a corner and went up to the bar.

"Whiskey straight," he ordered in German.

The bartender put the bottle down in front of Babyface and placed a glass beside it. The American secret agent tossed off three, then looked around. He saw a young, wan-looking flyer standing in a corner.

"Come over, comrade," Babyface invited. "Let us drink to the dawn."

The young German moved forward slowly. He smiled as Babyface filled a pony of whiskey for him, then suddenly grasped it in his hand and downed it.

Garrett kept feeding the drinks to the kid. They talked of Berlin, the retreat of the French, some months ago, and what effect the new

American "push", which was no secret to the Germans, would have on the morale of the infantry.

"I don't think it will be good," the young pilot said. He was forgetting his nervousness in the interest of the conversation. "They have been shot to pieces, you know. A lot of them were taken from school and put in the trenches." He took another sip of whiskey, then looked up, "Our only hope, Herr Oberleutnant, lies in Ritcher's fire guns." He shrugged, fear coming back into his eyes, "But then we may not have a full squadron of them rigged before the push. It takes time. We have only fourteen of the machines left. The rest will have to be shipped from Berlin, and that takes weeks—sometimes months."

"Yes, I know," Babyface Garrett said. He wondered if his ears looked as red as they felt at this moment. Fourteen liquid fire machines to rig on fourteen new Fokkers. He made a pointed thrust, holding his breath for the answer. "How much fuel is left?"

"Oh, the tank is full. We can be thankful for that," the Boche said.

They had been talking for some time. Jed Garrett felt it best to leave the subject for the moment now, and he turned to other things. He kept feeding liquor to the pilot, and it was almost three thirty—a half an hour before the dawn patrol left —that he swung back to the fire gun topic.

"I never did get the location of that tank right," Babyface said. "They gave me the wrong papers when I left headquarters." He shrugged. "Of course, it doesn't matter."

"It's just three kilometers over," the youngster said quickly. "Down in the middle of the pine tree woods. You know—"

"Oh, sure," Babyface replied. "Yes, I know where you mean."

Suddenly the door of the canteen burst open. Babyface Garrett had heard the mechanics warming up one or two of the planes for the patrol, and thought this was the C.O., routing the pilots out for a cold shower before they took off. What he saw before him now, however, was not what he expected, even though it was the short, stocky Boche. For with him, ragged and blood smeared, was the genuine Collins! He had evidently escaped!

"Click!"

The handsome German police dog leaped to its feet and raced to Babyface Garrett's side. The American captain whipped out the heavy

German Luger that had been substituted for his own automatic.

"That man is a spy!" the C.O. shouted, pointing.

"Get him!" Collins rasped.

Babyface careened forward. His Luger barked bullets, and one of them took Collins squarely between the eyes.

A blockade of Boche pilots stopped Babyface's exit. Leveling the Luger, Garrett shot two of them down. Others had their Lugers loaded and ready, but dared not shoot for fear of hitting their own companions. The lad who had given Babyface so much free information stared dumbfounded, then he unhooked his Luger and came grimly forward.

Click was in the midst of the officers, snarling, biting. Babyface caught a glimpse of the young pilot to whom he had fed drinks. The pilot raised his gun, but Babyface fired first, taking the lad in the shoulder and spinning him about. He whirled, plunged at the door. "Get back!" he rasped. His Luger spat twice more. Then he reversed it in his hand and plunged forward, hitting with the butt.

He landed outside on the ground with the pack of Huns on him like wolves. Babyface hesitated for a fraction of a second, then he commanded.

"Click—stay back!"

The dog whimpered.

"Stay back, I say! Fight them!"

With that, Babyface broke into a mad sprint for the hangar. Over his shoulder he saw the Germans piling out of the canteen; poor Click was doing his best. He hurled his furry body at the necks of the officers and herded them back, as though they were sheep. Finally, one lieutenant fired at the dog. He howled and lay over on his side. The Germans raced forward.

Babyface rushed across the tarmac and spied a large Fokker, its motor roaring. It was to be one of the ships in the dawn patrol. Babyface reached the mechanic and his fist lashed out. It caught the man on the point of the jaw and sent him reeling.

Quickly, Babyface hurled himself into the cockpit. He didn't want to leave without Click, but he had to. He had been with the dog for years—had him trained until he was almost human in understanding. Click, having done his best to hold back the Germans for a few precious seconds, had reeled purposely with the single gun shot and pulled one of the first tricks he had learned, "playing dead". Somehow, he'd snake his way back across the lines, just as the Boche dogs worked in No-Man's-Land for the Boche, without being hit by bullets. Babyface Jed Garrett knew this, and rolled the Fokker forward.

The first of the pursuing Huns reached him and held to the wings. Drunkenly, Garrett swung the ship into the air and laughed as the clinging officers were forced to let go.

As he mounted higher and higher into the sky, Babyface became conscious that the first light of the dawn was beginning to show over the horizon. He gazed at the compass and swung the Fokker back over the drome.

Already the Archies had been brought into use and Babyface thumbed his nose at the roaring guns. His motor and spinning prop carried him reeling across the drome and in the direction of the tank which contained the fuel for the fire-guns.

In another moment he was over the tank. He looked about in the cockpit and smiled his satisfaction at what he saw there. Several small hand bombs were fastened in place to the side of the cowling. Probably used, he thought, on low strafing patrols. He plucked one loose and dropped it at the tank. A second quickly followed the first.

Banking the plane in the wind, he whirled the Fokker about. He laughed insanely as he saw the tank blow to pieces.

In the next moment the laugh had disappeared from his face, for he saw that the six remaining planes in the German dawn patrol were already in the air!

The six machines were headed straight for Babyface! He gritted his teeth and gave his ship all the speed it would take. Then his eyes fell on a queer looking instrument where the Spandau guns should have been. Suddenly he rocked with delight, for by luck, he had gotten the one Fokker that had fled from the battle last night—the one German plane left with a fire-gun on it!

He nosed the Fokker up, his hands playing about the fire machine. Flaming liquid, was it? Babyface would give them a dose of their own medicine.

In another moment the Hun planes were on him, and Babyface circled and rolled crazily. He pulled back the handles of the fire-gun and red flames spurted out. They licked the wings of the nearest Fokker and the machine began burning!

Tac tac tac tac.

Tracer bullets slashed his guy wires. Babyface dove the plane, then jerked it up. The roaring motor labored under the strain he put on it. Again he jerked back on the handles of the new fire-gun and caught one plane squarely in the center of the body. Quickly switching his aim, he sent the red streaming fire to lick another Fokker!

The pair of Boche planes went down in flames, and Babyface turned his ship to the next. His face turned ashen. There was no more liquid in the gun!

More Fokkers were rushing across the tarmac of the air drome. They lifted into the sky, and the tracer bullets were cutting Babyface's ship to ribbons. He ducked in the cockpit and headed away from the attacking squadron, but they were after him—there was no getting away!

Tac tac tac tac.

The Fokker tracers chewed at his tail assembly and he felt the loss of full control. Grimly, doggedly, Babyface flew on. Then, looking forward, he saw a welcome sight.

It was the American dawn patrol from the 27th! Babyface was flying right into them and he spurred the ragged Fokker ahead! The German ships behind were overtaking him.

Then suddenly, at the speed both American and German squadrons were traveling, they came together. Babyface shouted and waved a wild greeting.

Acting Captain Tex Logan recognized Babyface and waved back. There was only a fleeting glimpse, but Garrett could see that the ex-cowboy's lips were tight and his face was grim.

Because the Fokker he flew was ready to collapse at any moment, Babyface couldn't linger to watch the combat. He had faith in Logan's ability to run the Boches to the ground—faith in the ability and the undying fighting spirit of the Yank pilots who were with Logan this morning.

And so the almost helpless Fokker carrying Captain Babyface Garrett limped toward the field of the 27th, riding the glory of the sun's first rays.

The

Dark Angel

What monster of the night was he whose name was Mr. Death—a relic from the grave who laughed at fear and the sting of Vickers lead—whose cruel and vicious cunning took its toll in the lives of men? Grimly Jed Garrett sought to bring him down, staking his life and honor against the man whose wine was human blood!

The
Dark Angel

Over No-Man's-Land the sky was red with a glow that might have been a bloody mist. Multi-colored bombs burst in mid air and came screaming down. A squadron of planes rumbled high over head, and Archies boomed away at them.

The war had produced queer things: wretched men without arms or legs; steel-jacketed planes that could not be shot down; liquid fire that was more dangerous than bullets; astute spies who roamed through every regiment. But the queerest thing the war ever saw,—the most dangerous, ruthless and hideous,—was "Mr. Death." He was never known by another name.

Back of the lines at the 25th American airdrome it was quiet, yet you couldn't help hearing the low moan of guns at the Front. And all the time, each moment or so, searchlights flashed through the heavens, spotting a plane, or maybe two, and then the roar of noise would begin again and the anti-aircrafts belched leaden death into the sky.

The trees that surrounded the 25th were not tall, yet they served the purpose of being a guarding fence which almost hid the drome. In the canteen you could hear the shouts and songs of the pilots who knew not when they were going for the flight that would take them "West"; but in the barracks, and along the rows of tents, and in the C. O.'s shack, all was quiet.

It was this night that he came, and it was the first time anyone ever saw him. How he arrived, no one knew. That black plane, whose motor made hardly a sound, was seen only as he escaped. For a long while he was alone, and he slithered in and out the buildings like the gruesome phantom he was. He was well over six feet tall, and stood very straight and rigid. He was gowned in long black robes that swept the ground when he walked. His face was just an ugly scar,—without emotion, without expression. There was a stump of a nose, two blotches for eyes, and a grim slit, without lips, that was his mouth.

His deplorable physical appearance was the result of an explosion in which every other man that had been present had been blown to bits. Immediate and expert surgery saved "Mr. Death" and they turned him out a tall skeleton of a thing,—he, who had once been a man.

And now he walked slowly behind the tents, and his robes swished behind him. His face, chalk white, without hair, was turned straight forward. He had no control of the facial muscles. He was headed in the direction of the "experiment" shack that the 27th had rigged since Bob Acres had arrived with new "ideas" for warfare.

Bob Acres was working late. He was garbed only in his boots, trousers and undershirt. Sweat stood out on his back. He was bending over a table on which there were many bullets. His blue eyes were gleaming happily, when suddenly, he heard the door open and spun about.

He stared. The hideous figure in black robes stood there, those great blotches of eyes staring squarely into Bob Acres' face. Who was he? Acres threw back a wisp of his blond hair.

"Hello," he said weakly, his voice trembling. He wasn't so much afraid as he was mystified.

"Your invention is finished?" the figure in robes asked. His voice was brittle, short-clipped.

"Yes—yes. I—" Bob's eyes shot up to meet the stranger's. "But who are you?"

That grim slit of a mouth moved a particle of an inch. The blotch-eyes were boring into Acres. Bob went for his service automatic, then his hand hesitated. He found himself staring,—staring into the eyes of the man, and suddenly he found that he was weak. He tried to shake the feeling off. But those eyes,—set in sockets in that horrible white, bone of a face!

"I am Mr. Death."

Bob nodded. Maybe he was crazy. Too much working. "You—"

"You are very tired. Very sleepy," Death said in a somber, soothing voice.

"Yes, I—I've been working, I—" "You are going to sleep." Death approached, the long robes sweeping behind him.

Bob Acres kept staring into the eyes of the ghostly man. He tried again to lift his gun and he found that it was very heavy. He looked up, hopelessly. The figure was coming closer and closer. Then suddenly, Bob saw the flash of a blade. A scream found its way to his lips, but it was choked as the knife pierced his throat.

Carefully putting the knife away, Death gathered up the many charts and plans that were in the shack. He took all of the sample bullets that were in sight and put them in a pocket inside of his robe. Then he turned and swept swiftly from the place.

He was walking hurriedly past the rear of the tents when he suddenly came upon a second lieutenant. The Yank, taken by surprise, jerked out his automatic. "Who goes there?"

Death kept on walking, he reached and passed the man as the lieutenant gaped up into the expressionless face. Then the American called:

"Halt, or I'll shoot!" Mr. Death did not halt. He kept moving, and gradually his black robes were being swallowed up in the darkness. The lieutenant stumbled after him. He opened fire.

Tac! Tac!

A spurt of orange leaped from the gun muzzle, and two bullets found the mark, but the blank-faced man never stopped, nor even hesitated. He kept going.

The lieutenant stared, bewildered. He fired again. Emptied his automatic.

Mr. Death was hit each time, yet he walked on and soon he had disappeared in the trees. A crowd of pilots rushed to the spot where the lieutenant was holding his smoking automatic limp in his hand.

"I—I have just seen a ghost!" he said weakly.

At that moment a cry went up. Someone had found Bob Acres and the drome leapt into action. Spads rolled out across the tarmac, lifted into the air. They saw the black metal plane of Mr. Death winging far ahead of them but it was going at such a terrific rate of speed that the Spads could not hope to compete.

Captain Jed Garrett's trim Spad was humming evenly as he winged his way across France. In a small space behind him there was a huge German police dog, "Click", the most famous on the lines. "Babyface" Garrett, called that because although he was twenty-five years of age, he still had the face of a sixteen year old youngster, had flown trick planes before the war. At the time, he had taken Click with him and taught him many tricks. Click was fast to learn and could do almost anything but fly a plane. Special orders permitted Babyface to keep Click with him in the war, and since the time the U. S. had entered, they had directed their trick piloting to tearing hell out of the Boches. Babyface's jaw was set tight. His eyes were staring straight ahead. His fingers were like iron bands around the stick. He held a roving commission, though he was officially a G-2 man. He was on an assignment now, the grimest job that he had ever been given. Babyface himself didn't realize the vicious cunning of the man that G.H.Q. had pitted him against. He knew only that his orders read: *Find "Mr. Death"—Kill him!*

The orders were vague. No one knew just where the mysterious pilot came from. It was up to Babyface to find him. He turned now, and patted Click's head. The dog looked up, his ears whipped back by the wind.

Jed Garrett's eyes scanned the horizon.

Far ahead of him he saw the familiar signs of No-Man's-Land. To his left, behind the lines, was the drome of the 27th. Babyface had no reason to go there; Mr. Death had struck at the 27th, but there was little hope that he would return there, for his mission had been a successful one.

Suddenly, Babyface saw a group of Spads winging back from behind the German lines. Jed drove his plane ahead faster. He tore through the sky lanes with his slip-stream blowing back in his face.

As his eyes remained on the fleeing Yanks, Babyface saw a strange sight. A sleek black metal plane was practically flying circles around them. Tracer bullets whirred from both the Yank ships and the black one, but the Spads were falling out of the sky in pieces.

Babyface arrived at the group of ships within the next two minutes. He whirled the Spad around and dove it toward the black plane. He saw the black ship zoom away from him, circle him, and then bear down.

brrrt .... brrrrt .... brrrrt

Chunks flew out of Babyface's wings. The tail assembly was wrecked. Grimly, Babyface gunned his Vickers. His tracer bullets tore after the black ship.

brrrt.... brrrt.... brrrrt

Flames spat from the muzzle, but the bullets only spattered against the metal of the ship and dropped away. They dented the side, that was all. The black plane moved so quickly that only a short burst was possible.

Jed Garrett's shop was tattered and torn when the black plane dove down and came up the second time. Babyface nestled back in his cockpit and from beneath the glass of his goggles his narrowed eyes took in the figure that was in the pilot's seat.

A cry escaped Babyface's lips.

"Mr. Death!"

The pilot wore no goggles,—wore no uniform. His black robes ripped in the wind that screamed about the sides of his plane. His face was a hideous white thing that looked like a thousand year old bone, like powdered chalk.

Babyface sent the Vickers' tracers streaming at the pilot. He heard the "brrrrt . . ." from the robed pilot's gun and saw a hole leap into his ship as the bullet reached it. What was he firing with? These were no ordinary bullets! They exploded when they hit!

brrrt . . .

Half the wing fell away. Click jumped up in his little seat. He was barking at the top of his lungs, but the noise was killed by the wind and the horrible, screaming noise of the falling Yank ships.

Babyface went into a nose dive. His plane whirled around and around and he jerked frantically at the stick. Cold sweat crowded over his face. His hands were icy cold and the hair rose on the back of his neck.

Was this Death?

He whirled down, the wind screaming about the canvas coffin, diving closer and closer to the earth. Then, through a miraculous stroke of fate, he managed to pull back; the last remains of what had been his tail pulled the ship up, stopping the doomed fall.

Babyface shifted the stick; rocked it to the left. He stared over the side and saw that the ground was dangerously close. A tree, whose leaves had been stripped and which stood like a reaching skeleton of nature, loomed before him. He guided his wrecked craft into it.

The prop caught in the bony branches of the tree, and the Spad fell sideways. Babyface had unstrapped himself, and now he fell down through the lower branches and landed on the ground.

Babyface lay where he had fallen, unable to move. Minutes dragged into a half hour. They were close to the lines and he could hear the shells exploding, dangerously close by.

At last Babyface struggled to gain his feet. His muscles were sore and aching; he had a splitting pain in his head, and his brain was still whirling around.

He found that he was more stunned than anything else and gradually, as he stood up, propped against the tree trunk, the numbed feeling of shock began to leave him. Click was whimpering softly from above.

"I'll be up in a minute, boy!" Babyface called. Then he fished into his flying jacket for a cigarette. He put it in his mouth and lit up.

It was with some effort that Jed Garrett finally climbed up into the tree and released Click. The dog had been pinned in, though not badly hurt. When they were both back on the ground, Babyface said:

"So we've met, Mr. Death, old fellow, and that ghastly gentleman had the honor of being the first damned Boche to ever down Jed Garrett and his hound! He's tough!"

The look in Click's eyes signified understanding and sympathy.

"But we're not exactly softies ourselves, are we, Click?"

The dog barked.

Major Smith of the 25th was a small, rotund man with a shiny bald head. Three days growth of beard smeared a red stubble over his face. There were lines under his dark eyes, and though he wore his full uniform, he wore it sloppily. He looked as if he hadn't slept since the war began. He poured two short drinks of whiskey and pushed one across the table.

"Here's to a long life," he said grimly.

Captain Jed Garrett picked up his glass, his baby face was solemn as he stared down at the cloudy liquid. Then he put it to his lips and drank.

"—And to Mr. Death."

"G.H.Q. was right in sending you here," Smith proceeded. "It's true that we've a captured Fokker, but the pilot doesn't look any more like you than the man in the moon. You could never double for him."

"All right," Jed said. "I have a Boche uniform; just get the Fokker warmed up and I'll take off."

Major Smith's round face became serious. He sponged sweat from his bald head. "Hope you get this bird," he said. "The way our squadron got wrecked today, by those bullets that explode when they hit the object, makes me sick. Absolutely sick. You can't expect these kids to go out and play with a black plane that shoots exploding bullets at 'em. And besides—"

"I know," Babyface said. "And the worst of it is that Lieutenant Bob Acres invented those bullets. The black Hun-plane has just adopted them."

"Yes, damn it," Smith rasped. "If it goes much further, the whole lousy German army will have 'em." He picked up the phone and snapped some orders to the men in the hangar. When he finished, he looked up, pouring more whiskey. "What's your plan to get this Mr. Death, captain?"

Babyface shrugged. "There's only one way. I'll hang around the German headquarters as a Boche pilot until this figure in black robes shows himself. He undoubtedly works out of headquarters, for they wouldn't attach a man like him to any one drome, d'ye think?"

The phone buzzed and Smith answered it. He looked up, his dark eyes a little sad, and his hands trembling. "Well, kid," he said, "your Fokker's ready."

Jed Garrett's face was grim, his hard eyes unflickering. "Okay," he muttered. "I'll hop over to a tent and get into my Boche uniform." He left the office. Click had been waiting outside, and when he saw Jed, he got to his feet and followed at his heels.

In a few minutes Captain Babyface appeared on the tarmac. The motor of the small Fokker was roaring. The Yank mechanic hopped out of the cockpit and Babyface climbed in. Click backed, then ran and leaped. He landed atop Jed, and squeezed down beside him.

Garrett raised a gloved hand. Major Smith, who was standing at the edge of the hangar, waved. The Fokker taxied forward over the smooth brown dirt, then lifted gently into the air, the motor humming evenly.

Soon he was past the Boche lines. The motor still throbbed evenly; the wind whipped about the sides of the ship. Click was squinting his eyes. Jed turned on the panel lamp and, laying a chart on his lap, figured out the directions to the newest German headquarters. It was with grim humor that he noted it was located a safe distance behind the front lines.

He looked down at the police dog. "Mr. Death's got our exploding bullets, Click," he said. "We're going to try and get them back."

The night was dark. There was no moon, and a few dead-looking stars glimmered high in the sky. Below, there was a dense thicket of trees. Babyface had made his course a safe one and he steered away from any known Boche dromes where there might be Archies or pursuit squadrons. Even though he flew a Fokker, he was taking no chances.

It was a good hour trip to headquarters. Babyface found a small clearing within a mile of it, and it was here that he made for ground. The task was a difficult one, for there were trees on every side, and just enough room for the Fokker's wings. He pulled the stick back; eased gradually down. Finally he slid over the tip of the highest tree and banked down into the clearing.

He taxied only a few feet, then brought the ship to a stop. Snapping off the motor, he hopped out. Click leaped to the earth beside him. Babyface straightened his German uniform, then began winding his way through the trees toward the German base.

When he arrived, he found it to be a larger place than he imagined. There was a company of infantry here, back behind the lines for a week's rest. Several official offices edged the small air drome. He was glad of the presence of the troops, because one German more or less didn't matter. He wasn't as apt to be caught up by not being able to identify himself.

Men always talked a lot when they drank; Babyface had found that out, so he headed first for the canteen. When he found it—a large place with a bar extending the width of it—he ordered Click to remain outside while he entered.

The place was crowded with Germans who were sopping up beer— singing, laughing and talking. Babyface's eyes narrowed at the sight of them. With the dawn they'd be out shooting down Yanks. He sought out the officer's section of the bar, leaned on the rail, and ordered a drink.

For many minutes he drank alone. No one recognized him and no one was anxious, apparently, to make his acquaintance. Babyface took the third drink in his hand and pretending to be drunk, staggered to a small table.

"Mind if I—" he spoke in German.

"Sit down, my friend!" a fat Boche invited. "Join us in drinking death to England, France and America!"

Babyface was forced to drink. He took in the fat Boche carefully. He looked like a typical bartender, which the idle conversation that followed proved he had been before the war. He had a drooping mustache and narrow, beady eyes. His fat face was dotted with beads of sweat. He talked a great deal, breaking in on the others' conversations, and he laughed at almost anything. The other men called him "Hans."

"And where are you from, my friend?" Hans asked.

"From down the line—one of the dromes that were blown up. I escaped. I'm waiting for assignment to duty."

"Yes, yes, my friend. I remember," Hans said excitedly. "Some American— a secret agent, blew it up. He had a dog with him, they say, a big police dog—"

Hans went into great detail telling of one of Babyface's narrow experiences behind the Boche lines. Jed was worried, for Hans would undoubtedly see Click, and put two and two together. He wanted to jump up from the table and go out and send Click away, but he dared not do it, for it might create suspicion.

"But, Herr Death!" Hans went on heatedly, wiping sweat from his fleshy face, his beady eyes gleaming evilly. "He will get even with these American swine. He has taken one of their precious inventions, exploding bullets! He is working on the formula for them. He stole that, too! Soon we will have them in our Fokkers—"

Babyface realized that Mr. Death had been testing the exploding bullets this morning; that he was now convinced of their worth, and was planning to make them for the whole German Army. He had to stop it!

"No one can go near his laboratory," Hans went on, never stopping for breath. "He works alone—secretly. He is a hideous man, wrecked by explosion. Have you seen him, my friends?"

"It's getting hot in here," Babyface said. "Hans, will you come out with me to get a breath of air? I like to hear you talk. Your wide knowledge of warfare interests me very much."

Hans wasn't particularly happy to leave the bar, but he sensed through the flattery that he was making an impression on the newcomer. Since the other pilots already knew him too well, and were sick of his long winded talks, he agreed to go with Babyface.

As soon as they had stepped outside the door of the bar, Click jumped to his feet. Hans leaped away from him. Jed Garrett jammed a gun into Hans' back.

"All right, Hans, get moving toward the forest or I'll blow your guts out!"

Hans' beady eyes grew very round, and his face turned deathly pale. He was as cowardly in the face of a gun as he was brave over a bar. He knew by looking at Click that Babyface was a dangerous American secret agent; he obeyed the orders silently.

When they had entered the thicket, Jed halted him. Hans turned around. He was trembling. Garrett's hard eyes were on him.

"Now where is this laboratory that Mr. Death is working in?"

"Gott in Himmel! I can not tell you that. They would—"

"I'll—"

"No—do not shoot. I have a happy family back in Berlin. I—"

"Take me to Death's laboratory."

Hans shook his head. "Herr Death does not permit anyone near it, even Germans. I—" He read the chilled look of death in Jed's eyes, then he nodded violently. "All right—I show you where it is, but —but then you let me go. I do not wish to die!"

The laboratory was a well constructed little hut a half mile away from the Boche base. Had Babyface known its location he could have reached it with his plane in less time than it had taken him to get to the headquarters.

Hans pointed. "It is there— Someone is on guard."

Babyface nodded. He reversed the Luger in his hand. "There is neither time nor ropes to tie you up, Hans. You're going to go to sleep for awhile." With that he brought the butt of the gun down on the German's head. Hans wilted to the ground and lay still. Click sniffed in the unconscious German's face. Babyface motioned the dog to stay a few yards to the rear, then he crept forward. The sentry on duty was standing by the door of the hut, his rifle on his shoulder. When Jed was almost close enough to be seen, he hissed:

"Sic him, Click!"

Click catapulted forward like a bullet and rushed the sentry before the man could bring down his gun. He ripped at his clothing, then disappeared around the side of the hut The German followed. Babyface ran up and stood at the side of the building as Click disappeared into the forest. The Boche returned and Babyface's swift gun hand cracked down. The sentry's legs buckled beneath him. Quickly, he went through the clothing for the keys. He found them and let himself into the hut. There was a blue lamp glowing in one corner, but Babyface groped for a light switch. He finally found it and the electric globes flooded the room with light.

There was a long work bench on which there were many bottles, tubes, and parts of various kinds of guns. A heap of bullets were piled at one side of the bench. It looked like the laboratory of a chemist. Mr. Death must have been that before the war, Babyface decided.

Beneath the bench he saw a drawer which he pulled open. Babyface immediately recognized the plans for the exploding bullet which Bob Acres had perfected. He snatched them out and put them in his tunic. He searched the place again, very carefully, to be sure there were no more.

Going to the door then, Babyface whistled softly for Click. The dog was nearby and came on the run. Quickly, Jed put the papers in the hollow panel in Click'a collar. He snapped the collar shut.

"Go home, Click!"

The police dog knew his way back to the American lines. He'd had to make the trip before. Babyface could not take the chance of getting caught and having the Germans regain the precious plans. Click whined, but Babyface repeated the order:

"Go home, fellow!"

Click finally turned and started through the forest, in the direction of the Yank lines. Jed Garrett sighed with relief. At least that was one job done. The Boches would never have the exploding bullets to hurl into Spads again. Instead, the situation would be reversed. The Americans who had invented it would rightfully have it.

Babyface returned to the hut. He went through everything that was in it, finding, among other things, several bombs. He realized that it would be best to blow up the little laboratory, then he'd be sure that whatever plans Mr. Death had been working on would be wrecked. After that, he'd have to hide nearby and await his chances with the mysterious, black-robed figure.

He took a bomb that had a long fuse. He didn't know how fast these burned, but he wanted to have time enough to get away from the laboratory before it went to pieces. Putting the bomb in a corner beneath the work bench, he stretched the fuse along the floor. He slid it back into a crevice so that is would be invisible to anyone entering the shack.

At last he struck the match and lit the fuse. He watched it for a moment and was dismayed to see that it worked so slowly. It would take a good twenty minutes. Should he break it off and start it closer to the bomb? Yes, this—There was a noise outside. The sentry coming to? Babyface straightened up and kicked the fuse out of sight. His hand crept back and grasped the Luger. He held it evenly. The door swung slowly and silently back. Suddenly, Babyface found himself staring into the hideous countenance of Mr. Death. Death stood there, his long robes about his tall, straight body; his chalk-white bone of a face without expression. The blotches that were his eyes were flaming; his slit of a mouth was curved downward.

"I have company?" he asked in German.

"Why, yes, sir. I—"

"You knocked out Hans Schmidt. You have put my guard into an insensible condition. What is it you are seeking?" His words were slow and deliberate. His hands were folded over his stomach in the manner of a priest.

Jed wondered why he was answering the German in such a dignified manner. His orders had been to kill him, hadn't they? He had a Luger in his hand and the figure in robes had no weapon in sight. What was the matter? Then, Babyface suddenly knew. The eyes! Those black blotches that were sunken in the sockets of Death's white face! He couldn't get his attention away from them!

Mr. Death began walking slowly forward. His face remained expressionless—white and horrible. His hands moved to his side and his long talon-like fingers clenched and opened.

Suddenly, Babyface jerked his gaze from the hypnotist and fired straight into Death's chest. Death stopped, wavered a moment, then continued forward. Sweat drenched Jed's forehead. The hair rose slowly on the back of his neck. He stared again into the great blotches that were Mr. Death's eyes. He fired the Luger again.

Again Death stopped, but the bullet had no effect and he started forward at his same, steady gait. Babyface emptied the gun. All of the shots ripped through Death's black robes.

Suddenly the robed figure sprang forward like a panther. He knocked the empty gun from Jed's hand and his great fist slammed out, knocking Jed back against the wall. Then a knife, springing from nowhere, was in Death's hand. The awful face was the same—without expression. The knife lowered and plunged toward Jed.

Captain Babyface writhed aside and the knife went into the wall. Babyface threw his fists into the stone-like face of Mx. Death. He rushed at him, grasping him about the waist. It was then that he felt the steel plates that covered Death's chest and back. Huge steel plates which surgeons are sometimes forced to put on a man to keep his body intact. Death's bony fingers gripped Babyface's neck and closed like a steel vice. Babyface choked, his face turning blue. Then he saw Death reach down and sweep up the empty Luger and it descended toward his head.

For a moment everything was black; but it was only for a moment. He had fallen to the floor, and now he twisted his body and stared up. The blank-faced vision of Death hovered over him.

"American, you will tell me things I want to know! I will not kill you—yet!"

Death reached down. His foot pinned Jed's body to the floor and the Yank G-2 man felt thin straps binding his wrists behind him. Then he was jerked to his feet. As this happened, he remembered that the fuse was still burning. In approximately ten more minutes the bomb would go off!

"I have various ways of torturing people," Death said in his brittle voice. "I will use them on you, unless you talk now. You see, I am a chemist, and an inventor. My rank in the German Army is a high one. I ordered the building of my own special plane, which you may have heard about. Before the war I was a monk. I had sickened of life, and giving up my chemistry and inventions, entered a monastery near Alsace-Lorraine. The monastery was blown up, but I escaped. I swore vengeance upon the Americans, and joining the Germans, still wearing my monk's robes, have started upon a campaign which may—" he sucked in his breath, "—win the war for Germany. German surgeons saved my life by operation, and I will give that life back to them through my schemes of destruction!"

Jed Garrett was bound securely and there was no chance of escape. He realized what he would have to do—keep talking with the hideous monk for a few more minutes, then die in the explosion with him. Captain Babyface's orders had been: "Kill Death." The orders did not specify that he was to save his own life in doing so. Mr. Death was a menace; it was worth Garrett's dying to exterminate him. He couldn't hear the buzz of the fuse, but he knew that it was burning, for the dry, acrid smell was in his nostrils. It was singular that Babyface should wonder —of all the things he might have thought about—what Click would do when he never came back. Babyface regretted that he would never fly again. He loved the air, and life—and now he had to leave it, all because of this gruesome specter who stood before him!

"Will you talk?" Death asked, folding his arms over the black robe.

"Do most Yanks talk?" Babyface spat.

The grim countenance of Mr. Death did not move. He stepped across the room, emptied the contents of a small bottle into a cup, then returned.

"This is acid," he said evenly. "I am going to throw it into your face—then it will be like mine—ugly, and without form or expression."

"Go ahead," Jed Garrett said.

"Brave?" Death laughed harshly. He tore back Jed's tunic, put a small brush into the cup, then daubed a spot of acid on Babyface's chest. It burned, stung, ate into his skin, yet Captain Babyface did not move. His lips were in a hard line. There was only three minutes left at the most; after all, he could stand it that long, couldn't he?

"Now do you want it in your face—in your eyes?"

"I told you to throw it," Babyface said grimly. His heart was pounding hard. His temples were throbbing. So this was the way it really felt before death, was it? He thought of a thousand things he could do if he lived—but he wasn't going to. The fuse was burning—burning, and only two minutes of life were left.

Mr. Death's hand drew back and the cup tilted. He was going to throw the acid!

Babyface's leg moved, quickly, mechanically. The acid spilled onto the black robes of the monk. Death drew back, the acid burning his hands.

Babyface leaped for the doorway, Death after him. Garrett, his wrists still tightly bound, squirmed out through the door of the hut, then he waited. He had to wait until it blew up! Had to die so that Mr. Death would die. The seconds were endless. There could only be a minute left now!

There was a hiss. It was the fuse burning the last foot, and Mr. Death suddenly realized what it was. In that second, he must have connected the hiss with the strange odor that had been faint in his nostrils. At any rate, a cry burst from his lips, and he raced out of the hut and away from it.

Babyface stumbled after him, but with his wrists tied, he couldn't hope to accomplish anything. Babyface was less than a hundred feet from the hut when it exploded. There was a great yellow flame that leaped high into the night air, then the shattered pieces began coming down.

Garrett hugged the earth. When he looked up he could not see Mr. Death. He knew he wouldn't return, and there was a chance that he was going for his plane. Babyface started running toward the place where his Fokker was hidden. His wrists still bound, he stumbled through the forest.

When he arrived at the plane he managed to cut away the straps on a sharp edge of the plane's metal. Then he climbed up into the cockpit, turned his switch, and getting back down, spun the prop. He was into the plane again when the motor caught, coughed twice, and then roared evenly.

He lifted into the sky with a feeling of satisfaction that he had at least wrecked Mr. Death's precious laboratory and had regained the exploding bullets for the Americans. He searched the heavens for the black plane of Death, but he failed to see it. Since there was nothing more he could do at the moment, because of the fact that the Germans would spread the alarm to find him, he winged back toward the

American lines. He had been flying for almost a half an hour when he saw something black zoom in front of him.

Mr. Death had seen the Fokker lift into the air! The Fokkers of the German division were too slow to catch him, but Death's plane traveled twice as fast. He had set out after Babyface. The robed monk knew no fear. Escaping death in the hut, he came after it again!

Angrily, Babyface jerked the Fokker about. He sent tracers streaming toward the black ship. He saw Death circle him, then cut beneath. Instead of keeping to his course, Jed deliberately dropped the Fokker down so that Death had to bank his black panther into the wind to escape collision. Babyface's Spandaus kicked fire again.

Brrrrt—brrrrrt—brrrrt!

He laughed insanely as he saw the sides of the black ship dented; saw Mr. Death weave back and forth in the cockpit. The black plane came up and zoomed over Jed. Babyface nosed the Fokker toward the heavens, but again the black ship banked away to avoid a collision.

Brrrrt.

A stream of bullets missed Jed's ship entirely, and he jerked back the Spandaus. Bullets tore into the black ship, and some of them ripped across the front of the prop. Jed heard the black ship's motor coughing and sputtering. He circled and aimed for the fuselage.

Brrrrt—brrrrrt—brrrrt!

At last Mr. Death was forced to turn back and limp toward the German base. Babyface spun his Fokker about and his grim-set eyes watched the disappearing form of the black plane. He knew that later he would have to meet Mr. Death again—would have to carry out his assignment to kill him. The robed monk with the hideous white face was no ordinary foe, and Captain Babyface had finished his work for one night, at least.

He turned the Fokker in the direction of No-Man's-Land. He would fly high over it, giving the Archies a good time missing him, and then back to the 25th Airdrome for a good night's sleep.

Death
Laughs
Last

Grimly, Captain Babyface thundered his Hisso into the Heavens— knowing full well that high in the clouds lurked the figure of MR. DEATH— the monster from the grave who stole the blood of the living! And now before the Red Gods of War, these two were to fight so the finish—Lead and hate are the weapons they carry, and the loser pays off with his life!

Death Laughs Last

The German hangar was a large one. Within the vast shed and on the surrounding tarmac there was great activity as the shiny, mirror-like, tin plated Fokkers were wheeled out. The grease-smeared Boche mechanics milled about, busy getting the ships ready to take off for the experiment flight. There was a tense, strained excitement in the atmosphere. Pilots spoke in low tones; high commanding officers strutted about.

Mechanic Ritcher stayed in the background, his narrowed black eyes observing everything. He was bundled up in coveralls, and wore thick, oil stained gloves. He was one of the juniors in the hangar, and looked to be no more than a boy just out of high school. He watched the new shiny planes as they rolled out into the sunshine— dazzling, glittering pieces of flying machinery.

Next he turned and went into a small office where mechanics often stayed on their all night matches. The small compartment was empty at this important time. Ritcher slipped inside, closed the door, and jerked down the flimsy, crudely made cloth shade. He moved across the room swiftly, shoved a small desk to one side, then bent to the floor. He slid back two of the boards and reached down to a shiny new portable radio set.

His fingers flew as he spun the dials, then he picked up a pair of ear phones and put them on his head. He heard the "come in— we're listening" call of American G.H.Q. The mechanic's hand touched the radio buzzer, then thumb and forefinger moved quickly as he clicked out the Morse code:

EXPERIMENT SQUADRON OF SUN REFLECTING FOKKERS WHICH I REPORTED ON IN DETAIL YESTERDAY ARE TAKING OFF IMMEDIATELY PERIOD ADVISE TWO FLIGHTS NEAREST THESE LINES BE THOUSAND FEET ABOVE BOCHE SUN SQUADRON WITH ALL YANK PILOTS WEARING GREEN GOGGLES TO OFFSET BLINDING REFLECTION OF FOKKERS
CAPTAIN JED GARRETT, G-2

Working like lightning then, Babyface Jed Garrett, who for a week had been "Mechanic Ritcher," drew the boards over his secret set, shoved the desk back, and turning, left the office. All of the planes were out on the tarmac by now, their motors roaring into the air. The German officers were out with them, while the pilots of the squadron were standing in a straight line, as though waiting for someone.

Captain Babyface slipped quickly out of the hangar and stopped near the tail assembly of the nearest Fokker. Here, he watched with slitted eyes. They thought they were going to blind the American pilots, did they? A grim smile creased Babyface's thin lips.

Suddenly, the Germans snapped to rigid attention. Across the field, Babyface saw the reason for it. A tall, hideous figure cloaked in long black robes was walking toward them. This was the desperate, cunning man who had concocted the mirror planes—the bloodthirsty monk who had entered the war with a vengeance, and who was feared by almost every Allied soldier—the horrible genius of destruction—known to all only as—"Mr. Death"!

Mr. Death had been in a monastery which was blown up, and he alone had survived the awful disaster. But he was no longer a man. He was a hateful figure, ugly, repulsive, mysterious—even to the Germans for whom he worked. In the explosion his entire face and upper body had been blow away, so that now, steel plates covered his chest and back, and his countenance was just one hideous blotch of white, parched, scarred skin. Holes in that skin—like crazy shaped chunks of coal—were his eyes. They were glittering blotches of things. His nose was but a stub, and his mouth a lipless slit. And now he advanced, his black robes sweeping the ground.

The Boche CO. snapped to attention and saluted.

"You have a wonderful scheme in these planes, *Herr* Death," he said. There was a trace of fear in his voice; fear in the presence of a figure so ghastly.

"Very elementary," Death replied, his words crisp and brittle. "Have you ever flashed a mirror in the eyes of a companion when you were a child? These planes will only be useful until the American swine devise a way of being able to look at them, and fire, without being blinded. However," he continued—his scarred face was without visible emotion, for his muscles were dead and human expression was beyond his power— "the sun squadron should deal much destruction before the Americans recover from the shock of seeing them. Have the flight take off!"

"Yes sir!"

The pilots were told to get into their ships. They turned and started. Babyface Garrett was watching Mr. Death carefully —he and Death had met before. If Death saw him—

Suddenly he was conscious of those horrible, black, blotch-eyes resting on him. It was uncanny how Death had spotted him, greasy-faced, and in the mechanic's garb, out of the countless other men on the field. But he did. Babyface saw a Luger slip from the sleeve of Death's black robes.

Quickly, realizing that he had no chance against the entire hangar force of Germans, Babyface ran for the nearest mirror plane. He knocked the pilot away, then leapt into the roaring ship. He taxied down the tarmac, wild shots following him.

Death broke into a run. His Luger was aimed and shrieking gunfire as Babyface pressed back on the stick. He edged down into the cockpit. Bullets whizzed by his neck, thudded into the dash board.

At last Babyface's Fokker lifted into the air.

He circled, climbing rapidly for altitude, but the other sun planes were lifting into the sky behind him. Six against one! And Babyface had no green goggles to save his eyes from the mirror ships. He was trapped!

Streaking like a comet out of hell, he headed toward the Yank lines as the wind screamed through the silver colored guy wires. The prop buzzed like an electric saw, and steam slipped back from the racing motors. Babyface dared not to look back. He realized only too well that the Boches would be on him like hounds on a hare.

His eyes turned to the carpet below—a carpet of trees, broken ground and shell holes—whirling, whirling away as his bobbing wings sang the song of the air. Babyface Garrett's lips were tight. It was now or never!

He nosed the ship into the clouds. As he did so, the pursuing Fokkers caught him. Spandaus guns cracked like a thousand angry whips. Bullets tore into his wings. Part of his tail assembly was torn away.

He could not escape. He had to fight— a useless fight of six against one. He had to hold them off. Soon the Yank squadrons would be swooping down. How soon, he did not know. One minute, maybe two, maybe five! But he could not hold out five minutes. A mere second was prolonged eternity in an air fight.

He had altitude on the six glittering Fokkers, but they were climbing up after him.

Brrrrt... brrrrrt.... brrrrrt!

Rasping, ugly little tracers cutting through the frail tin of the mirror ship. Canvas blowing in the wind— Higher, Babyface climbed. Then, his teeth gritted tight, and hurling an insane curse of hatred, he bore down.

His ship screamed out a siren wail as he drove down, down, down onto the attacking Fokkers. One ship banked madly to the right to avoid collision. Another turned, nosed down in a hall loop. Babyface's ship roared headlong for the third.

Brrrt .... brrrt .... brrrrrrrrrt!

The Spandaus gun spat steel-jacketed nails of doom into the ships. But Babyface was flying crazily. He could watch for only a moment at a time against the intensified sun cast from the ships. His eyes watered, smarted, burned.

Brrrrrt .... brrrrrt .... brrrrt!

He hurled another volley of tracers into that third ship. Suddenly, he shouted with grim delight. The Boche pilot stood up, his mouth running with blood, his eyes glazed and glassy. His gloved hand went up in what was meant to be a salute. But he never finished it. His plane leapt from his control and went screaming toward the earth.

Two more Fokkers rushed in, trapping him in a crossfire. Hemmed in, he turned the Fokker doggedly upward. A roaring Boche ship missed his prop by inches. Babyface filled its belly with tracer lead.

Still cursing and laughing madly, Babyface drove upward. Where were the Yanks? Why weren't they here to aid him?

Brrrrrt ...

A Fokker chewed greedily into his tail assembly. Babyface rocked the stick hopelessly. He continued trying to climb, but he found himself losing speed. He glanced at the instrument panel. The Fokker followed up after him, the Spandaus gun blurting grimly.

"All right, damn you!" Babyface oathed into the roar of fire. "If I go—two of you go with me!"

Deliberately—all hope of Yank rescue gone—he turned his ship, drove down at the ship that followed. The tip of his wing touched, and was torn off.

Brrrrt .... brrrrt .... brrrt!

Babyface cut a crimson streak across the chest of the Boche pilot, sent it dropping out of the sky. It turned over and over like a broken kite. Babyface turned toward another plane.

At that moment he saw the familiar sight of Spads zooming down from the heavens. Their motors roaring, the American pilots tight in their cockpits, they were coming down to destroy the Fokkers!

The Boches saw this threat of death at the same moment. Almost immediately they jerked their ships about in the wind, began high tailing it for their airdrome, and the protection of their Archies.

Babyface swung in the other direction. He saw two Spads split and start after him. My God! They thought— Grimly, he laughed. The situation was not a new one. It had happened countless times on the lines—Yank mistaking another Yank in an enemy ship. And Babyface had thought he was free!

It would be impossible for any of the men in the Spads to realize the truth. Babyface was a G-2 man and most of them knew him only by reputation, not by sight. The remaining Fokkers had fled, since the Americans outnumbered them almost four to one.

Babyface simply had to outrace the Spads, which seemed impossible. He could not turn and fire on them. He was sick with apprehension. His wrecked wing was blowing wildly, and the Fokker was losing altitude with every moment that passed.

Looking about again, Babyface suddenly saw a strange sight. A lone black Fokker—metal body—winging with thrice the speed of an ordinary Fokker or Spad —was hurling through space toward Captain Babyface Jed Garrett and the two Spads that were chasing him.

Jed knew the black ship only too well. It was the machine that "Mr. Death" used—the only one like it in the war!

His wings torn, his tail assembly all but wrecked, it would be useless to try and fight Death at this time. It was only a matter of minutes before he would be forced to the ground, and by that time he wanted to be on Yank soil.

Mr. Death's black plane overtook the Spads with ease. Babyface saw the grim, blotch-eyed figure in the black robes, jerk back on his Spandaus guns. The Yank Vickers' returned the fire instantly.

But it was all over in only a moment or so. Death, flying circles around the Spads, ripped them to holes, sent them rocketing down through the sky in flames—ugly yellow coffins of doom!

It was more than Babyface could take. Knowing that there was no hope for him, realizing the monster of the air that he was facing in combating Mr. Death—he wheeled his tattered Fokker about.

He rushed headlong toward the black ship piloted by Death. He saw the grim, white-faced figure begin to jerk back on the handles of his Spandaus guns. Then suddenly, Death's hand went up over his eyes, his ship lurched crazily, went car-reening upward. His own diabolic invention was blinding him!

Brrrrrt.... brrrrrt.. . .brrrrrt!

Babyface's tracers bit into the metal of Death's ship.

"Killed two of our boys—just like it was nothing at all!" Babyface spat. "You lousy skeleton of a Boche, you—"

In the next instant he saw a blur of black in front of him. Mr. Death sailed his ship just over the top of his wings. Before Jed Garrett could bank his ship out, Death had turned about. His Spandaus shrieked as they hurled lead into the silver Fokker.

Captain Babyface lost control. He turned the stick madly, but his Fokker was dropping down, down. He reached the bottom of the cockpit. He jerked an emergency cord to the tail assembly— another little thing that Mr. Death had installed in Boche planes. Death's own invention was going to save an American!

With the aid of the emergency cords attached to the tail assembly, Babyface managed to bring the Fokker out of the fall and into a glide. He cut off the motors, coasted down toward a field of gaping holes. He landed with a thud, the plane turned over. Babyface hurled himself free, and turning, he watched it burst into flames.

He looked up and saw Mr. Death's black Fokker winging back toward Boche-land.

Stars were hung across the sky in glittering abundance as Captain Babyface left the canteen of the American 25th airdrome, and started toward the C.O.'s office. At his heels, following happily, was a huge German police dog.

"Sorry I had to leave you here the last few days," Babyface told the dog laughingly. "But, surer than hell, Click, if I'd taken you with me, they'd have recognized me a lot sooner!"

Click barked. He was delighted that his master had returned. Babyface and Click were almost inseparable. Before the war Jed had operated a flying field of his own, and he and Click had done air stunts that a willing crowd paid well to see. When the war came along, special orders permitted Babyface to bring Click along with him—for the dog was no ordinary police pup. He had almost human faculties for understanding, and knew so many tricks, that he was of invaluable aid to Jed in his ramblings.

Jed Garrett, attached to G-2, was on one important assignment. The orders read simply: "Kill Mr. Death!" But the feat was not to be done quite as easily. Death was a worthy foe—the most feared man on the lines—he laid traps, worked with unusual brilliance. Jed's job was a grim, responsible one—but he intended getting it done. Although he was 25 years of age, an expert flyer, and a fighter who was like the devil himself, he was one of those men whose faces had not changed since youth. His countenance fooled men —made him look like a sixteen year old. So they had nicknamed him "Babyface," and he and Click were famous in the Allied air forces.

Babyface arrived at the C.O.'s office. The adjutant was not present, so he entered and walked back through to the C.O.'s room. The tall, blond haired major was sitting at his desk, a grim look on his face. His blue eyes took Jed in carefully, with almost a trace of pity.

"Sit down, Babyface," he said.

Jed Garrett sat down, and Click, after sniffing about for a moment, lay down at his feet, his beautiful pointed ears whipped back.

"I have news from G. H. Q." the major said. "You reported on a large German ship which intends to fly over soon, under the command of Mr. Death, to send exploding torpedoes down upon as many Yank dromes as possible."

"That's right—they may try it tonight."

"And—"

"Those torpedoes—" Jed Garrett said evenly, his babyish face tense, "they aren't the usual kind. They explode when they hit, and blow everything for yards around, galley west. Death, in his new laboratory behind the German lines, has mixed various kinds of powder and has found a blend that is far worse than anything the Boches have yet used."

The major nodded, frowning. "You know where this new laboratory is—what I mean is, you discovered that while you were over there?"

Babyface nodded.

"Fine—you will give me exact directions. G.H.Q. is going to send two of our best G-2 men over to—"

"Two others," Jed gasped, "but what about me?"

The major coughed, reddening a little. "You are to be given a furlough—" he smiled, "—a chance to go to Paris for a couple of weeks."

"What do you mean?" Babyface demanded. "My assignment was to kill Death and—"

"But you have been temporarily relieved," the major said, "you see—"

"Quit beating around the bush."

"Well, Captain Garrett—" the CO. began, becoming very formal, "it seems that G.H.Q. has learned to respect the threats of Mr. Death. He has succeeded in carrying out so many of them, you know. Frankly, you are too good a man to lose. We feel—and they do, that if you are out of the picture for a few days—"

"Out of the picture? Why?"

The major opened a desk drawer and brought out a letter. "A black plane flew over G.H.Q., escaping the ground guns. This was dropped." He shoved it across the desk. The paper read:

I HAVE SWORN OUT PERSONAL VENGEANCE UPON YOUR MAN CAPTAIN JED GARRETT. IT IS MY INTENTION TO BRING HIS BLOODY CORPSE TO YOU, AND TO DROP IT UPON ONE OF YOUR AIRDROMES. I HAVE NEVER FAILED IN A PERSONAL MISSION AND I SHALL NOT THIS TIME. I WILL NOT REST UNTIL CAPTAIN GARRETT IS DEAD
"MR. DEATH"

"No doubt infuriated that you tricked him in giving us the information about the mirror planes," the major said hurriedly as Babyface read the note. "He is the one Boche genius in this war. Sometimes I doubt that he is human, for he seems to be a devil brought out of hell to wreak havoc on us."

Babyface Garrett looked up slowly, his face a grim, tight mask. His lips were firm, and his eyes shone with a hard glow. He stared at the major for a moment, then rose to his feet. Folding the note "Mr. Death" had written, he placed it in his tunic.

"Tell G.H.Q., major," he said evenly, "that Captain Garrett has gone to strike first."

The C.O. leapt to his feet. "Why you can't do that, man! It'd be suicide. I advise—"

"Sorry," Babyface snapped in a brittle voice, "I can't take your advice. I am sorry also that G.H.Q. doubts my ability to account for Mr. Death!"

"It isn't that—it isn't like he was an ordinary man. He has hypnotic powers— a plane better than anything we can conceive! He—"

But Jed Garrett strode from the office, with Click following close on his heels.

He rode high. The air was cold, but there was no immediate danger, now that he was alone with the stars. The beating motors were bearing the trim Spad across No Man's Land and behind the German lines. Click was in his special compartment in the cockpit.

Babyface had not wasted any time in starting, for the orders from G.H.Q. which had meant to be kind to him, had filled him with wild fury. It was true that Death was dangerous, almost inhuman, but that was no reason why Jed Garrett should run and hide from him! He felt the note in the pocket of his tunic, and his face flushed hot. He'd show the major—and G.H.Q.—he'd finish the grim assignment to "Kill Mr. Death"— tonight! There would be no time wasted, no usual precautions taken, he was going straight to the lair of the genius of war. It would be a show down!

While behind the lines he had learned the location of the new laboratory where Death invented his murderous weapons, but there had not been time to investigate it, without giving away his identity. He had learned also that Death was chartering a huge bomber from which he would drop his new torpedo shells upon Yank dromes. That too, would have to be stopped, and the torpedo shells with their formula, destroyed!

He checked with compass and chart, and when he was over the place where he knew Death's laboratory was hidden, he cut the Spad's motor. Circling, he made an almost silent landing. The laboratory was on the other side of a clump of trees that hid the Spad from view.

Captain Babyface climbed out of the ship. He was not disguised now. He had been too infuriated when he left, to change his American uniform. Click was released from the ship. The police dog trotted ahead of Jed, his fur bristling, his ears pointed, sharp and alert.

Babyface crept forward. He saw the long, flat building in the distance.

"Click!" he whispered.

The dog came to his side. Together they moved slowly forward. Babyface's spine tingled, his temples throbbed. He felt his skin turn hot, and then go cold. There would be no preliminaries. A light showing from a window indicated that Death was in the laboratory. He allowed no other German soldiers with him. A tall sentry was standing at the door.

Babyface strode across the stretch of ground. The guard saw him, called out a challenge. There was a streak of brown, moving forward. The sentry howled with pain as Click sank his teeth into his legs. Babyface rushed the guard, slamming his automatic butt across the man's head.

His heart increased its beat. He turned to the door of the laboratory. Slowly, his hand moved to touch the knob. He found that the door was not locked. He pushed it open, hovering outside, waiting for an attack. None came. Click stood behind his master, growling.

It was now or never. Captain Garrett swung in through the entrance of the door and stared straight across the room...He saw the dim outline of the ghastly figure in long black robes. A gun was leveled on Babyface.

Tac ... tac..., tac ... tac.

Four bullets from Jed Garrett's automatic screamed across the room and thudded through the head of the figure he faced.

No blood came.

Babyface just stared, his eyes wide with terror, his skin crawling. Was Mr. Death human? Or was he a grinning ghost— the devil from hell that the major had spoken about? You could not shoot his chest or back because of the steel plates— but his head—!

Click whined, then barked sharply.

Babyface snapped his remaining shot into the head of the black robed figure. Nothing happened.

Then Click turned and leaped across the room. Babyface spun around; he saw the bony white scar of a face of Mr. Death, saw a blunt instrument whip out and lash across Click's head. Babyface took in the figure at which he had been shooting.

It had been a trap! What he had fired at was a corpse in black robes! A corpse so dead that the blood had clotted and would not run.

When he again stared at Death he saw Click lying helpless at his feet. He saw the grim monk of murder striding toward him, his burning black blotches of eyes staring through him, his slit of a mouth even, his hairless head hideous beneath the small light on the work bench. A Luger was in Death's right hand.

Babyface's automatic clicked on an empty chamber.

Weird, rasping laughter issued from the throat of Mr. Death. It echoed back from the four walls of the laboratory— chilled Jed Garrett's blood.

"You came—Captain Garrett—just as I planned you would!"

Babyface moved forward.

"Another step, captain, and your brains will be blown from your head!"

The Luger was pointed straight between his eyes. Babyface stared into the hypnotic eyes of the monk. He was repulsed by the blotched white face. He had to kill this man, no matter what the cost. But how?

"I sent that note over, knowing that you had secured the location of my laboratory," Death said in his crisp, dead tones, "and knowing that you would return without taking precautions. Return full of your American rage and walk into my trap. I give your courage credit, my friend; but I meant every word I said in that note!"

There was an appalling silence and doom hung heavy in the atmosphere of the room. Click was rolling over. The dog's head was caked with blood.

"Your scheme was a very clever one," Babyface said evenly. "I came here to kill you. I intend doing that."

Again that horrible, burned-out laughter issued from Mr. Death's throat. He came forward, his black robes sweeping the floor.

"I am the one who is executioner and—"

Babyface leapt forward. His hand slapped down at the Luger and at the same moment it exploded into the wall. Garrett's right fist whipped up into the bony white face of Death. His left hand clutched the throat of the Boche monk.

Death jerked back with strength that was almost inconceivable. He snarled. Then the Luger sounded again, and this time it creased Jed's head.

Blackness swirled in his mind. His knees caved in. As he sank to the floor he heard the evil laughter of Mr. Death above him.

It was cold, very cold, and there was the sharp sting of the wind, the roaring rush of air, and the throbbing of the heavy motor of a German bomber. These elements combined brought Jed Garrett back to consciousness.

He opened his eyes to stare down, horrified, at the faraway puffs of red. They were flying high over No Man's Land. Babyface was strapped in a netlike bag beneath the bomber. His wrists and ankles were bound. Tied next to him was Click, whining, and each few minutes, howling pitifully.

It was another few moments before Babyface could fully comprehend the diabolic meaning of this situation. The wind ripped at his clothing and screamed in his ears. The bomber was bearing steadily toward the American lines.

Mr. Death was making good his threat to deliver Garrett's body to the Yanks. He intended releasing the strap when they were over an airdrome, so that both Babyface and Click would fall, headlong, and be crushed to death when they hit the top of the hangar, or smashed on the ground!

Foolishly, Jed had stumbled into the careful trap laid by Death; because his Yankee temper had gotten away from him. Now he was in the power of the man he intended to kill! Perhaps G.H.Q. was not so wrong in rating Mr. Death as they did. He was a monster of murder who calculated his movements far in advance, and knew each step he was going to take. To successfully combat him one could not rush in, blind with rage, and expect to defeat him. Plans more carefully laid had to be used. So far the game had been on the side of the murder monster.

And now he was in the clutches of Death. Only quick, daredevil action could save him. There was no time for plans. No time for anything. In a few more minutes the straps would be released. Babyface and Click would go tumbling through the air.

More than that, Death would continue in this bomber, dropping his deadly torpedo shells on American dromes. He would wreck the Yank aviation Front— cripple it, smash hundreds of planes, and kill countless Yank pilots asleep in their tents!

There had to be a way out—but where was it? Time was too short to find the answer!

Babyface wriggled, he squeezed his wrists together and pulled hard to escape his bonds. But the cords were tight. Click howled again, a long blood-chilling howl. Jed kicked his feet; they too were well secured, and the way they were arranged in the flimsy net, he could not possibly reach down to them.

Again he stared at the moving ground a thousand feet below, reeling by like so much film. The barking field guns were like faint echoes, drowned in the roar of the wind and the pounding of the bomber's motor. Minutes—minutes ticking by.

Frantically, Babyface turned, twisted, fought to get his arm free. Tighter and tighter the cords seemed to draw. They were flying over American territory now.

Click whined again, and the sound was lost in the din of screaming wind. The bomber's prop was whirling, the big ship of death was nosing on and on, toward the inevitable ending for Babyface and his dog.

Three more minutes passed. They were ghastly, endless things, those minutes. In that time, Babyface waged a terrific battle with the cords that bound him, and he felt them weakening, but they would not free him in time. He knew that. And even if he were free, what could he do? The bomber was case-enclosed, a bulky thing. Death and the pilot would both be in it, and possibly a third Boche.

His eyes burning from the sting of the wind, his muscles aching, Babyface kept up his valiant struggle. It all seemed so hopeless though. The reward of war was death, and had he not accounted for himself on the Western Front?

He had, but not sufficiently. He could not die satisfied with himself, for he had been ordered to kill Mr. Death. It would be leaving the earth with a job unfinished.

Closer and closer, the ship drew toward the goal of destruction.

Babyface's aching eyes took in the four strands of cord that held the net to the bottom of the plane. They disappeared up inside the cabin. At the crucial moment they would be cut, and that would be the end. There would be no more of anything then.

His brain throbbing, Babyface suddenly came in possession of an idea. Quickly, his wrists still bound, he reached up, grabbing the net. He hooked it onto the undercarriage of the ship. He hooked the net again and again, in as many places as possible.

Now, when the cords were cut from above, the net would not drop.

There was faint hope in that—hope that Babyface could free himself and somehow get into the cabin of the plane. What would happen once he got there, he did not know. Click howled again. The wind was growing colder and cutting with the sharpness of a knife.

Four more long minutes dragged by. Babyface jerked his wrists free. He looked down and saw that they were traveling over an American drome. Clutching the undercarriage of the plane he looked up. The cords that came from inside the cabin suddenly sagged. They had been cut!

The net remained intact. Death could not look directly down from his position in the cabin. He would not know that Babyface and Click had not fallen! His fingers frozen to the iron of the undercarriage, his blood surging hot within his veins, Babyface clung to his place.

At that moment he saw a little trap door open forward. A small torpedo-like bomb dropped out. Babyface's eyes followed it to the ground. He saw half of the huge, smooth tarmac, blown to bits. Again that little trap door opened. Babyface lunged out, grasped the torpedo bomb in his hand.

The bomber was moving fast, the wind was trying to pull him off. His clothes ripped and tore in the pressure of the air. His hair was blowing wildly, but Babyface Garrett clung with one hand in the net that was protecting himself and Click. With the other, he caught hold of two more torpedo bombs being dropped through the trap door.

He put them in the net, but they were heavy little things and added to the weight. The net, insecurely attached to the undercarriage, was beginning to tear. Presently it would be loose. He had to get rid of the torpedoes!

He looked down, they were passing over a forest now. Babyface dropped one of the torpedoes. He saw trees blown up in the air.

And then, just above his head, a larger trap door opened. The Boches were investigating to see what was wrong with the torpedoes—why they had not landed!

A head and a pair of shoulders looked down through the torpedo outlet. Babyface reached out his arms. He jerked down. The net was tearing, giving. The Boche, taken by surprise, was pulled out of the plane. He somersaulted out, hung in the air, holding to Jed Garrett's neck. Jed worked himself free, let go of the German.

The Boche fell earthward, screaming wildly.

Quickly, his legs still tied, Jed worked himself up into the trap door through which the Boche had come. Click was left in the net which was secure enough to hold the dog's light body.

Sweat bathing his face, wind tearing at him, Babyface Garrett climbed up into the cabin of the bomber.

He saw the pilot ahead in a small compartment by himself. But facing him was Mr. Death, his hideous white face set, a Luger gripped in his right hand.

The moment was a tense one. No words were spoken. The wind screamed below them, and the trap door lay open like a gaping coffin hatch. The little torpedoes were lined up in the plane.

Mr. Death's black robes made him look more somber than he ever had before. His huge black eyes were staring, as though he were insane. His slit of a mouth was twisted down.

"You are hard to kill, my friend," he said.

"Most Yanks are," Babyface replied evenly.

Again there was a silence, this time unbroken. Then Death moved forward, the point of his Luger unwavering, his horrible mask of scars glowing in the dim light of the plane.

"There will be no mistake this time. I will put a bullet in your head, then drop you. I wanted to drop you still alive, but you have made that impossible."

Babyface said nothing. He edged away from the trap door, toward the side of the plane where the torpedoes were laid.

Death brought the Luger up. His hand was steady. His finger tightened a little on the trigger.

"It will be all over soon," he said. "Goodbye, Yank."

"Goodbye," Babyface said grimly.

And then suddenly he held up one of the torpedoes. Death moved forward, Babyface motioned him back.

"Shoot me," he rasped, "and before I die, this torpedo bomb of yours will be smashed into the floor of the plane. It will explode with all of us!"

"Death's slit-mouth, moved until it was a straight line. He took Babyface in carefully, saw that the situation was an impossible one.

"Put the Luger down," Jed said evenly.

"That I will not do."

"Then we all die. I am not afraid of death—particularly if it means killing you with me—and smashing these infernal torpedo bombs of yours at the same time!"

Again there was silence, like that of a tomb, a silence made more ghastly by the howling of the wind, and the even throb-throb of the motors. The pilot was watching his course, he was shut off from the compartment Death and Babyface now occupied.

"I believe you will do that," Death said.

"You know I will," Jed snapped. "There is only one way out—put your Luger down, and order your pilot to land on an American field."

Mr. Death laughed that awful laugh of his, then became very somber.

"Do not speak foolishly," he said. "I may as well blow up with you in this plane as to allow myself to be captured. I would be as useless to Germany imprisoned, as I would be dead. Smash your torpedo down, Captain Garrett. Blow us up. I refuse your orders!"

Now the two arch enemies looked directly into each others eyes. Babyface was grim, resolute. If this meant his finish—well, it also meant the end of Mr. Death. He didn't want to die; there was much to live for; and a smoldering heap of ashes that was once his flesh, cast to the winds over Flanders, was not exactly a happy ending. Even so, Jed Garrett saw his duty clearly.

His eyes remained riveted upon the gruesome, ghastly countenance of his enemy. Death simply stared, striving desperately to effect, if possible, the spell of his hypnotism. Even now, Jed felt his senses reeling beneath the weird, inscrutable glare.

But now Babyface did not hesitate. He began to slam down with the torpedo.

"Wait!"

Jed hesitated, looked up.

Mr. Death threw his Luger to a corner of the plane. He reached a voice tube.

"We are captured. Make a landing or the plane will be blown up." He turned back to Garrett. "Your orders were to stop this plane, to destroy my new invention—the torpedo bombs. Is that right?"

Babyface nodded.

"In that mission," Death said, "you have succeeded. But this is far from the end. I am working on a new invention, I—"

He turned, drew something bulky from a locker, threw it over his shoulders, and put his arms in it.

"Just a moment," Babyface shouted, "you jump and I'll—"

But it was too late. With the clumsy parachute on his back, Mr. Death stepped through the trap door. Babyface saw the white 'chute spread and float gently toward the ground. In a moment it was swallowed up in the night air.

The bomber was circling to make a landing. Jed Garrett reached down through the opening and dragged Click up into the cabin. The dog shivered still, but wagged his tail. Jed nodded at him grimly.

"Again we lose, old fellow, we've won by capturing the bomber, and we have the torpedoes that murderous monk invented; but we'll have to return again to get Mr. Death!"

Click barked.

The wheels of the Boche plane skidded to a stop. Somehow, their screeching, and the shouts of the Yanks running toward them, sounded to Captain Babyface, strangely like the shrill and ghastly laughter of Mr. Death.

Death Rides Alone

Once again the flying monster of murder lurks alone in skies of dripping blood—Mr. Death, the human vulture, is waiting for his prey! Climbing now to the tune of his roaring Hisso, comes Babyface Jed Garrett—eyes piercing the clouds for his mortal foe, fingers tight against the trips of his Vickers. Mr. Death has asked for a sky duel; Jed Garrett intends to let him have it!

Death
Rides Alone

T EN minutes before dawn, and the shrieking howl of the wind had died down, leaving the stillness of death in the crisp morning air. There was tension in the atmosphere which forewarned the new day of horrors rapidly approaching—a new day of men strung on barbed wire with their guts spilling out, while the sun ate their eyes in their sockets. A new day of gun fire, bloodshed and gore, smeared over the Western Front. In a half second more, new dawn patrols would lift into the sky to rain their leaden death.

Perched like a flimsy canvas kite in the half light of early morning, flew a lone Spad. Its cargo was Captain Jed Garrett —and his faithful police dog, Click. The youthful American whose commission was a roving one, and who, because his face had not aged when he himself grew older, was affectionately called "Babyface", winged slowly, his white countenance set grimly, gloved hands hard on the controls. Black eyes stared straight ahead; lips were in a straight line. The jutting cheek bones in his countenance made him appear, though young, rugged and unafraid. Somehow, there was courage in that face of his, courage that made the medals he had won seem like cheap tin. And this morning, of all mornings, he was on a mission no single man on the Ally Front would dare try alone.

A few weeks ago he had been commissioned to kill the most horrible menace on the air front. Twice Babyface had the Boche master mind at the point of destruction; but in the end, his lone enemy had escaped. This time the arch aces of the war—Babyface and the German "Mr. Death", had themselves arranged a duel—a test of honor between the two; a duel until one was dead.

This was the morning. Captain Babyface's Spad droned through the dark air lanes, while Click shivered in his specially designed compartment. His small, homemade goggles fitted half over his furry face, and his sharp ears were whipped back.

In Captain Babyface's tunic pocket was the scrawled note:

I HAVE MARKED THE MAP WHERE WE SHALL MEET,
THE TWO OF US ALONE. IT IS OBVIOUS THAT
NEITHER OF US CAN PROCEED ON OUR MISSIONS OF
WAR WHILE THE OTHER LIVES. ONE OF US MUST DIE.
"MR. DEATH"

Five hundred feet above the Spad, in a trim black metal plane, sat Mr. Death.

He was staring down with bubbling hatred shining in his blotch eyes—watching Captain Babyface, contentedly—making no move to attack.

He was a monster, sitting there, cloaked in his flapping black robes which covered the steel plates on his chest and back. His head was a gruesome bone of a thing, white and without hair. His mouth was only a grim slit. He had no nose, and only scars showed where his ears should be, and no human expression could register on that hideous countenance.

Mr. Death had been a monk, and a bomb had blown up the monastery. A genius of the world of chemistry, which profession he had followed before becoming a monk, he had joined the Boche air service to wreak a bloody revenge on the Allied ships which had left him the physical wreck he now was.

In those glittering black holes of his scarred face—the things most men called eyes—there was power that few possessed; the power of hypnotism, the strength to command men's minds. Above all, there was murder in his soul.

He looked up as the sun began climbing over the horizon, then nosed his black ship down, a death-like glimmer in his blotch-eyes, his lipless mouth fiercely contorted. He jerked on his Spandaus, and the teeth of the gun, clattered across Captain Jed Garrett's tail assembly.

The Spad spun into action. From the easy pace at which it had been traveling, it banked out, cut a loop through the wind and began nosing upward. Vicious Vickers' tracer lashed into the belly of the black metal ship.

Brrrt . , . brrrt . . . brrt.

A shrill, ghastly laugh issued from the parched throat of Mr. Death as he rained his bullets down, and slit a hole in the side of the Spad. Whirling his ship away from the lifting Spad, he cut back, pressing down on the Spandaus again.

Brrrrt. . . brrrrt.

Babyface's grim eyes burned. He rocketed his ship, and tore in blazing lead and hate. Click raised his brown head and howled wildly. The dog crouched down, growling his loyalty to his master.

Suddenly something strange happened. Babyface had been aiming at the motors of the black plane, and now he could hear them coughing furiously. Mr. Death was rocking back and forth in the cockpit.

Captain Garrett rushed in for the kill— like a fighter who has his opponent weak, and getting up from the floor. His wings roared in the wind, his prop spun like merry hell.

Brrrrrrt . , . brrrrrrrt . . . brrrrrrrt!

Death returned the fire, but weakly. His ship began losing altitude. Now Babyface was on him. He cut the sides of the black plane and rode its tail, slamming Vickers' lead toward the monster in the cockpit.

Then Mr. Death held up a gloved hand, and pointed toward the ground.

Captain Babyface signaled back, then followed close behind the black plane as it circled to make a landing.

Babyface released Click from the cockpit as soon as they settled on the ground. In a flash they reached the black plane, even before Mr. Death, his black robes trailing behind, was out on the ground.

For a moment, the American ace simply stared at his hideous opponent, his automatic trained upon the ugly head. It was a moment of great victory for Captain Jed Garrett. Click stood behind; his hair bristled and he growled.

Slowly, Mr. Death raised his hands over his head. His expressionless face was set, his black eyes boiled within their crazy-shaped sockets, his robes blew back in the breeze. It was defeat.

"This has been coming for a long time," Babyface said.

"My friend," Mr. Death replied in a brittle tone, "it was my intention that I would hold the gun, and that your hands would be raised."

"Yanks don't often do that," Babyface reminded him grimly.

"So I have heard," Mr. Death returned sardonically. "What do you intend to do with me?"

"Lock you up for the rest of the war at least. But no tricks, Mr. Death; I'm warning you that your first false move will make me pull the trigger. And as you may have also heard, these American automatics spit lead fast, and they would make many ugly holes through your head."

Mr. Death did not reply. Babyface marched him back to the Spad. Death was silent while the American bound him securely, and lashed him to the body of the ship. Click was arranged facing him, so that if he moved, the dog would bark. Then Captain Garrett took off.

Two weeks passed, as the news flashed up and down the Allied Front. Details of the capture echoed from every American, English, French and Italian newspaper. Captain Babyface and his dog Click were the heroes of the day. Every doughboy's lips mentioned his name in awe; pilots who had known him, bragged of it.

And now Jed Garrett, his tunic recklessly open in the front, sat with his feet cocked up on a table, a row of Champagne bottles before him. Click was in a high chair provided by the management, a cock-eyed paper cap on his head, his eyes blinking sleepily.

Captain Garrett's Paris leave was a gay one. French girls were swinging glasses, rolling their eyes and singing:

Oh, Mr. Death is in the jail, Oh, Mr. Death is in the coop He'll never get out, his ship to sail, Alles, alles, alles OOP!

It was a crazy, drunken song, climaxing the gayety. One honey blonde with an arm about Click, sang the lyric joyfully.

The dog looked up every now and then to lick her cheek, just to show his master that he appreciated feminine pulchritude and charms. *Oh, Mr. Death is in the jail, Oh, Mr. Death is in the coop He'll never get—*

A high pitched scream shrilled through the room. All activity ceased as Babyface looked up groggily.

A French peasant woman was rushing by the waiters and sweeping aside tables. Her eyes were popping and her face was dead white. She arrived at the table, and the young girls scattered. She broke the Champagne bottles, slapped Click across the snout, then laughed hysterically.

"You think you captured Mr. Death— you and the Americans think he is in your jail. But last night I saw him—" her voice trembled as she confessed this "—I saw him, you understand?"

Her words poured forth violently in heavy accent.

"—I saw him last night. He killed my husband and my little boy, and my father, He killed them all, but I escaped because I ran—I ran—"

Her words struck with a tone of utter sincerity; nor did the horror in her eyes suggest insanity. Babyface believed her. He shook from his stupor, staggered to his feet.

"Did you report that to—"

The woman, her hair down about her shoulders, shook convulsively. "I told them—and they showed him to me in his cell. Showed him to me there, locked up—"

A waiter rushed in. "Monsieur, I am truly sorry, permit me to evict—"

"Leave her alone," Babyface snapped.

"Others had been killed," the woman went on miserably. "For two weeks the villages behind the lines have been plagued by this figure in robes. Oh, it is horrible. You must come back, do something!"

Captain Garrett stared at the woman another moment, searching her face and her eyes. Then he pushed the table back.

"Come on, Click!"

He strode through the gay dining hall with a hundred pairs of eyes gaping after him. Click trotted at his side; the paper cap had already fallen from his head.

"Monsieur," pleaded the head waiter, "you are not going, yes?"

"I am going," Babyface said acidly, "back to finish the job I thought was finished."

Enroute back to the Front, Captain Garrett's orders had been flashed for him to return, so that his arrival was not entirely unexpected. He had been ushered straight back into the offices of General Headquarters the moment he reported.

The general's white van dyke beard was straight and pulled, the Old Man's blue eyes were clouded with a dismayed look. He was pacing back and forth. Click's head and eyes followed him from one end of the room to the other as he walked. Babyface sat back quietly awaiting the barrage of words to begin.

Finally he turned about. "I tell you, Captain Garrett, that man is unholy. There is something about him—like there was Rasputin—that you cannot get around. He is like a ghost, not a human. My guards have watched that cell of his all night, they have never opened it. Yet, these French people report seeing him; report murders that he is said to have committed. Now what sensible reason would a man like Mr. Death have for going around the villages murdering—" "Doesn't his alleged trail circle most of the American dromes, giving a wide arc, sir?"

"That is true, but—" Captain Babyface's eyes glittered. "My capture was too easy," he said simply. "What I can't understand is—" "They would pick a man like Mr. Death," Babyface continued as though he had not heard. He nodded, "Yes, I think I see it all now."

"Blast it," the general roared, "see what?"

"The biggest thing of the war. A plan that would wipe out the entire American lines. Kill half of the Allies. Do you hear what I am saying, general, half of our men! Do not laugh, it would be impossible for an ordinary man to do that, but Mr. Death is a murder genius. He is cunning. He is the "brain" of the war. We must kill him, or—"

"I don't follow you, Captain Garrett—"

Babyface got to his feet, his jaw set tightly. The general pulled on his van dyke.

"What has happened," Babyface said crisply, "is that Mr. Death has been planning this for weeks. One by one he has sent Boche spies over here with faked orders; spies who wormed themselves into being prison charges. The few who are Yanks were taken care of by Mr. Death himself. These spies acting as prison keepers allow Mr. Death to get out each night. They put a decoy in his cell to fool the sergeant of the guard."

"But why does he want to get out? Why doesn't he go back to his own lines while he has the chance then?"

"He was captured by me because he wanted it that way; he wanted to be lodged here behind the lines so that he wouldn't have to slip over from Boche-land each night. His work here is undoubtedly taking him a long time. If he is here, all that is necessary, is to release him from his cell so that he works during the darkness. Some new and horrible scheme is festering in his mind, General—"

"We should drive a spike through his head?" the high officer oathed.

"Since he has gone this far," Babyface said grimly, "it would be foolish of us to show our hand and reveal that we know of his activity. Let things go on as they have for the present. Don't let on we know of the spy system in the prison—that is, not until you hear from me."

"But—"

Captain Garrett held up his hand. "Don't you see, that whatever they are doing is perhaps almost finished? That if we at this point of the game killed Death and his men, that other Germans would come over and finish the job—a job that we know nothing about and could not prevent?"

"I see what you mean."

"I'll wait outside the prison. When Mr. Death comes out tonight I'll follow him. I'll see what he is doing—what his scheme is. Then, when we discover it, we can destroy his plans and whatever he has built thus far, and destroy him, too. To kill Death without knowing—"

"I see, then I'll leave this up to you?"

"Do nothing, sir," Babyface said, "until I have made my report."

It was one minute past midnight. Mr. Death walked grimly back and forth in his cell, his robes sweeping the floor, his bony face hideous in the light of the moon that shone in through the bars of the window.

A lock clicked. The door opened. Dark shadows crossed the walls, then a slim figure stepped inside. He whispered hoarsely:

"All is ready, master!"

"That is good," Mr. Death answered.

"Captain Jed Garrett has returned from Paris," the other continued, "be wary."

Death nodded, then made his way to the door. Quietly, he slithered down the long corridor. The Boche spies on guard nodded as he passed. Mr. Death was fully aware that he had honeycombed the Yank front with more spies than he had ever been able to get since the war began. These spies were his helpers. They had the principal guard positions in the prison here; others dwelled in peaceful French houses behind the lines, while still others, mingled with the officers. But at the stroke of midnight they reported to work to the "master of murder" who was the ghastly monk, Mr. Death!

The device of destruction that he and his spies were completing— the latest invention of massacre—would soon go into effect. Already well-laid pits and dugouts, hidden by innocent looking debris, were filled with tanks of heavy deadly gas which would be released when the wind swept back toward the Front. Thousands would die!

They would die like dogs and there could be no escape. It was a gas Mr. Death himself, in his laboratories behind Boche lines, had concocted. It would make the crude masks that had been invented, useless toys! It would seep through anything; eat the skin from men's faces. It would wipe out half the Allied troops!

The "duel" arranged with Captain Babyface Garrett had been a cunning ruse to effect Mr. Death's capture. To put him into an American prison which was run by his own German spies!

Mr. Death left the prison, swept out into the cold night air. He lifted his ugly head as three men came toward him and saluted. Mr. Death gave them low orders, then added:

"I shall linger behind; this impudent puppy, Captain Garrett, will no doubt be waiting to follow me tonight. I will trap him so he cannot find our hidden gas pits. You will find him in the center of the controls pit when you go there tomorrow."

The men were off. Mr. Death, his monk's robes flowing behind his tall, arched body, walked calmly toward the woods. He fingered a huge Luger that was secured in a holster made in one of his sleeves.

Babyface Garrett lay on the limb of a tree under which Mr. Death passed. Click was crouching somewhere farther back in the forest.

When the tall, robed monster of horror was a safe distance beyond, Babyface swung down from the tree. He snapped his fingers. Click appeared from nowhere. The dog stood at Jed's side, his body tense.

"There he goes, boy," Babyface said, "this time we'll find what he's got up his sleeve, and make our capture a good one." He didn't know when he spoke, that the Luger was up one of Mr. Death's sleeves. Warily, Babyface and the dog followed, step after step, twigs breaking at times, lurking behind trees lest they be seen, following the huge figure of Death. They walked a mile, then two, and Babyface wondered what the game was, for Mr. Death met no other men, nor did he engage in any activity.

At last they arrived at a bombed wreck of a town. It was ghostly and quiet. The structures of grenade torn houses stood in skeleton.

Mr. Death suddenly bent over and swept back some clay walls that crumpled to the ground. He jerked open a trap door, then hesitated. Finally he descended down a pair of steps and disappeared.

Captain Garrett rushed to the place. He stood at the open mouth of the underground room. Should he go in after him? Was it a trap?

Still Garrett hesitated. He had been trapped by this monster of horror before. Perhaps if he waited until he came out; if he investigated after Death returned to his cell—

He did not see Mr. Death open a trap door behind him and come up from the pit from another entrance. He did not hear the padded steps of the tall figure in robes.

Click turned, growling. Babyface spun about. He saw the Luger pointed at his heart, saw in the half light of the moon, the hideous white face of Mr. Death.

"Do not move, Captain Garrett."

There was a tense moment of indecision. Then Click charged forward, leapt for the Luger.

Babyface jerked out his automatic, he leveled it and began firing.

Orange spurted in the night. Death twisted away from Click, the dog's teeth tearing his robes; he shot at Babyface.

A bullet took the American in the shoulder and spun him about.

Weakly, Jed pulled the trigger of his automatic again. The bullet flattened against Death's steel plated breast.

Another shot roared from the monk's automatic. Babyface toppled over backwards, a blackness rushing into his mind. He could hear Click charging, growling, tearing to get at Mr. Death.

The place was a low, slimy floored basement, fetid with the fumes of death. Broken bits of skeletons that had once been men were spread across the dirt floor. One low hole for ventilation was somewhere near the far corner.

Captain Garrett lay there bound with wires. Click lay beside him, his front and hind feet fastened. They had been here for three days, and Hun spies had forced poor, spoiled food down their throats. They had not seen Mr. Death since regaining consciousness.

Along one wall there was a black ebony panel disclosing many levers and wheels. Babyface knew by now that these would operate the gas tubes. Why Mr. Death had chosen to spare him and his dog he still did not know—unless it was to gloat when he stuffed up the one hole so the gas could not get in, and turned his panels to kill off half of the American troops.

Babyface's muscles shrieked with agony. His face was pale and drawn, and his black eyes had lost their luster. Three days ago he had been a celebrated hero, and now the tables were reversed. He was being kept to watch the Boche inventor succeed with his horrible plans.

The blood in his bullet wounds was caked and dry, and he throbbed with pain. Yet, normal strength was gradually returning to him. With blood-shot eyes Jed looked up and stared at Click.

"Click!"

The dog whined, writhing at his bonds, but he could not escape them.

Babyface threw his body a little forward, so that he fell on his face in the muck of the floor. He knew that Mr. Death's traps of gas would be released as soon as there was a good Western breeze; he had learned these things from the Germans who fed him. Unless some miracle allowed him to escape, countless thousands of the Allies would be wiped out!

Babyface tried to crawl forward by means of twisting his body. His wrists were bound behind him, but he could use his elbows to some extent, and also his toes. His face became covered with the ill smelling filth, but he had to reach Click. Somehow, he and the dog had managed to get away from every other close encounter, and they had to manage it again.

Bitterly, Jed recalled his stupid party in Paris; his heroism in bringing Death back as a prisoner. In reality he had been made a fool of; he had been cutting the throat of the Allied powers by allowing Death to be put in a prison where he could soon command the guards. Those blotch-eyes of his staring into their faces, and those slit-lips giving them commands.

Inch by inch Babyface made his way through the slime. Twice he had to crawl over dried skeletons that crackled like sticks beneath his weight. Once those skeletons had been living men like himself. Would he and Click be left down here to mingle their bones with the others?

He was halfway when weakness and a sudden short spell of unconsciousness made him stop. He lay there without moving for more than an hour. He opened his eyes when he heard Click barking.

Again Babyface began to crawl. His muscles ached, his stomach felt as though it was on fire, and his head acted as though a hatchet was stuck into it. Eye balls burning, slime clinging to his neck, chest and sides, he reached the dog.

Jed rolled over so that he could use his bound hands. His back to Click he reached, groped for the wires that were about the dog's legs. Quickly he twisted off the one on his front feet, and then the back.

"Don't move, Click!" he commanded, "dead dog." Click whined. "Dead dog, I said!" The whole success of Captain Babyface's wild scheme lay in the hope that the Germans who came down to give him food would not know that Click was free. If Click could escape when the trap door was opened; could escape without being shot down, then he could go back to H.Q. and get aid—lead them to Babyface!

The dog understood much; Jed had raised him from a puppy. Yet, the trick of going for help for his master, was not a new one. Collies, police dogs, even terriers had been known to save lives in that way. This time it was Click's turn to save not only his master's life—but the lives of thousands of Allied men.

In the next hour, Babyface managed to crawl back to the place where the Boche spies had left him. Click still did not move and he looked as well secured as ever. There remained nothing now but to wait. There were many more hours of waiting. At times Babyface felt as though he could watch no longer, so filthy was the floor of this lair in which festered the schemes of Mr. Death.

At last the first trap door began to open. Jed tensed, then snapped a low command to Click. The dog got to his feet, his fur bristling. He shook himself, then crouched, his ears straight up.

The door opened fully allowing a crimson shaft of the dying sun to rush into the blackness of the pit. Babyface Garrett whistled low. Click rushed at the door. A German jumped down into the pit, and at the same moment, before the second Boche could frame in the entrance of the trap door, a bundle of brown fur sped through the air; Click leapt into the opening. He was gone before the Germans could realize what had happened.

Jed breathed easier. The Boche spies checked to see that Babyface was well tied, then without a word, they left the pit. They had to report the accident, Jed figured. In their hurry to get away they had dumped the salt pork they had brought him for supper, down into the dirt and slime.

Now if only Click could get back safely and manage to lead the officers from H.Q. to this pit! This was one time when it was impossible for Babyface to effect his own escape; more than once he had risked his life to save Click—and now it was Click's turn again.

"Thank God," he mumbled hoarsely, "they gave me a special order, letting me keep him; without that dog—" his words trailed into a thin whisper. He was weak from his bullet wounds, his hours of inactivity, from starvation, and sick to his stomach with the awful stench of Death's hell hole. He closed his eyes and his brain throbbed with pain.

What if the Germans caught up with Click and shot him? What if the officers at H.Q. would not understand Click's barks and attempts to lead them here? What if the dog who had never failed him before, somehow lost interest, got off the track this once and failed to help him? There were so very many things, and worst of all, so many men's lives depended on the dog's success.

Mr. Death stood in the midnight darkness. His bone-white face, blotch-eyes, and slit-mouth were hard and even. Three spies stood before him, humble, yet eager.

"The dog escaped, master; but that is of little consequence."

"Yes, the time is ripe; the breeze is a good one. We must open our tanks and let the fumes blow back. The other spies have already been notified to return to their stations on our own territory," the second spy said.

The third added: "You are a genius, master. Thousands will die tonight. Die in horrible convulsions. It is the vital stroke of the war; the blow that will win for the Fatherland; the blow that will crush the Allies!"

Mr. Death said nothing. His bony arms were folded over his steel-plated chest. At last he turned, strode to the trap door of the pit and waited while one of the spies opened it for him. He climbed down; the others followed.

Lamps which had been placed in niches in the wall, were lit. The ventilation hole was blocked up, and made impregnable to gas. Mr. Death strode through the pit, the slime sliding and crunching beneath his feet, his robes trailing in the muck, and stood over Captain Jed Garrett.

A hoarse, burned-out laughter issued from his throat. He kicked his heavy boot into Jed's side. The American looked up with burning eyes, but made no sound.

"Too bad that the Allies do not give me a worthy opponent. You and your dog, captain, are amateurs who blunder at every turn!"

Jed Garrett's eyes were red and sore, but they gazed up unflickeringly.

Was it true, Jed asked himself frantically, had Click been shot, captured, or in any way detained? The Yanks should have been here to the rescue hours ago!

"There is no time to waste, master," one of the spies said.

"I have saved you to watch this, Captain Garrett," Death said in his brittle voice. "You shall watch my hand turn the wheels and pull the levers that will send gas tumbling across the fields and into the Allied trenches, dromes, and rest camps."

With that Death strode across the room to the panel of controls. He turned back, his slit-mouth even, his blotch-eyes glittering madly. His hand reached up.

Jed Garrett dared not move. If Death turned those wheels—! Where was Click?

Slowly, Mr. Death began turning the first wheel.

Captain Babyface wriggled, twisted, trying to escape the wires that were bound about his wrists and ankles. But the more he moved, the tighter the wires became.

Mr. Death pulled down one of the levers. He chuckled satanically. His left hand reached up; he spun another wheel.

Mr. Death concluded his operations and turned about. "Your comrades are dying, Captain, and you shall soon join them."

"You are a butcher," Jed said evenly. "If your gas is so powerful, what makes you think it will stop traveling westward when it reaches our trenches?"

There was a moment of appalling silence.

"It will travel on over," Jed continued, "and kill your bloody Boche friends as well!"

The three spies stared at one another incredulously. Mr. Death merely placed his hands together in front of him and said in a low voice:

"The gas, after traveling a certain-number of miles through air, burns itself up. That is why I had to plunder far behind the lines, through French towns, to lay my tanks. Had to get it far enough back so that it would not travel to the German lines."

Death strode forward and picked him up. He set him back against the dirt wall. Then his iron-like fingers wrapped about the Yank's throat.

"Your murder will be performed personally, Captain. It will be a pleasure."

Bound, helpless, Babyface could do nothing as the fingers tightened. His face turned blue. His eyes bulged from their sockets. In a moment, just one more moment, and life would cease for Captain Garrett. . . .

Suddenly there was a faint sound of a dog barking.

Death stepped back, whirled around. The spies looked up.

"But all life should be ended," one of them said, "the gas—"

"The gas did not work," Death screamed insanely. "Some trick—"

The trap doors, both of them, were opened. Yank officers tumbled down into the pit. Mr. Death's Luger leapt into his hand. A bundle of brown fur careened in through one of the openings.

Shots blazed through the pit. Click leapt toward Mr. Death's throat but, the monster of murder swept him down.

An officer rushed over to Babyface and began unbinding him.

"Click led us here," he said, "but we thought to find the gas trunk lines, and the electric currents leading from here which would open the tanks. After we destroyed them so that Mr. Death could not release the gas, we came down to get you."

"Then no one is dead—" Jed gasped,

"No one," the officer said.

Babyface stared at the back of Mr. Death's robes. He saw Americans in front of him, holding their revolvers level. Suddenly something strange happened. Two of the Yanks seemed to grow dizzy, they wavered. Two others fired but stupidly, not knowing, they fired into Death's steel plates. The black robed monk leapt for the trap door. He was out of it just before Click leapt after him.

"He's hypnotized them!" Jed Garrett shrieked. Weak though he was, he rushed after the Boche, crawled up through the trap door.

The roar of a plane's motor throbbed into the night air. Click's barking noise was lost in the din. Babyface arrived at a broken down villa in time to see Mr. Death's plane taxi out of the secret hiding place the Boche spies had placed it in.

He caught onto one wing of the metal ship, saw Click back of the cockpit, tugging at Death's garments. The plane lifted into the air as Babyface swung onto it.

The wind screamed around him as Jed crawled across the wing. Mr. Death leaned out of the cockpit fighting Click who was holding on for dear life.

Babyface Garrett reached the body of the plane. He grappled with a guy wire, swung himself up.

Death let go of Click and fired at Babyface, but he missed. Babyface edged toward the cockpit. Death reached out and tried to push him from the plane. But Click sank his teeth into Mr. Death's neck.

The black ship was falling!

Desperately, Babyface and Click fought with the monk of horror.

From out of the darkness they suddenly saw the close flare of guns in No Man's Land. The plane was only a hundred yards off the ground.

A tree loomed from nowhere. There was a crash.

Babyface's hands were wrenched loose, he went tumbling through the branches which broke his fall.

He regained consciousness a moment later to see the wreck of the plane beside him, and Click limping toward him.

A multi-colored bomb flared from the German trenches. In its light, Captain Babyface could see the silhouetted figure of the ghostly black robed Mr. Death retreating back to his own lines.

Death in the Dawn

A roll of the drums; a last glance at the sky, and a Fallen Eagle looks into the guns of dishonor. . . . Captain Babyface has lost. Death is his reward for serving his country well, a traitor's grave his resting place. Yet high above the shrieking Gods of War have planned another fate— Herr Death rides on— a mocking, rampant curse to men!

Death in the Dawn

ISTER DEATH, the hated master of murder, rode the sky lanes on this bitter cold morning. He rested easily in the cockpit of his black metal plane as the growling motor pulled him through the crisp morning air. His black robes flapping wildly in the wind, concealed the steel plates with which his chest and back were covered. The bony horror of his face was set and even, the blotches that were his eyes, glittered savagely; the scar of his nose and his lipless slit of a mouth, expressed defiance.

In the viciously cunning mind of the mysterious monk of hatred there was born at this moment a scheme of vengeance that could only come from a mind such as his—a mind like a brewing pot on a witch's fire, giving off fumes of human blood—the stink of long-dead corpses, the odor of burning skin. It was a mind clouded with the insanity of hate; a mind that knew no reason.

All of Death's hatred this morning, was centered upon Captain Jed "Babyface" Garrett and the despicable police dog companion the Yank pilot carried with him in his Spad. Mr. Death, with the ruthless planning for which he was famous, had laid a fool proof trap for the American. He would not merely kill him, he would make Babyface Garrett suffer. Too many times had Death planned clever attacks against the Allies only to have them wrecked by Garrett. Now Garrett would be removed, but not without suffering the tortures of the damned.

The sun peeked timidly from behind a cloud. A shaft of its rays slid through the sky, lighting the black, specially designed ship of Mr. Death in a blaze of shimmering gold. The flapping robes of the monk with the hideous face were silhouetted against the sky line. The slit-mouth of the murder monster twitched down a little. In the distance, he saw a small speck.

Advance information had let him know that this speck would be a plane. That in its cockpit sat one man—Captain Jed Garrett!

Mr. Death's bony fingers touched the handles of his long-nosed Spandaus. The jagged pools of his eyes bubbled with a fiend's anticipation.

Captain Babyface leaned back in the cockpit of his Spad. A warm smile crossed his lips and his blue eyes sparkled beneath his goggles. It was going to turn out to be a fine day. He reached back and patted the head of the police dog he carried with him.

"Well, Click, we'll just get the lay of the land for a report to H.Q.— so they can plan their drive. Then we'll go back to the 25th and spend an easy day. We need a rest after that last scrape with Mr. Death."

The dog, bundled in a specially made little leather helmet, lifted his head; his sharp ears whipped back with the wind. Jed Garrett had flown with this dog back home before the war in the pioneer days of aviation. When he entered the war, a special order had granted him permission to retain this faithful dog. Now Jed was a G-2 man, with a roving commission. His face, though like that of a boy, had lately become a little creased; still, he looked more like a lad of eighteen than a man of twenty-five. His friends called him "Babyface", but his latest assignment had been one of the grimmest ever given to a Yank pilot. It was simply this: "Kill, or capture, Mr. Death!"

And now Babyface's iron-like fingers were on the stick of the Spad. He banked left in the wind, his guy wires humming, the slip stream blowing back at him. It was about time to turn about and go back. Today, the Front below, was unusually quiet, even Archie refrained from casting his lead into the sky.

But suddenly, Jed's heart increased its speed; blood froze in his veins. In the sky before him he saw the black panther ship of Mr. Death winging toward him at a terrific speed. The rag-like robes of the murder

monk flew ominously about the bony-faced pilot. In the next moment
there was a burst of tracer fire.

Babyface Garrett ducked down in the cockpit. He drew the stick
back; sailed into a nose dive.

Click howled. He stretched his neck beneath the red white and blue
collar that French H.Q. had presented less than a week ago for his service with Babyface at the Front.

Jed maneuvered the stick dangerously. The canvas of the Spad howling in the wind, he brought the plane groaning back upward. He
pressed back the handles of his Vickers.

Brrrrt . . . brrrrt . . . brrrrt.

Yellow hell, leaden and lightning-fast, screamed from the barrels,
and cut through the air. Bullets flattened against the metal of Mr.
Death's Fokker.

Babyface swerved his ship to the right, almost ripping the wings off
with the frantic effort. His slip-stream spurted from the fuselage, like
hot steam back into his face. Death was diving toward him, his
Spandaus chewing across his left wing.

Babyface's stunt piloting was never put to better use. He nosed
upward in an almost vertical position; then he turned about, the ship
screaming in protest to the heavy reverse. Again he jerked back on the
Vickers.

Brrrrt. . . Brrrt. . . Brrrt.

Mr. Death waved his arms wildly and commenced diving. Jed
Garrett followed on his tail, the Spad's ripped wings roaring in the
mighty wind of the prop.

Death banked out. Babyface slid by him, narrowly avoiding a collision. Tracer lead screamed through the air, two inches from his head.
Again Jed banked the Spad around, his Vickers barking without mercy.

Brrrrt. . . Brrrt. . . Brrrt.

Mr. Death ceased firing and again dove toward the ground. But this
time he kept dropping without trying to turn back. The wheels of his
ship skimmed over the top of a tree, then he settled in a three point
landing in a small clearing. Jed Garrett landed almost beside him.

He cut off the motor and leapt from his plane, releasing the dog.

Automatic in hand, he rushed to Mr. Death's plane. Suddenly he saw the bony-faced monster point the Spandaus toward him. The hooded countenance of the murder monk was grim; the slit-mouth twitched downward.

"Halt!"

Babyface realized that he could be cut down in an instant if he did not obey. He came to a stop. Click, however barked shortly and catapulted forward. With the wild whine of a savage beast, the dog leaped for Mr. Death.

But in the next moment, other guns blasted out. Babyface Garrett looked up to find himself surrounded by Boche soldiers, their rifles leveled straight upon him. Click had been hurled to the ground by Mr. Death.

Death climbed slowly out of the plane. He walked with a long stride, his glittering eyes like ebony.

"Well, Captain Garrett," he said in a short-clipped, brittle voice, "you've played right into my hands."

"Have I?"

"Yes, and it is most fortunate, since I have a very interesting future planned for you. However, I doubt that you will enjoy it."

Death laughed hoarsely—the burned out laughter of a monster. Then he turned about suddenly, and lifting his heavy Luger, fired a bullet at Click.

Babyface leapt forward in fear. He saw the dog leap into the air, howling, then drop prone to the ground, his fur now covered with blood. Babyface ran to the dog and knelt by him.

He breathed easier when he saw that the bullet had not pierced his head; it had only creased the dog's back. His collar was bloody, but unharmed.

"Play dead," Babyface whispered hoarsely, "play dead, old fellow, then when they've gone, try and get home. I know you're hurt—but try—try!"

The dog twitched.

Fear swept Babyface. Click understood what it meant to play dead but the excitement of a new wound—the tense situation. Perhaps this time he would not obey!

Mr. Death strode forward and jerked Jed back.

"Get up!"

Click rolled over, opened his eyes, then struggled to his feet.

Death aimed his Luger again.

"Home, boy, home!" Babyface shouted.

Click's eyes were pleading; he growled low.

Jed Garrett did something then that he had never done before. He did it to save Click's life. His booted foot reached out and kicked the dog.

"Home, Click! Back to the lines. Go home!"

Click turned and started trotting off. Death aimed the Luger again and fired. The bullet missed. Click was fast approaching the trees of the nearby thicket. Death fired again, cursing. Click stood still, twitched, then whining pitifully, fell. Babyface started toward him, but two Boche guards stopped him.

"Your hound is dead, American," Mr. Death said in a brittle voice, "and you are my prisoner. These are circumstances which you may later find unpleasant!"

His wrists cuffed behind him, Captain Jed Garrett, faced the fat German major to whom Mr. Death was talking. The office was a small one which had two windows, a threadbare rug. A tall Boche guard stood at the door.

Babyface had been stripped of his clothing and was dressed in a soiled private's uniform, recently removed from the corpse of a German.

Presently the door opened and a young German entered, wearing Babyface's uniform. Behind him came an army surgeon and a police dog which looked exactly like Click. The young officer stood back for inspection.

A grin creased the fat face of the major.

"It is perfect, Herr Death! He looks exactly like the prisoner."

The medical officer dry washed his hands, his beetle-like eyes gleaming. "I have done a good job, have I not?" He bowed to the robed figure of Mr. Death. "But I could not have accomplished it to this perfection if you hadn't concocted that mixture of liquid which we placed over Herr Garrett's face to harden. It formed a mask so thin and perfect in line, that it will never be detected. Von Elt wears it well!"

Mr. Death folded his bony arms. His blotch-eyes were glittering.

"Von Elt, you have all of Captain Garrett's private papers?"

"Yes sir," the Hun snapped. "You have learned the little personal habits exercised by Captain Garrett, so that you can take his place without arousing suspicion?"

"Yes sir. I am sure that my disguise is perfect. And as for being Garrett in manner, Herr Death—in Berlin, they hailed me as the stage's greatest impersonator."

"Then the trap is a perfect one, von Elt. You will follow your instructions to the letter. The Spad which has the special cockpit for the dog, is in the hangar ready for you to take to drome 25."

Von Elt clicked his heels and saluted. A grim expression played about the lipless slit of a mouth in the hideous explosion-wrecked countenance of the murder monk.

Babyface Garrett was for once speechless. Even he was forced to admit that the disguise of the German representing himself was without flaw. With Click dead out there in the field, and a clog to take his place— inwardly, he shuddered. Outwardly, his face was a grim, defiant mask.

Von Elt 's duties were simple, yet deadly to the American air force. Captain Babyface's irreproachable character made his activities possible. Each morning, before the dawn patrol departed, von Elt would wait until the ships had been inspected. Then, walking about and through them casually, he planted a bomb beneath each ship. They would take off, and ten minutes later the whole squadron would be blown to hell. One terrific explosion—seven American pilots blasted into horrible eternity!

At the end of the first week G.H.Q. was in turmoil. The 25th was drained of ships and more were being rushed. The new, green pilots arriving to be sent up, quaked in terror, for their comrades never had a chance to fight. They were unable to defend themselves. And the recruits knew that they would meet the same fate.

Major Smythe, in charge of the 25th, was the verge of going mad. Each day he had sent seven kids out to be killed. He felt like a butcher, yet he didn't know what to do about it. It was obvious enough that there was a spy working on the drome. Still, he had shaken down every man mercilessly—every one, that is, except the famous Babyface Garrett.

It seemed too fantastic to believe at first, but now, as the husky, blonde haired, brown-eyed major sat in the C.O.'s shack, drinking whiskey to control his nerves—he could no longer reason with Babyface's past reputation. In a moment the G-2 man and his dog would be before him.

Smythe pounded on the desk, rubbed his unshaven face. His bleary eyes took in a straight figure at the door.

"Babyface," he snarled.

"Yes sir?"

"You're the one—damn you!"

"Why—why, no sir. I don't see what you mean."

"You've been acting damn calm about all these explosions. You've seen our pilots shaken, their nerve gone; you've seen kids go crazy and hysterical and refuse to fly—yet—yet" the major gulped down another drink, "—you've shown no emotion. By God, Garrett, I'm going to court martial you!"

Von Elt had known that the showdown would come sooner or later and his orders were to return to Bocheland when that time arrived. He jerked out his automatic.

Smythe stared up at it, blinking.

"Then you are—by God!" he lunged across the desk.

Von Elt wanted to kill him, but he had been ordered to reveal Babyface as the traitor, then to flee. He cracked Smythe with the butt of the gun and left the office.

He hurried across the tarmac and nervously ordered a mechanic to get his machine in order. A police dog whined at his heels. He helped the animal into the plane, then climbed into the cockpit himself. The mechanic spun the prop.

"Contact!"

He taxied across the brown field and lifted into the air. Von Elt looked back at the American drome, chuckling.

Babyface Garrett paced anxiously back and forth in his cell. He wondered why he had not been killed. It was the usual treatment given to G-2 men. A long week had passed. He wondered if Click had died, or had lain out on the field suffering?

Presently there were footsteps. In the next moment, the huge, robed figure of Mr. Death was at the cell door. A guard unlocked it, and Death entered with Jed's clothing.

"Put these on!"

"What's the—"

The monk's horrible face was as expressionless as ever, but his slit-mouth twitched upward; his blotch-eyes burned sadistically.

"I am sending you back to your own lines."

"What's the trick, Death?"

"There is no trick. Your plane is waiting. All you have to do is return—if you have courage enough!"

"Courage?"

"That is what I said Herr Garrett. You are going back to answer for the death of forty-nine American pilots!"

"What do you mean?" Jed growled.

Death's bony arms were at his side. "You will find out soon enough. When you foiled my plans in the past, I swore a vengeance against you. You played right into my hands. Your name will forever bear the name of traitor—the war's greatest traitor! Your own comrades will shoot you down like a dog!" He sucked in his rasping breath. "I am sorry that I can think of no death more horrible for you."

"What if I don't return!"

Death shrugged. "That is up to you. The Americans will get you sooner or later. They already believe that you have fled their lines!"

With that, Death turned, his black robes sweeping the floor, and departed.

Captain Garrett realized the difficulty he would have in proving his innocence. With grim dread he anticipated the court martial board that awaited him. But he could not fail to return. There was one hope and one hope alone of proving his case.

He landed his Spad in the spot where he had been captured, and getting out, began a search for Click's body. He was both relieved and terrified when he did not find it. His hope to escape the charges against him lay in Click. The fact that he was not here, proved that he had tried to crawl back to the American lines. The trip was miles. There was every possibility that he had died further along the way.

With heavy heart, Jed went back to his plane. He fixed the motors, then spun the prop. At last he made contact, and climbing in, taxied slowly forward. He lifted from the ground, skimming over the top branches of a tree. His saddened eyes swept the field below him as the patches of land slipped away and the heavy hum of his motor, and the whistling howl of the wind through his canvas wings, drummed the song of the air into his ears.

He landed at the 25th and was immediately seized. Major Smythe's fist cracked across his jaw.

"You yellow swine!" he swore.

The men of the drome crowded about, shouting and cursing. Babyface submitted to the handcuffs. He was marched off. Smythe, a bandage on his head, gave him a quick questioning. He laughed at Jed's protests that a German impersonated him.

"Don't you think I know you! It was you, all right. This bloody mess is at an end!"

"If it was me—and I hit you like you said, why should I return?"

"Because you have the damn gall to think your past record will clear you! It won't!"

"You're a fool," Babyface snapped, "If you'd listen to me I could explain—"

"I'm through with your explanations! You've caused the worst break in morale since the war began. You'll submit to an official court martial immediately and you'll be shot at dawn!"

"Tell me something: what kind of a collar did Click wear?"

"None—he never—"

"You didn't know that the French presented him with a red, white and blue collar, did you? That dog that was here was another. Click has been wounded. I don't know where he is."

"Talking isn't going to do you any good, you dirty skunk," Smythe barked, "I don't want to hear you any longer!"

Babyface had not realized what serious damages von Elt had done. He could see that the major was unreasonable, because of the strain he had been under.

In the next moment, Yank guards marched him off. An hour later a Colonel from G.H.Q. sentenced him to death.

Waiting—that was the worst of it! Waiting for death to come! He was in a small, six by six cell in the basement of the canteen. Above him the racket of the noisy Yank pilots never ceased. His feet crunched the mud of the floor. His sore eyes searched out through the tiny window; searched the field. A week had passed and Click had not shown up — there couldn't be hope that he would appear now. Yet, Babyface clung to the possibility as a drowning man clings to a log. The collar, that was the one thing that could sway the evidence his way and grant him a reprieve.

It was four A.M. now, and they would soon be down after him. Mr. Death, back behind the Boche lines, would have his grim laugh. His would be the triumph over the American who had been commissioned to kill him. It was bitter, painful, to have to face a firing squad of his own countrymen, after the many battles he had waged for them. With red, white and blue on his wings he had gone into hell; his Vickers lead had screeched; teeth bared, face drenched white, he had gunned out Boche after Boche. He had smashed Mr. Death's fiendish schemes to poison the Allied troops with gas; three times in the past he had thwarted the murder monk's gruesome tricks to butcher the Allied soldiers—and this was his reward!

With trembling hands he lit a cigarette. The end of it glowed in the dark.

It was not sweet to die at his age. He had faced death a dozen times, but the anticipation of the rolling drums of dishonor, the realization that America would despise him as a war traitor, ate into his consciousness. Yet, there was now no escape. The court martial had been brief — to the point. Captain Babyface would stand against the wall and be shot!

Feverishly, his eyes crept to the small window. He saw a crack of light slipping up over the horizon. His blood raced in his veins. Sweat crowded over his youthful face. He dropped the cigarette and stepped on it.

He walked to the window, and staring upward, he uttered a prayer that someway, somehow, Click would come through. That they would grant him some short reprieve during which he could prove the fraud.

Steps . . . steps coming down after him. Babyface straightened up. He jerked out the package of cigarettes again. Once more he lit up.

Outside, the light of dawn was spreading rapidly. The dusk of the sky was turning to gray.

Silent men appeared at the cell door. The lock clicked back. Babyface walked out through the door. Two men—they were young, nineteen year old lieutenants —stood at his side. Without a word, then, the procession moved forward.

They climbed the steps and walked across the soft and cool earth. Sweet dew lay on the dirt and it crunched beneath Babyface's heels. How good the air was to breathe! There was a sweet scent of day in the atmosphere. The drome was quiet, picturesque, with its vari-colored drome, the planes, motors dead, being lined up for the dawn patrol; the trees fringing the background.

The death party moved slowly on. Pilots coming out of their tents halted and watched. Wistful eyes, some with hatred in them, some with pity for the brave American daredevil ace, followed his marching feet.

Jed Garrett's shoulders were back. The cigarette dangled between his lips. His burning, restless eyes, took in the singular sights that he passed.

Finally they reached the low adobe wall. It was the remains of a French house. Babyface went over and stood against it. The captain in charge offered a bandage for his eyes as a gesture he knew to be useless. Babyface would die with his eyes open!

Presently the squad lined up before him. They were youngsters, their faces white and grim.

Babyface looked up and over their heads. In the distance he could see the stars and stripes being pulled up the pole. The flag furled in the breeze.

And then the even humming of the motors of Spads that would go on the dawn patrol burst into the cool silence. Babyface's cigarette was becoming short; he lit another on it. He puffed.

"Squad, attention!" the captain snapped.

The men drew rigid.

"Shoulder, arms!"

Flag waving in the wind . . . motors of Spads that would go on the Dawn patrol, humming the song of the sky lanes . . . the drome in the gray shadows of the dawn.

"Ready…"

Babyface Jed Garrett threw away his cigarette. He straightened up. A smile crossed his thin lips.

"Shoot straight, fellows," he said.

"Aim. . . ."

Suddenly the tall Texan captain waved his arms. "Order, arms!" He turned to Babyface. "Damn you, you saved my life—got me promoted to captain! Somebody else can take this job! I won't! Not if they bust me for it!"

Major Smythe presented himself a minute later. He eyed Babyface and breathed easier. Behind Smythe came one of the commanding generals from G.H.Q., and with him was a private, carrying a furry bundle.

"Click!" Babyface shouted.

The dog was no more than a skeleton. He looked up at Babyface with dark eyes.

The General was speaking. "I'm granting you a reprieve, Garrett. After all you've done for the Allies I cannot believe you guilty of this charge. I just returned from Paris last night to hear of your plight. They told me they were sure you are guilty and I—I well, when someone finally mentioned something about a police dog that had been picked up in No Man's Land with a red, white and blue collar on him—"

"How long ago was he found?"

"Two or three days. But no one recognized him as Click. Even now we can not be sure. Dogs look pretty much alike."

"But Click was awarded—"

"Yes, I know," the General snapped, "I found all that out. But it is not strong enough proof to free you. I am granting you a reprieve on the condition that if you bring back Mr. Death, you go free!"

Babyface straightened, then saluted. "Yes sir!"

He took the dog from the private's arms and held him close. Tears crowded into his eyes. Then, with the eyes of the General, the Texan captain, Major Smythe, the firing squad and the general's orderly upon him, he turned and started slowly off to the tarmac of the drome.

Babyface Garrett and his sick dog tore through the air in their Spad. Garrett was a flying maniac, bent on one purpose alone. His hatred knew no limit, and his courage no end. He drove the humming plane straight back across the German lines. He rocked back and forth in the cockpit. Then, circling to where he had been held prisoner, and where he knew Mr. Death kept his headquarters, he zoomed for a landing.

Ground guns spat at him. Babyface catapulted from the plane. He left Click in it, and left the motor running.

Huns ran toward him. Garrett's automatic chopped them down. In the next moment he was safe within the office of the drome. He ran back through a corridor; he heard the Germans scrambling after him. He arrived in the Major's office. The fat Boche was drinking a cup of coffee.

Babyface's automatic hurled its last bullet through the major's forehead. The portly officer fell forward, his mouth spurting blood.

Babyface reloaded. Germans crashed into the door. Jed opened one of the windows in the room and leapt out. He wanted to draw Mr. Death into the air and this was enough to do it. Running as fast as his legs would carry him, he sped back to the tarmac.

Boches were going toward his plane. He shot them down ruthlessly, leapt into the cockpit and taxied forward.

Those who had followed him into the office and through the window were arriving at the field. Bullets screamed after Jed Garrett as his plane lifted into the air. He stared down at the field.

He saw the tell-tale black plane of Mr. Death roll out across the tarmac. A moment later it taxied forward, before other Fokkers took off in rapid succession.

Babyface had a lead and he throttled the Spad back toward the American lines. He knew that one plane alone could catch him—Mr. Death's specially built metal ship. He was crossing No-Man's-Land when a spray of Spandaus lead told him that Death had caught him.

Garrett wheeled his Spad around. Banking out in the wind, his carriage creaking, the motor groaning in protest, he jerked back the Vickers handles.

Brrrrt. . . Brrrt. . . Brrrt.

The black robed monk laughed harshly, but the sound was lost in the roar of the firing. He pressed down on his Spandaus.

Garrett zoomed up and under him. He streamed bullets toward the gas tank. Death barrel-rolled out of the firing line. In a moment, they were flying side by side. Jed turned toward Death.

The murder monk rose quickly to avoid collision. Once again Babyface shot lead into the gas tank. Click whined happily.

Presently a happy sight greeted Babyface's sore eyes. The black ship burst into flame.

Mr. Death—one of the few men in the war who always wore a parachute—leapt out. The silk cloth that he himself had designed, opened up. The black robes flapped about him wildly.

Jed Garrett began following Death downward, but at that time, the pursuit Fokkers shot out from their lines and surrounded the avenging Yank. Jed raced on toward the Allies' trenches, skimming close to earth.

The Spad's wheels touched the earth; then, in the next moment, they caught in a shell hole. The plane turned over and caught fire.

Babyface squeezed himself out of the cockpit. Frantically, he unleashed Click and lifted him to safety. Then he crawled on his stomach, away from the hungry flames.

His eyes searched the blotch of land for Mr. Death. He stared upward and saw the Fokkers lifting back into the sky ..to meet an attack of the Yank Dawn patrol.

Babyface searched again to catch sight of the illusive monk. At last he spotted him, hopelessly caught in German barbed wire. He started racing toward him.

Tac . . tac . . tac . . tac . . tac.

Babyface, holding Click, fell to his stomach. A German machine gun was cracking at him. The men in the trenches had been stirred into action by the drama that had just taken place before their eyes. Allied soldiers returned the fire of the machine gun.

Jed Garrett and Mr. Death were both caught in a cross-fire between trenches! Babyface crawled forward to a jagged hole and tumbled in.

Machine gun bullets hummed over his head. The whine of rifles snapped from the lines. A grenade dropped within fifty feet and sprayed dirt over Babyface.

"Hell of a war, isn't it, Click?"

Tac . . tac , . tac . . tac . . tac.

Babyface peered upward and saw Mr. Death struggling to free himself from the barbed wire. The steel plates that covered the robed figure's chest and back would enable him to stand a lot of shots that Garrett could never take—but he couldn't stand one through the head!

Suddenly an idea struck Jed. He brought out his automatic. His lips in a thin line, his burning eyes straight on the monk of horror, not a hundred yards away from him, he took aim.

"Dead or alive . . ." the general had said. He fired. The shot missed.

Tac . . tac . . tac . . tac . . tac.

The machine gun bullets ripped dirt off the edge of the hole. He crouched down. After a few moments he risked taking aim at Mr. Death again.

Suddenly there was a gigantic roar as everything seemed to explode at once. A grenade had landed so close to them, that for a moment, Babyface thought he was being blown into hell. Then darkness engulfed him mercifully.

Click moved closer, whining. He licked Jed Garrett's face, but the Yank ace did not move.

Babyface Garrett came to in a hospital bed with Click lying at his feet. The first thing he became conscious of was the beaming face of the general.

"You're cleared—cleared plenty! After the performance you made—rushing right over after Mr. Death. We owe you an apology! An agent in German lines sent over by myself after you came back, investigated and made the report that an actor named von Elt had impersonated you. . . ."

Jed Garrett's eyes flickered. "Yes sir, that's fine," he moved his arm, "but—but what about Mr. Death?"

"You did damn well," the general answered evasively. "I'm sorry to say that in order to get you back we had to make a treaty with the Germans that they could take Mr. Death from the barbed wire if we could come and get you."

"Foolish, sir," Babyface murmured, "you should have killed him . . . hell with me. . .

"What do you mean?" the general barked. "You're one of the foremost agents we have, Major Garrett!"

"Major?"

"That's right—from now on you're a major with a roving commission—assistant in charge of G-2. You'll get your new buttons as soon as you get up!"

Babyface relaxed. He was thankful for his promotion, but he was disappointed that the monk of murder had not been killed.

Back behind German lines the hideous face of Mr. Death, cloaked in the filthy black robes he always wore, twitched cruelly. The huge blotch-eyes stared down at something on his laboratory desk. He rubbed his bony hands together, chuckling hoarsely.

"Next time—" he said, significantly.

The Brand of Death

Hideous and heartless, an avenger whose veins run blood of ice, Mr. Death is again in the skies! His mission nobody knows—his challenge but one man dare accept! Major Jed Garrett is armed with his brains and his courage, yet these are but little things when pitted against the Murder Monster of the skies—skies that have given their human birds that a fiend's lust might be satisfied— skies that mourn and thunder in protest against this pitiless scourge called MR. DEATH!

The Brand
of Death

BARRY KELLY was only eighteen and had arrived from the pool just yesterday. But now that he was climbing into the Spad assigned to him for his first taste of gun fire, he was proud. Major Jed Garrett's smooth words of encouragement were still in his ears, and before him stood the six other Spads of the noon patrol. The other kids—seven in all—were envious that he was the first replacement to fly into enemy skies, and they stood on the edge of the tarmac now, their eyes upon him. Barry Kelly saw the leader's ship roll swiftly down the smooth course and lift into the air. The second ship followed in his wake. The kid adjusted the goggles over his eyes. His eager, trembling hands groped happily for the stick. He sucked in his breath, then tucked the good-luck scarf his mother had sent him, about his neck.

In a moment he was moving swiftly over the tarmac, waving to the fledglings left behind. Then he eased the stick back and lifted the red, white and blue marked wings gently into the air. The roar of the motor was sweet music in his ears. The blue of the sky thrilled him. He swung neatly into position, lifting higher and higher into the air.

Soon the drome was just a black speck on the reeling brown earth behind him, while the ship slid speedily on. The guy wires of the Spad hummed in the wind; the grim handle of his Vickers gun protruded just before him.

Beneath his goggles, Barry's wide gray eyes were sharp and observing. They had been the keenest eyes in the training school and he was proud of them. They were big eyes, alert, and bright with youth. The Yank Squadron swept droningly over No Man's Land. Barry looked down at the puff balls of Archies and a boyish laugh broke from his lips. His good-luck scarf was flapping in the wind now, and the fresh, crisp air that swept through the canvas of his wings was healthy and invigorating.

Suddenly he noticed the signal from the leader. His eyes scanned the horizon ahead and he saw the wedge-shaped group of Fokkers flying out to meet the Yank challenge. Barry eased down in the cockpit. His blood raced high with the thrill of anticipation. His lean fingers groped for the Vickers' handle.

In another moment the Fokkers were upon them, green, black and brown ships.

Spandaus lead screamed through the clear afternoon air.

Tac ... tac .. tac ... tac ... tac!

Barry Kelly's ship raced toward a nearby green Fokker. He pumped the guns, saw the Boche pilot wave a gloved hand, then twirl toward the earth, eaten by his own flames.

"One down!" Barry laughed. "What son of the Kaiser is next?"

But even as he shouted his words of victory into the wind, his gray eyes spotted a different sort of a ship hurtling through the sky lanes toward him. It was a black plane and it glinted like metal. Its pilot seemed garbed in flipping black rags.

Bravely, Barry plunged toward the oncoming ship. Then he suddenly saw the face of the pilot. A ghastly, bony white countenance, blotches for eyes, a grim, lip-less slit for a mouth. A cry of apprehension escaped him. Then came the splitting nails of the black ship's guns.

"Mr. Death!" Barry muttered.

Many tales of the grim flying monk of murder had reached the training school. Stories as ghastly as was the face of this skeleton pilot. How Major Babyface Garrett had been fighting him for two months; how he had been wrecking all of Mr. Death's hideous schemes of destruction to the Allies, and yet had never been able to capture successfully nor to kill Mr. Death.

Even as he pulled back on his Vickers, as the leaden pellets of doom barked from his flaming gun muzzles, Barry Kelly recalled the history of the Boche Monk of Murder. He had been in a monastery where he had retired after a successful career as a famous Berlin chemist and inventor. The monastery had been bombed and Mr. Death had been dragged out. The only way they could save him was to baste steel plates over his chest and back. Now his face was a horrible mess. The disaster seemed to steal away his soul, so that now he was less a man than a living monster. Allied bombs had brought this horrible fate—and now Death was determined that Allied blood should pay the price. Only Major Babyface Garrett had dared to block him and Mr. Death had sent over a warning that he would kill Babyface. Babyface's orders were, on the other hand, to kill Mr. Death!

And now Barry Kelly, a fledgling on his first flight, was facing the most horrible menace of the war!

Tac . . . tac . . . tac . . . tac . . . tac . . .

He saw part of his right wing tear away and shreds of the canvas scream in the wind. Hot steam slipped from his fuselage and whipped back into his face. He gripped his Vickers gun, tried to pour damaging tracer streams into the monster's metal plane. It all seemed useless. His bullets flattened along the side of the ship, leaving only dents. Mr. Death seemed to have singled him out and he drove on toward him, surely, inexorably.

Barry weaved back and forth in his cockpit. He felt the Spad losing altitude. Grimly, madly, he jerked on the Vickers handle.

Tac . . . tac ... tac ... tac ... tac . . .

Now his other wing was dropping away and his plane was beginning to spin. He looked down and saw the earth rushing up to meet him. Frantically, he jerked back on his stick, tried to straighten the wrecked ship out. His throat was dry and burning. His gray eyes were livid.

Death. He was plunging to his death. It wasn't fair. They hadn't given him a chance to fight.

Then, all of a sudden, he pulled the Spad level. He skimmed over the top of trees and miraculously made a smooth landing on a little clearing below. He cut the motor, whipped off his goggles. He sucked in his breath.

In the next moment his eyes almost popped from his head. For shooting closely over the top-most branches of the trees was the shimmering black metal of Mr. Death's ship. He saw it bank down, then bump to the ground almost beside him. At the same time, Boche gunners appeared from the thicket of trees. Barry Kelly was surrounded.

His body frozen and numb, he simply stared as Mr. Death climbed from his ship. He saw the hideous scar of a face without expression—the blotches of Death's huge, hypnotic eyes were upon him—the mouth, without lips, pulled grimly taut. Death's head was hairless and his robes swept across the ground as he walked. He was a living figure of terror!

"My aim was good," he said, "I did not want to kill you."

Barry's tongue seemed glued to the top of his mouth. He wet his lips and felt his throat. His fingers felt through the silk of his good-luck scarf and he smiled grimly, mirthlessly.

"So you—you planned to capture me like this, Mr. Death?"

"You are the new flyer from the 27th, are you not?" the monk of murder asked, folding his black-robed arms over his chest.

Had Barry thought twice he would have denied the truth that he was a fledgling, but he was excited, feverish.

"Sure, I'm new. Eighteen years old and that was my first taste of gun fire. Aren't you proud that you downed me? Big shot ace, eh?" He laughed harshly. "I heard a lot about you all right, but now I know you're nothing but a lousy coward. A stinking, rotten, yellow-bellied skeleton. You didn't want to fight the aces, did you? You had to land on me!"

Mr. Death strode slowly toward the cockpit, his bony white face set in a mask of bitter contempt.

"I downed you purposely," he said in brittle, short-clipped words. "Your fledgling friends will be waiting for you to come back. Well, you'll go back all right, Yank pup. You'll go back to tell them about your visit—a visit they'll make, too, if they ever take the air!"

Barry shrunk in his seat. Mr. Death was so close now that he thought he smelled a peculiar acrid odor about his clothing. He loathed the sight of the black garments.

"Send me back, hell—kill me, or throw me in the putrid war jails—I lost and I'll take my lot!"

"You'll take your lot," Mr. Death said evenly, "but it will be more than you expected!"

Barry stared curiously as the hideous monk of murder laughed—a dry, burned-out laughter.

Major Jed Garrett drummed his fingers on the old mahogany desk in the C.O.'s shack of the 27th. His babyish face was twisted into a deep, thoughtful scowl, and his eyes were brimming with hatred. At the major's feet sat the huge, beautiful brown police dog which was famous up and down the front lines as Garrett's flying companion.

Jed Garrett and his dog Click had been together in days before the war when they stunted for the anxious crowds. They had piled in the cash hand over fist. When the war came it was a natural for them, and Jed enlisted with the special understanding that wherever he went Click accompanied him. There had been some fuss at first, but good pilots were few and G.H.Q. had finally given him a roving commission. In the months that passed he went from second lieutenant to first, and then to captain. A week ago he had been commissioned major. His new duties were command of the 27th, plus an order to "Kill Mr. Death," so that his mission in the war was two-fold.

Jed Garrett was twenty-five, but his youthful face had given him the nickname of "Babyface." He looked at the thin-cheeked lieutenant adjutant who stood before him now.

"Four came back from that patrol, eh? That's all right." His fists tightened. "But what has me furious is that Mr. Death should fly in, and of all the pilots, to pick one, knock little Barry Kelly out of the air. That's going to give the other fledglings a good scare. I was hoping especially that Barry would come back today."

"He was a good kid, sir," the adjutant said, "a lot of us hoped he would return."

Babyface Garrett's eyes dropped a little and he stared absently across the desk. "He was wearing a scarf his mother gave him. Said it was good luck and that he couldn't fail so long as he wore it."

The adjutant stood patiently by, his fingers working in and out nervously.

Babyface looked up. "You may go."

"Thank you, sir."

When he had departed, Garrett looked at Click; he reached down and petted the dog's head.

"Mr. Death's been pretty quiet for a week or so," he said, "I wonder what he's going to pull on us next, boy?" He was silent for a minute. The dog looked up, his brown eyes affectionate. His ears were sharp and straight. "We'll have to go out scouting for him again soon," Babyface went on reflectively. "By God, Click, some day I'm going to tear those steel plates right off that—"

The adjutant rushed back into the room, his face livid. "Barry Kelly's come back! He walked back!"

"What?"

"Barry—he's in front of the canteen! You'd better come out and see him, sir!"

Babyface leaped to his feet and strode out of the office. Click padded squarely behind his master's booted heels. They swept into the night air. Garrett broke into a run toward the canteen. There was a large crowd around Barry Kelly. Most of them were the fledglings who hadn't yet gone up into the fire of Spandaus lead.

Someone called "attention" as Babyface elbowed his way through. The men stood back. Major Garrett stopped dead in his tracks and stared. Sweat cropped out on his brow and trickled down his face. A chill raced up his spine.

The husky eighteen year old pilot stood before him, his trembling hands groping blindly. In the places where his large gray eyes had been, there were now only gaping sockets. Burned-out holes in his face. Stamped in searing red scars on his forehead was a hideous skull and bones, and the livid letters:

"The Brand of Death!"

For a moment Babyface Garrett could not move. He felt something hot in his throat, choking him. He was unashamed of a tear that dropped across his cheek. He saw the floundering, blind fledgling come toward him. Saw the ragged remains of the silk scarf his mother had made for him—his "good-luck" scarf!

A fledgling behind Babyface screamed and suddenly fainted away.

"Kid," Babyface stuttered, grasping the pilot's arms and holding him. "Barry Kelly—you poor kid!"

"I want to go home," Barry said tremulously, "home to my folks, major." His white fingers held the ragged ends of the silk scarf. "Tell me, is this torn badly?"

"No, not badly," Babyface said in a strained, far-away voice. "Not badly at all."

THE General's face was white, and his eyes were staring as if he had suddenly seen too much of the war, too many unspeakable horrors.

Babyface Garrett sat at his desk, pounding an empty cordial pony on the top of it.

"Your visit here is warranted, sir, as you have already seen. Mr. Death is striking in another, a more vital way. Dying, you can, after all, account for. There is a shred of glory left in it—of going West and fighting like Almighty Hell. The kids aren't afraid to go up and face Spandaus bullets. They'll take their chances with the next one at fighting Fokkers, and being burned down—of having their bodies scorched to a crisp. But when they see one of their buddies come back with holes where his eyes once were—"

He tremblingly poured himself another drink and gulped it down.

"You see, sir, the whole idea is to break the morale of the kids moving up from the schools. To whip our air force before our planes can even get off the ground. At the very sight of Mr. Death's ship now, they'll turn tail and run for their lives. It's not because they're cowards, but because they'll see the picture of Barry Kelly—see that and nothing else. There's a difference between cowardice and foolishness. It would be foolish for a fledgling to try and combat a metal plane flown by an ace like Death. They have every right to turn back. Unless something is done, in another month, our green pilots from the school will be a corps of shattered nerves—a useless bunch of kids who'll be too scared to climb into a plane!"

The General finally caught his breath. He looked squarely at Babyface.

"There's one answer," he said slowly.

Major Garrett rose to his feet. Click, who had been crouching on the floor, got up also. Babyface reached back into his locker and drew out his leather jacket which he quickly put on. He gripped his goggles and helmet in his hand.

"You're right, general, there's only one answer."

The superior moved forward. "Garrett," he said, "don't you come back with that mark, and your eyes burned out. If seeing a fledgling like that affects the men so, what do you think the sight of one of our aces—such as yourself—would do? It would not only weaken the recruits, but the other aces as well, I—"

"If they brand me," Babyface said evenly, "I won't be back. Good evening, general."

He left the office, Click trotting behind him. He sucked in the cool night air, then headed toward the tarmac. A mechanic was warming up the plane that he had ordered out. He reached it, and putting Click up in his special place, climbed in.

"Contact!"

The Spad rolled swiftly over the tarmac and lifted into the air.

He flew over the crimson-lighted fields of No Man's Land, and headed into the star-streaked heavens of enemy territory. He knew that as dangerous as it might be, he had to get Mr. Death tonight—had to bring him back, dead or alive. It was the only thing that would save the morale of the Yank air corps.

He knew from previous engagements with the monk of murder where his headquarters lay. Babyface knew he would probably not return alive, but he had to take the chance. Perhaps Mr. Death would not be expecting him tonight. That would help some.

Jed Garrett thundered on, while Click lay huddled in his place, blinking through his specially made little goggles, his sharp ears whipped back in the wind.

Babyface arrived at the forest just ahead of the dromes and head-quarters village housing Mr. Death. Circling once over the dark ground, he glided to a smooth landing. He cut the motor and stared about him. The trees were like tall, silent sentries. Babyface leaped from the plane, unhooking Click as he did so. Thus far, his approach was undetected.

They crept forward through the trees and edged close to the out-skirts of the villa. Babyface's smooth countenance was hard. His thin lips were tight as he glanced at the dimly lighted huts, the three huge dromes, and the solid block of official offices. On the other side of the village, apart from the offices, there was a long shed-like shack.

"Come along, boy," Babyface whispered.

The dog trotted a little ahead of him as he wound his way clear of guards and sentries and drew near the experimental laboratory of Mr. Death. Here he waited and drew in his breath. Then, taking a chance, he lifted his automatic. A guard stationed outside of the laboratory spotted him and leveled his rifle.

Babyface fired. A spurt of orange cracked in the night air. The guard crumpled. Garrett raced forward with Click barking at his heels. He threw his weight against the door of the laboratory. It gave.

Plunging inside, he found darkness. Quickly, he reached for the lights. They came on with a rush of illumination. Babyface Garrett saw Mr. Death rolling from a cot on which he had been sleeping. Behind the cot was the long table of bottles and test tubes, and the cold branding iron.

"Don't try to move!" Babyface rasped. "I'll send a slug through your head!"

Mr. Death rose to his feet. His black robes clung to his body, his blotch-eyes blinked sleepily, then hatred welled in them. His slit-mouth was curled back.

"So you—"

"The very unexpectedness of this attack," Babyface snapped, "the daring of intruding into your territory, and the speed in which I have done it, catches you in a moment when you're off guard, Death. And that moment is going to cost you your rotten life!"

The monk stared with hypnotic eyes. Babyface laughed.

"You can't put me in a trance—you ought to know that by now!"

"Swaggering swine," Death cursed, "in all our dealings, you have, for the first time, the upper hand."

"Never mind the lip sputtering," Babyface growled. "The shot I used will attract other guards. Get going—out of this shack. And if you don't move fast, I'm going to kill you. Go on, Death, get ahead of me. Remember I have this automatic leveled right at your neck."

Words and threats did not have to be wasted between these two. Their pledged hatred for one another was sufficient. Mr. Death realized that if there was anyone in the American, or for that matter, the Allied forces who could come near besting him, it was Major Babyface Garrett. He knew that Babyface would shoot and do it gladly. He had been taken by surprise and he was willing to admit his error. Staying alive was his only hope for making a break in the future.

He walked out through the door. Babyface saw Boches running from the villa toward the laboratory. He could spot only their silhouetted shadows, but he aimed his gun and clipped off two of them. Then he prodded his fist into the steel plate covering Mr. Death's back.

"Snap now—this way, and make it fast!"

They rushed along through the trees. Babyface was exultant. The horrible, black-robed priest of horror was at last at his mercy! So simple, it had been, after their bloody conflicts of the past!

They made a grotesque picture rushing through the forest toward the Spad. Babyface holding the gun level with the monk's neck, and Click rushing madly ahead, breaking twigs with his sure, four-footed steps.

They reached the Spad. Mercilessly, Babyface brought the butt of his weapon down on Mr. Death's head. The monk spun about, the crimson flowing down over his face. His mouth was open, his blotch-eyes horrible.

"You—you tricked me—"

"I haven't any rope, and if I'm to carry you, you must be unconscious," Jed yelled. With that he lashed again at Death's forehead. He saw with burning eyes, the figure in black robes sink before him.

Quickly then, he lifted his bulky weight and managed to throw it over the body of the plane. He tore his strap from the cockpit and made Mr. Death fast. Then he climbed into the plane. Click leaped up to his place. Babyface managed to get the motor roaring after one or two unsuccessful ventures back and forth between the prop and the cockpit.

He glanced back, saw the still form of the murder monk strapped to the body of the ship. Then he taxied forward and lifted into the air.

MR. DEATH opened his blotch-eyes as soon as the Spad was in the air. What Babyface Garrett did not know was that he was able to withstand thrice the blows of an ordinary man. It was this power which had allowed him to live through the monastery explosion while the others were torn to shreds. Realizing that Babyface would keep slugging him until he was unconscious, Death had faked it. He stared now at the American pilot's neck and at the dog crouched behind him. A thin, ugly grin creased his slit-mouth. He felt his own black robes sweeping about his body.

Looking down he saw the blackness of the earth below. Even for him, a fall would mean certain death. It was unfortunate that the stupid guard outside his laboratory had allowed Babyface to get in while he slept, for Mr. Death did not have a gun. He thought vainly of his parachute—the one in his metal ship. He had nothing now to break his fall if he slipped off the plane. Yet he knew he was going to have to capture Babyface while he flew —before he could get behind Allied lines!

The wind screaming about him, his ghastly bone of a face set in an expression of hatred, he silently oathed that he would wreak a vengeance worse than death on Babyface—a vengeance he owed him for past interference with his plans. He despised the American's courage, and had utter contempt for his wits.

Mr. Death unhooked the strap that held him to the body of the Spad, crawled forward an inch, then two. His robes were still flapping and whipping about his face. His blotch-eyes were steady, watching the movement of Babyface.

Once, when Garrett turned about, Death closed his eyes. But as soon as Babyface returned his attention to the controls, Death crawled forward again. He kept looking down at the distant dark cover of trees and German dromes. One little slip, one false movement, and he would be plunging down to smash like jelly on the ground!

Breathlessly, Mr. Death moved forward. His bony face was set toward the American pilot. It took four minutes—four minutes of daring movement, of hanging, agonized, to the flimsy carriage of the ship. But at last he was nearing the cockpit.

The prop spun like a cyclone wind. The guy wires in the wings flapped and hummed. A tiny spurt of water escaped the slip-stream of the fuselage. The canvas fluttered in the changing winds. Click moved uneasily, his shaggy head turning back towards Mr. Death.

Death wrapped one bony arm about the dog's neck and choked him. Click could not howl, could not move. Holding to the plane with one hand, the fingers of his other shut off Click's wind pipe. He pressed without mercy, his hideous face twisted in a scowl. The dog went limp.

Mr. Death squeezed his knee into the small place where Click lay. He grasped the edge of the plane. He was ready now. He had to let go with both hands and throttle Babyface Garrett. Had to take a chance of tumbling five thousand feet to the ground. But it was his only opportunity to escape!

Wind screaming! Prop whirling! Wires humming! Mr. Death braced himself, stood half erect. His black robes wrapped tightly about his huge body. His slit-mouth was straight! His blotch-eyes horrible!

He struck! His fingers entwined Babyface's neck. He slipped half of his body into the cockpit, one leg hanging over the side of the ship. Quickly, while Babyface struggled with the controls, he jerked the automatic from Garrett's holster.

"Circle—land!" Death yelled above the roar.

Face white, Babyface Garrett cursed desperately. "Go to hell!" he answered.

"You—"

"We'll land all right," Garrett blurted, "both of us, Death!"

He plunged the plane into a nose dive. Mr. Death slammed the automatic across Babyface's head with terrific power. But even as Babyface slumped, let loose of the stick, Death had reached the controls. He jerked the Spad upright and leveled it off. In another moment he was coming close to the ground, skimming over tree tops.

The wheels touched bumpy ground and the plane skidded to a stop.

The monk of murder laughed a ringing, triumphant laughter. He climbed from the plane, dragging Babyface Garrett after him. He let the unconscious American fall to the ground, then dug his booted foot into his side. He glanced at the still form of the dog in the plane.

He leaned his robed figure down and picked Major Jed Garrett up. He carried him several feet from the plane, then returned. His blotch-eyes were on Click. He saw the dog move his legs. Consciousness was returning.

"Click, they call you," he hissed, at the animal. "You'll get your hell right now!"

He struck a match and threw it across the canvas wing. A small flame spurted and flickered red against the dark night. Presently it leaped in size, began consuming the Spad. Click wriggled, uncomfortable in the heat, yet not sufficient awakened to realize the situation.

In another minute the plane was roaring inferno of flames. The furry figure of Click struggled to get free.

But now Mr. Death was walking through the thicket, the silhouette of his black robes dancing against the light of the burning Spad. On the monk's shoulder was the unconscious form of Major Babyface Garrett!

His voice was hollow, like that of a corpse, but at the same time it had a grating ring that could not be mistaken to mean that anything but torture was to come. It was this—Mr. Death's voice— that Babyface Jed Garrett was first conscious of. He heard it even before he opened his eyes, even before he felt the pressure of cords about his wrists, and the solidity of the wall to which he was strapped, legs and body.

"You'll recognize this place when you open your eyes, Garrett. It's my laboratory where I was sleeping, until you came over, meddling again, and looking for trouble. You're going to get worse than trouble this time!"

Babyface opened his eyes. His vision was dim, but he saw the grim, awful face before him. He saw the black robes of the monk of murder. Behind him there was something burning. Then he saw what it was. The branding iron was being heated. It was already red hot!

A dim light burned in the laboratory and it cast little shadows over the bottles, tubes and tools with which Death made his devices of destruction against the Allies. The floor was covered with threadbare black rug. An open window behind Death blew in a breeze which bathed Jed's blood-caked face.

He struggled hopelessly for a moment with the cords that held him. They were tight, cutting his blood circulation. His head throbbed with pain. Again his eyes fell upon Mr. Death. His thin lips twisted.

"Where is Click?"

"In a better place than you're going to be," Death barked shrilly.

"You mean he's dead?"

"Burned in your plane!"

"You—you did that? I hardly think it was necessary. After all, it's me you want to hurt!"

"You're sorry he's dead, aren't you?"

"Yes," Babyface gasped, "but—"

"That's why I did it!"

Words caught in Jed Garrett's throat, stiffened, and slid out unspoken. His countenance became as tight as a drum, his eyes drilling, steely optics of chilled resentment. The color left his cheeks. His heart pumped faster, harder against his side.

Mr. Death's blotch-eyes turned and took in the sizzling branding iron, now glowing red hot in the oil stove. He faced Garrett again, his slit-mouth firm.

"Did you like that boy I sent back to you?"

"That's another thing that isn't decent in war," Babyface spat. "You might better kill him than to send him back to the States scarred, burned with your brand, you—"

Mr. Death chuckled. "Your consternation does me good, Garrett. I blinded and branded that pilot to break the morale of your school graduates. You probably guessed that. It had not occurred to me to capture you and return you in the same condition, but since you've played right into my hands—"

"You can brand me," Babyface snapped, "but you can't make me return!"

"Can't I?"

"No. I'd kill myself before I'd go back and let those kids see their major—"

"With my skull and cross bones on his forehead, eh?" Death interrupted brittily. "Well, you won't have a chance to kill yourself until you are safely delivered to your drome. They'll see you before you have a chance to do it!"

"You filthy pig—!" Jed Garrett oathed, suddenly losing his self-control.

"Take a good look at me," Death taunted meanly, "—at my robes, and my straight fine body and my ugly face. You won't see me again, Garrett. You won't ever see anybody again—the sunshine, flowers, planes—not anything!"

A shudder shook Major Jed Garrett; it was a shudder that tingled down his spine, made sweat break out on his forehead and drench his leathery face. He knew that nothing would stop Mr. Death in his scheme to brand his head and burn out his eyes!

The robed figure turned about. He grasped the wooden handle of the branding iron and turned it over. Babyface's feverish eyes were on the searing, red-hot metal. He thought bitterly of Click.

Neither Babyface nor Mr. Death had seen the dog crawl out of the burning plane and lie panting, a safe distance from it. Nor could either of them now know that Click, following the scent of his master and Mr. Death, was at this moment running through the forest to reach Babyface's side.

Grimly, Jed Garrett struggled with his cord. He stared down in front of him. There was a tight piece about his waist— if that were off he might be able to get his arm free. But it was not off. Sweat drenching him, his face white, he stared at the monk.

Mr. Death waited a moment for the iron to heat on the other side. He moved to his bench and picked up a long handled prong which he also placed in the fire.

"That is for your eyes," he said slowly, "—the eyes come last. That is the most horrible and it will give me the greatest delight. Jamming the blunt end of that prong into your eye ball, and listening to the sucking, sizzling sound as the eye is burned out. It doesn't bleed, you know, because the intensity of the heat sews up the wound—melts it together!"

Jed Garrett squirmed in his bonds. He felt his heart crashing against his side. His tongue was like a heavy leaden thing. His eyes were on the steady little blue flame of the heater, and the two bulky pieces of iron which were in it.

"Your fledgling flyer screamed his lungs out," Death went on solemnly. "He screamed for his mother. Tried to break loose from the bonds. He didn't like it very much. He cried and begged for mercy!"

A low laugh escaped the monk.

"I recognized you as a terrible enemy to the Allies," Babyface muttered brokenly, "but I didn't know you were a fiend, Death. Didn't know—"

Death laughed hideously. "It is only my revenge—for this—" he clawed at his explosion-wrecked face. "This ugly, unrecognizable mass of living scars that I must call a face!" His blotch-eyes blazed. "I am but evening a score. That is why it will do me good to hear you scream out your lungs, Yankee swine!"

He had been incensed and he was savage now, not unlike a ghastly black-clothed beast. He turned angrily toward the oil flame, jerking out the branding iron on which the skull and bones, and the words: "The Brand of Death."

The iron was almost white in its heat now. The dim electric light illuminated Mr. Death's contorted bone of a face, his gruesome slit mouth, and his grotesque bald head. He lifted the iron.

"On your forehead, Major Garrett. My brand. You shall carry it with you for life!"

Babyface's face was glistening with sweat. His lips were a thin, tight line. His eyes were as hard as ebony. His nose, straight, his nostrils quivering, were somehow defiant.

"Brand and be damned, you stinking dog!"

"Oaths cannot touch me as this iron will touch you," Death lipped harshly.

He drew closer with the iron. Babyface's glaring eyes were upon it. He saw the blistering heat in the end of it—saw it come within six inches of him!

Mr. Death was sucking in deep, husky breaths. His slit-mouth was pulled down, his blotch-eyes boiling.

"Another half second—"

He came within an inch. Babyface felt his skin beginning to curl beneath the intense heat in the iron. He struggled to break loose from his cords. His wrists were almost free. If only that cord around his waist were off.

"Here it comes!" Mr. Death screamed, "and may it scorch your soul into hell Babyface Garrett!"

Babyface writhed frantically. Winced. Tried to duck. The branding iron was coming at him!

A bundle of bristling brown fur careened through the open window with a wild howl. In the next moment Click was digging his white teeth into Mr. Death's neck!

The iron fell, lowered. The burning brand seared through the cord around Babyface's waist. In a wild jerk, Jed freed himself and slid out from the position he had been in. He slammed his fist into Mr. Death's face, then leaning down, quickly unbound his legs.

The iron fell to the floor. Babyface kicked it back beneath the laboratory bench. Mr. Death hurled Click from him and the police dog went sailing to the corner of the room. He rose quickly, however, limping. Baring his even white teeth, he prepared to leap.

Mr. Death grabbed up a Luger and aimed it. Babyface crashed the gun from the monk's hand. At the same time Click leaped, digging his teeth into Death's throat. Blood spurted in a wild stream!

Again Death threw off the dog. He stumbled to the other end of the laboratory and jerked down on a cord. A screaming siren started booming from outside the place. Death turned about, his hideous white face contorted, mad.

"Damn your begging, putrid hide, Garrett. I'll see you and that dog in hell!"

"You aren't going to see anybody else in hell," Babyface shouted. "I'm putting a bullet through your head. No capture this time. I'll bring back a corpse!"

The shrieking siren was wailing into the night air, bringing the dromes, the official offices, the sentries and guards into action.

Babyface pressed the trigger of the Luger. Mr. Death moved like a streak of lightning from its mark. Babyface swung the gun around and fired again. He heard the bullet clank into Death's steel-plated breast. Without hesitation, he jerked the trigger for the third time!

He had creased Death's head!

He cried out happily, and fired again. But he missed. Mr. Death had reached the far wall, was jerking down a lever. A trap door swung open. His robed-figure disappeared!

Babyface tossed the gun aside—it was empty. "Click!" he called.

The dog came to him. Babyface peered outside. He saw many dark figures rushing for the laboratory.

"There's just a bare second to escape, Click!"

Quickly, they dashed in the opposite direction. Through the brush and around the trees they went. Major Garrett heard the cries of Germans on the trail after them. At last he leaped for the low branch of a tree. He called Click. The dog backed, then ran and leaped up to where Babyface caught him. Babyface swung himself to a higher branch. Here, holding Click in one trembling arm, clinging to the tree with the other, he silently watched the Huns passing beneath him.

The escape had been one of Babyface's narrowest. He clutched the dog close.

"You saved my life, old fellow," he whispered. "You haven't got a nose for the trail for nothing, have you?"

The dog whined.

"Later on," Babyface mumbled, half to himself, half to the dog, "we're going to come down out of this tree and get ourselves a plane— then we're going to get Mr. Death. And we're going to kill him!"

Click growled—almost assuringly.

FREDERICK
BLAKESLEE

Death's Screaming Wings

The sky is weeping with the blood of those about to die; and trembling with the horror of the fiend whose wings it must support! Mr. Death returns!—returns with the lust that has made him what he is—a black robed Satan who feeds on the pain and the misery of the human flesh. Yet even he cannot go on unchallenged. For there are men in this War—men whose spirits carry on!—though their bodies lie cold in the silent grave.

Death's Screaming Wings

CHAPTER ONE
The Wrath of Death

HE WAS STRAPPED to the wall, and his hand was in a vise. The knife that was going to slash off his thumb was within an inch of his skin. But he wasn't going to talk—Bill Carter was a Yank! Yet, he could not help but feel a sickening horror rise up within him. His heart was beating madly; his burning eyes were on the knife.

For a flickering second, Bill stared at Mr. Death. With a shudder he regarded the horrible face of the Boche. He saw the contorted expression of hatred in that bony countenance, and he saw too, the gleaming cunning, the ruthless brutality in Mr. Death's blotch-eyes.

In the next moment Bill Carter's eyes were on the knife again. Suddenly he drew in, clamped his mouth shut tight, and closed his eyes in blinding pain. When he looked down again he saw hot blood spurting over him. There was a throbbing numbness in his hand. His severed thumb had fallen to the floor!

The blood splashed across the filthy black robes worn by Mr. Death, but the ghastly genius of murder did not seem to mind. He coolly wrapped a rag about Bill's hand to check the flow of blood.

Then he stepped back, wiped the knife with his grimy hand and laughed.

"You will soon learn, Carter," he said in a crisp, brittle voice, "that I mean business."

The American pilot stared at Death. He knew the story behind those monk robes, and more than that, he knew the gruesome history of Mr. Death in the war. It only made Carter more determined to allow himself to be slashed to pieces before he revealed the plans of the Allies. They were plans that meant the winning or losing of the war.

Bill shook his head. "It's useless. I mean business too, Mr. Death— else I would have preserved my thumb by talking. You'll have to get what information you can from your spies."

Mr. Death threw the knife to a table. It was a table covered with devious instruments used by men of science. There were siphons, bowls, test tubes, intricate little machines. All of them had been designed to manufacture death. The ugly, deformed creature who now wore the blood-soaked robes had once been a man outstanding for his scientific discoveries. Berlin had hailed him, the world had saluted his genius. Then, for reasons unknown to all, he had suddenly given up scientific research, inventions, and all work of the outside world and had entered a lonely monastery. Years had passed, and the world which had cheered the cunning of his brain forgot him and gave their cheers to others. Alone, working in singular oblivion, he had perhaps found solace.

Men could only guess why he gave up his position in Berlin. A German physician had claimed that the scientist, through the feverish strain of working, had been slowly losing his mind. After which he sought peace in the monastery.

But everyone knew what happened after that. The war had come. The Allies had, through error, or otherwise, blown up the monastery. Almost all of the monks within were immediately killed. But Mr. Death was dragged out—his skin torn from his body, his face a mass of blood and bones. An immediate operation had been performed. Steel plates—which he still wore —were laid across his chest and back. His face was patched as well as anyone could patch it—but still it resembled the face of some hideous Frankenstein. Able to walk again, the explosion-wrecked monk pledged himself once more to science—this time the science of killing! He joined the German air force, a master commander. His fiendish inventions had almost whipped the Allies.

Death turned. "My spies," he said bitterly, "have for the most part been captured and shot down like dogs. The Allies have a scheme which they are putting into use almost immediately. I want to know what it is, Carter. And I'm going to find out—even if I have to pull you apart piece by piece!"

There was harsh fury in the cold words of the monk. He walked the length of his laboratory, returned with a cold branding iron, then discarded it.

Bill Carter watched. He could not keep from speaking the words that forced themselves into his mouth.

"Know why your spies were captured? Know why you haven't any information this time? Major Babyface Garrett learned every source of information you had the last time he was here. He stole papers listing the names of every spy in your employ. He—"

Death spat a shrill oath, and leaping across the room, picked up his knife. He slashed a deep wound across Bill's cheek. Then he stepped back.

"Garrett," he breathed, his steel-plated breast rising and falling.

Bill Carter knew the reason. There had been only one man among the Allies who had proven a match for Mr. Death—that was Major Jed Garrett, a G-2 pilot especially assigned to "get Mr. Death." Garrett traveled fearlessly back and forth over the lines. He had met Death in hand to hand conflict half a dozen times. Garrett had pledged himself to kill Mr. Death; Mr. Death had pledged himself to kill Jed Garrett. Thus it remained, a constant, burning hatred.

"This time," Death lipped, "I have an invention that will kill all of you!" He tore back a curtain, waved his bony hand outside the window. "See..."

There was a long, flat building still being erected by Boche carpenters.

"That is the top—a camouflage top to my new underground workshop. It will be explosion proof. And down there, I will make a powder that will destroy the Allies!"

"Bill's hand was paining him now. The numbness was wearing off, and the grim reality of being without his thumb shot through him. He gritted his teeth, yet the white of his face, the cords that stood out on his throat, gave clue to the agony he was suffering. Blood was seeping through the rag that Death had applied. It dripped the crimson life fluid of the captured Yank to the floor, made little puddles there.

"A powder that will destroy the Allies," he mumbled after Death. "Your latest invention, I suppose."

"And my greatest—one that your Major Garrett will not stop—"

"One that you hope Garrett will not stop!" Bill spat.

Mr. Death dropped the curtain over the window, turned back to the American. He was savage, fury pounded beneath the steel plates of his breast.

"One that I know will defeat him—and kill all Allied soldiers!" His slit-mouth twisted cunningly. "Perhaps you would like to know more about it,—know how simple it will be to put this powder into use. With the wind blowing in the direction of the Allied Front, I have but to release it from a balloon, five thousand feet in the sky. It will sweep back in ten million little particles—more deadly than gas because just one invisible little grain of it will kill a man—will eat through his clothing and his skin like radium, and work its way to his heart. Released from that altitude, it will spread for miles, carried by the wind. It will choke and stifle your American buddies, Carter. It will win the war for Germany!"

"I can well believe what you say is true," Bill grunted, "but Garrett will stop you before you have a chance—"

"Your childish confidence in Major Garrett is utterly ridiculous!" Death oathed. "He is but a lucky young fool who, traveling with his giant police dog, has blundered into my schemes and ruined them. But not this time—"

Bill writhed at his bonds. Mr. Death caught up his knife again, advanced.

"Are you going to talk now—tell me what the Allies have planned, or—"

Bill Carter laughed shrilly. "You think your plan is clever. The Allies' plan is perfect! It is the Boche Front that will be wiped out, Death!" He laughed again, almost hysterically. His eyes were on the knife that had slashed off his thumb.

Mr. Death grabbed Bill's little finger, raised the knife.

"Talk, Carter, or—"

"Go to hell!" Bill screamed.

At that moment there was a pounding on the laboratory door. Death turned, strode to it and swung it open. A tall German officer saluted.

"Thirty more bodies have just arrived," he said.

"Only thirty?" Death spat. "I want a thousand more before the sun sets!"

"We are doing all we can, Herr Death," the officer reported. "It is difficult to pick up corpses from No Man's Land."

Death meditated for a moment, while Bill Carter watched. The murder monk's hideous face twisted, his blotch-eyes seemed to look through the officer.

"Have you thought of having ghouls rob the Allied graves in Flanders?"

The tall Hun looked surprised, his face was a bit strained.

"But sir," he said, "there is a certain honor in war. Certain unwritten rules that the dead shall remain dead. That the dead shall be respected by both sides. It is a matter of human decency—"

Mr. Death broke in harshly. "Decency? Honor in war ?" He slapped his bony hand smartly across the officer's face. "You talk like a school boy, I tell you I want a thousand bodies before the sun sets. Get them for me. Rob the graves, if you must, but get them. If you report back without them, I shall see that your eyes are burned out, Herr Major!"

Trembling, the German saluted. He turned and made off.

Mr. Death slammed the door and turned back to the American prisoner.

"You're rotten," Bill Carter whispered, "worse than rotten, Death. You would rob the graves—"

Mr. Death grinned an awful, wolfish grin. "The powder I spoke to you about," he said, in a deep, brittle voice, "is made from the bones of human beings. The bones of men, Carter. Ground to a fine, fluffy substance. It is then mixed with another powerful solution of my own conception. The chemical reaction causes the powder to become deadly. Charges each little speck with the power to kill!"

Bill Carter shuddered.

Mr. Death picked up his knife again, strode towards Carter, reached his little finger and slashed down. Bill's hand throbbed violently. He cried out in pain.

"The next to come off," Mr. Death said, "will be your whole hand, cut from the wrist. Are you going to talk?"

Bill Carter was sobbing with the agony that racked his soul, but he managed to turn his burning eyes up into the bony face of the hideous monk. He managed to move his clay-like lips and to slide a word off them, a word that sounded hollow, and dead, and yet somehow had great strength. The word was "No!"

CHAPTER TWO
Suicide Squadron

THE BABYISH FACE of Major Jed Garrett was fresh. The hell-bent ace who commanded the 27th American drome, was hunched forward over his desk. A huge police dog lay at his feet. The pair were inseparable. They had flown in stunt planes before the war. Permission had been granted for them to fly together in the war.

A clicking tube on the desk in front of Major Garrett kept signaling, on and off. It was tapping out the Morse Code. The signals were coming from General Headquarters.

"*Calling all commanding officers. .*" it tapped, "*the big parade has begun. A thousand trucks loaded with men are underway from Marseilles. . All relieved battalions behind the lines are moving to the Front. . All air-dromes are keeping but a slim patrol in the skies. .*"

It went on like that. It had been going on like that all morning—Ever since the brazen sun had poked its head up over the horizon. Babyface, his dark eyes hard, his well-shaped jaw out a little, and his short-clipped black hair standing almost straight on his head, had been listening, waiting for the orders that were to come to him personally. He glanced down now at the dog.

"It's on, Click," he said in a tense voice, "the big push, old boy. The neat, final stroke that'll win us enough territory to cinch the war. A million men are moving forward—French, Italian, British, all the Allies, Click. ."

The dog was panting, his tongue sticking out, as though he were laughing at his master. He looked up, closed his mouth and moved his cold snoot into the cup of Jed Garrett's hand. Babyface patted him, then leaned back toward the clicking tube.

It continued:

"*. . The zero hour comes at one minute past midnight. The combined forces of the Allies will then sweep forward into enemy territory. . . A preliminary push will be made at high noon by the suicide squadron of the American army air force. . . Major Jed Garrett will plug in on telephone line Y to G.H.Q. at once.. Major Jed Garrett plug in at once. .*"

That was what he had been waiting for. Jed caught up the phone, thumbed down on the hook, waited.

"This is Marshall," a tense voice said.

"General Parry," Jed snapped, "this is the 27th, C.O. talking."

"Oh, Garrett, okay. Here's the line."

A moment later a gruff voice came on the wire. Jed could visualize the burly, gray-haired general as he spoke.

"This is what you wanted," General Parry said, "you're to command the suicide squadron."

"Very well, general."

"But remember—you are to return to our lines. We need you too badly to lose you. Keep in mind that you can do us more good alive than you can dead. Anyway—" he added with a chuckle, "—you can't die until you've wiped out Mr. Death. Those are orders!"

"But I'm to take the suicide squadron up," Babyface said, "what are the orders?"

"The planes will be loaded with dynamite," Parry answered quickly. "Dispatch one to each German drome. In the case where you can find two or three dromes together, have the pilot dive at the middle one. The load of dynamite will be enough to blast the three of them to hell. If you can make twelve good hits with the twelve suicide pilots I'm sending you, it should be enough to put a damned serious crimp in the Boche air front. That'll make the big push tonight a little easier."

"It's pretty tough on the Yanks—having to plunge their planes like that, and die in them." Babyface said.

"Of course it's tough. But they have volunteered—all twelve of them. They're good men, Garrett. They don't make 'em any finer. I'm sorry it has to be done this way, but you can see for yourself that it accomplishes far more than a hundred bombs would. One plane will have more damaging power than six squadrons of ordinary equipment!"

"I understand," Jed said dully.

"The idea is to do your work quickly, before they can send up planes to get you. A Fokker ripping her tracer lead into that dynamite would mean ruin. It would explode in the air,"

"All right," Jed said, "I'll do the best I can."

"I'm sending the men right now," General Parry went on, "treat them well. If this push of ours is a success—they will be the real heroes."

Babyface hung up the receiver. He was glad that he had been given the command of the suicide squadron, but it grieved him to see twelve American boys go out and so gallantly give up their lives, without hope, knowing they were going to their doom.

He rested his chin in his hands for a moment and stared at the dull polish on the desk. The clicking Morse Code of the tube was still drumming in his ears..

"*. . . French will buckle up on the left flank. . Expert machine gunners will be needed at center of drive. . Instruct men to pick off snipers in going through the Argonne forest. . All pilots not engaged in patrol will take this opportunity to rest for the night drive. . Plane mechanics will see that all ships are in good condition. . Five hundred German spies were shot at dawn this morning, news of this push has not yet reached Bocheland. . Four hundred trucks have stopped at La Poret for rations of food to the men.. Sixth regiment of marines just reported arrived in front line trenches. .*"

He could stand it no longer. Babyface rose to his feet and left the shack. Click trotted at his heels.

In the fresh morning air, the major sucked in his breath. The sky was blue and the sun was high overhead. The usual rumble of guns was quieter than he had ever remembered hearing it. The drome was glistening. The planes were on the tarmac, some of them being warmed by the mechanics.

And just a few yards away, there were trees; there was life. Wild flowers were growing, and fish were swimming in a stream of water that wound down through the war torn earth. Babyface headed in the opposite direction. He went into the bar.

The young, vivid-faced pilots were toasting the success of the forthcoming push. Someone called attention as Babyface entered. He eyed the men solemnly, looked into their eager faces, saw the worry-wrinkles about their eyes.

"Sop up all you want to drink for the next twenty minutes," he said, a little gruffly, "then make off to your bunks—all of you. You're going to have work tonight, and you'll need clear heads for it."

He went over and ordered a straight gin. The white-clad soldier who tended the bar leaned forward and grinned.

"Don't look like the war will last much longer, does it, sir?"

Babyface lifted his glance. The gin glass was between his fingers and he put it to his lips.

"Doesn't it?" he asked.

Suddenly the gin slipped from his hand and crashed to the floor. The bartender stared down. Babyface eyed him grimly.

"We're having the biggest drive in the war tonight," he said, "but remember that little incident, will you—that there is sometimes a slip between glass and lip!"

The door behind him crashed open. A messenger who had just arrived in a motorcycle, stepped in. He was very excited.

"The suicide squadron is arriving, sir! They were right behind me in two cars. Here are their orders."

The crowd of pilots became suddenly silent. Men moved back toward small tables, into corners. Babyface leaned back against the bar.

"Have them come in here," he said.

The messenger saluted. Babyface's body tightened, his face burned with a peculiar pain, and his heart was suddenly heavy. He watched the door, watched the men troop in through it. They looked tired, wan. But there was a certain gleam in their eyes that could not be mistaken. Some of them were captains, some majors, and others were second lieutenants. Their boots were all shined, as if they were going to a dance or a party, instead of to their deaths. They wore clean whip-cord trousers, and heavy brown tunics, with golden wings across the breast.

"Will you have a drink, men?" Jed Garrett asked in a steady tone, "I am sure that the 27th wishes to drink to all of you."

"Sure, we'll drink," a captain of the death squadron said.

Babyface turned about to the bartender. "Cocktails," he said, "Devil's hoof cocktails. And make them potent!"

It was a long, long time later, twenty minutes later to be exact, when the twelve pilots were climbing into their ships and the men of the 27th were standing about the tarmac, watching them with grave eyes. Jed Garrett climbed into the Spad at the head of the others, while a mechanic lifted Click to his regular place. The dog was now wearing a specially made pair of goggles which protected his eyes from the wind.

Major Garrett peered out over the side of the cockpit. Contact was established, his motor roared. He stared back at the grim faces in the other planes. Then, with a wave of his gloved hand, he suddenly throttled forward. The wheels of the trim Spad raced across the tarmac. The canvas wings lifted, the ship left the ground.

One by one the other planes slid across the smooth dirt and took off. The Yank pilots waved their last goodbye to mother earth. The dynamite loaded planes fell into position behind Jed Garrett's Spad.

Babyface was dividing his glances between the altitude panel, the stick, and the ground below. His motor was humming evenly, the taut wires on the wing were singing in the wind. Below, like a weave of brown and green, the earth slid by, and trees and dromes and flat fields all became a hazy mirage, apart from the cold world of the afternoon sky.

Babyface didn't like his job. He felt like a devil, taking these twelve men to their deaths, signaling them down to certain doom, one by one. But this was war, and he had his orders.

But back in Garrett's shack, the little tube tapping out the Morse Code continued, a little frantic now, slower then, and again frantic. The dots and dashes spelled out:

"Major Jed Garrett, 27th airdrome, change plans, reverse orders, get in touch with G.H.Q. A German spy cut in on your phone conversation with General Parry. He phoned Mr. Death, and was caught and killed in doing so. Mr. Death will take to the air and try to destroy our dynamite suicide planes. . Garrett, call G.H.Q. at once to change plans. . ."

But Jed Garrett and the twelve men on their way to hell, could not hear the warning back in the shack. They were already high over No Man's Land.

CHAPTER THREE
Black Wings from Hell

BABYFACE ROCKED back and forth in his cockpit. His hand reached down instinctively and he felt the steel of the stick, felt the security of the undercarriage beneath him. From behind the panes of his goggles he looked out over the horizon and saw a clear sky. The changing air currents rocked his wings up and down, sang through his taut guy wires and rustled ominously against the canvas sides of the ship. Beside him, Click moved his furry head, stuck his nose up in the wind. A mirror revealed the twelve planes of the suicide squadron in formation behind.

Everything looked beautifully clear, yet Jed Garrett sensed there was something wrong. A queer premonition of disaster racked his soul. It was as though he were suddenly afraid of something he could not see. He felt danger in the clearness of the sky, death in the mist of the hanging clouds. A feeling of horror hung over the plane.

The sun glistened against his wings as he banked to the left, then cut through the screaming wind to head towards the South. The other planes followed. Babyface stared at the ground, thousands of feet below. He saw that they were passing from the long, slim lines of trenches and were hurtling their airships into Boche territory. A thrill shot through him. So far they had come safely. They were passing now over clear brown fields.

He looked over the horizon again. He stared this time, rubbed specks of dust from his goggles. His blood froze in his veins. Not because he was afraid for himself, but because he knew that so much as a single charged bullet would explode one of the dynamite-loaded planes behind him. And on the horizon there was a ship. A long way behind it there were other ships. Fokkers.

For a moment Babyface did not know what to do. His lips tightened into a grim line, his face flushed hot. He could not make these twelve men plunge into a conflict, it would mean the ruin of the entire squadron—ruin without having accomplished their purpose! Death for nothing!

In a moment he could see something that shook the foundation of his courage. The lead Fokker was a sleek black ship coming at them with terrific speed. There was only one ship like that in the war. It was the specially constructed metal plane in which flew the monk of murder—Mr. Death!

Jed felt the handles of his Vickers. His lips were pressed so tightly now that they were white. He rocked frantically in his cockpit. And then he knew there was only one thing he could do.

He signaled to the other planes and ordered them to land. He watched with burning eyes, saw confusion. Then the first began dropping from the sky and circling over the field below. Another plane followed suit. Soon the entire squadron was dropping from the danger of the tracer lead.

That was fine. That saved them all, those men who had left intending to die.

But it left Babyface Garrett alone in the air to combat not only the super-ship of Mr. Death, but the three or four Fokkers behind it. He pulled his leather jacket around him and shifted his booted feet. He stretched his gloves tight, and patted Click's head.

"It's going to be worse than hell popping this time, boy," he said softly.

After that he was tight-lipped. He throttled his Spad forward, heard the wind rip through the wings, then saw the black nose of Mr. Death's ship. In another minute—

Jed Garrett's days as a trick pilot before the war had taught him how to handle a plane to best advantage. He knew tricks that only an experienced pilot could know. Tricks that only years of flying would teach a man. He was therefore safer in the arms of the foe than the average American ace, yet he was no better equipped to battle a metal ship, or three additional Fokkers, all at the same time, than was any other man. The odds were against him. Fate had stacked him up this time as the joker!

He saw Death's ship ahead of him now. It was like a heavy black comet. He saw the flapping robes of the murder master who was steering that ship, and the gruesome, hideous bone of a face behind the glass shield of the cockpit. Even as he saw it, Babyface gave the first jerk of his Vickers.

Brrrrrrt....

Yellow-blue flame spat from the muzzles; screaming lead cut through the sky lanes! Steel messengers of death flattened on the snout of the black plane!

Babyface had no sooner discharged the first volley when he ducked his nose toward the earth. He felt the wings tear as he catapulted downward at a dizzy speed; but he was no sooner below Death when he rolled his protesting Spad to the right and crawled up under the belly of the black Fokker. His agonized eyes were searching for the gas tank. He spotted it as the speeding black coffin of hell sailed over him.

Brrrrt . . . Brrrrt. . .

Two short sputters of yellow-blue hell, but he had missed, and he was climbing for the ceiling now with desperate haste, before Death could swing about. Like a steeple climber, his plane reached into the clouds, his prop roared and pulled and yanked to get him back at level flying with Death; his wings were screaming in protest against the wind.

Babyface wheeled the Spad around just in time to see Death plunging down at him. He saw the flame fly from Death's Spandaus—could almost see the invisible little chips of steel hurl through the air at him.

Tlrrrrrr... tlrrrrrr. .

Death's gun had been tampered with, had been fixed for extra power and speed, and it made a different sound from the sputtering Vickers. Babyface had to bank away to avoid collision. He saw ragged little holes in his wings.

Tlrrrrr. . . tlrrrrr. .

Death was on his tail now, chewing into the precious assembly. Babyface lifted toward the heavens. His hideous face twisted in a snarl, Mr. Death lifted after him. Babyface was desperate. He felt clicking slugs tear into the back of the cockpit and rip about the fuselage.

His screaming motors red hot, he suddenly rolled into a loop. The ship came out of it, the motor still pounding, pounding.

Jed had Mr. Death on a side angle now and he ripped in savagely. His face white and bloodless, his heart pounding against his side, he punched the Vickers' handles.

Brrrrt. ... Brrrrrrrrt..

This time the coffin nails tore along the bottom of Death's black ship, ripped little holes in the metal, and tore away part of the fuselage. Something started flying in the wind. . The gas tank was leaking! Another load. .

Brrrrt. .

But Death's plane had swerved away from the line of fire. In a moment it was over Babyface's top wings, plunging down.

Tllrrrrrrrrrrt. .

Tracer bullets crashed all about him. His instrument clock was shattered. Mad hatred purging his soul, Babyface rolled away from the flying monk. He saw the black ship keep coming in the nose dive. It dropped far below the range of fire, was hurtling toward the earth as though Death could not bring the ship out of the spin.

Then suddenly the metal plane righted, began climbing again. Babyface saw green Fokkers a short distance off. A moment of indecision possessed him, then he dove after Death. His torn wings howling, his prop humming, he aimed straight at the cockpit in which Mr. Death sat.

Brrrrrrt. . .

Death was having trouble! He rocked the stick back and forth, then began heading toward the ground. Babyface followed him down. The green Fokkers were beginning to chase him now, but he couldn't let Mr. Death charge his tracers into the dynamite loaded ships which were landed on the ground below.

The sight in the sky was for a moment grotesque. The black metal ship driven by the bony monk of murder, nearing the ground, was leveling off. The wrecked Spad which Babyface piloted, roared after it, while the three green Fokkers pursued him madly.

Brrrrrrt. . .

Fokker lead chased him from long range, and bullets tore again across his tail assembly. Babyface leveled his ship.

He saw that Mr. Death was not going to charge fire into the dynamited Spads. He was ready to lift his torn plane into the sky again, to stave off the green ships, when his eyes met a familiar sight—a squadron of Spads that had been sent out after it was discovered that Babyface had left the 27th without the information about Mr. Death. The Fokkers were climbing rapidly to meet them.

On the Hun horizon more Fokkers were winging out to join the fray. Babyface lowered his ship, the wheels touched, rolled along, then suddenly the ship jolted and turned over.

He unhooked Click, and scrambled out. The dog was at his heels as Babyface ran across to where Mr. Death's ship had landed. He saw the bony-faced monk standing beside his plane, his blotch-eyes awful, his slit-mouth tight. There was a huge black Luger in his hand.

"Don't come any closer," he warned. Babyface stopped in his tracks. Beyond Death he could see the Spads that were loaded with dynamite. The pilots were still in the ships and the motors were still running. The whole awful air fight had taken but a few minutes.

"My gun jammed," Death went on, "or I wouldn't be down here now." The breeze was whispering through his dirty black robes.

Suddenly Babyface snapped a short order. Click catapulted forward like a brown streak. Mr. Death fired at him, but missed. Babyface rushed forward in that moment. Death fired again at the dog, and Babyface reached the monk. He crashed his hands down on the gun wrist. The Luger fell to the ground.

Death drew back, snarling. He lifted his foot and jammed it into Babyface's stomach. The American grabbed his waist, grunting. Click was tearing at the monk's robes.

Mr. Death hopped back into his ship, leaned over the side.

"I'll be back for you later," he said, "your pilots over there are coming after me now. I'm going back to Germany. When I do return for you, Babyface—"

Jed Garrett scrambled to his feet. The black ship slid quickly across the ground, lifted into the air.

In the next second three of the suicide pilots had reached the spot on which the metal ship had been. Babyface looked up at them, then stared into the sky. The Spads and Fokkers were dog-fighting.

"We've got to hurry with our mission," he said. "We'll take off and fly low, beneath that battle, until we get really back into the Boche strongholds. If we work fast—"

"But your plane is wrecked," one of the men interrupted.

Babyface glanced over at the overturned Spad. Then he eyed the suicide pilots again, his words were like a low throb.

"One of you will have to stay here then," he said, "or get back to the Allied lines as quickly as possible. I'll fly one of the dynamite ships!"

"But you'll be killed," the officer said, alarmed. "The orders were that you were to direct us! They need you to keep fighting! Us," he waved his hand bitterly in the direction of the suicide squadron, "we're either so old and war weary that we're nuts and no longer any good, or we're so young that we don't know what it's all about yet. But you—"

"I'll fly one of the dynamite ships," Babyface said. "Let some kid stay behind." He turned. "Come along, Click. We've got to lead our suicide squadron out of here."

The pilots stared at him as he strode toward the nearest airship.

CHAPTER FOUR
Dynamite Death!

THE SPAD was heavy with its deadly cargo, but under the expert hand of Babyface Jed Garrett, it rolled over the bumpy field and hopped into the air. A moment later the wheels touched ground again, jumped. Babyface pulled back the stick, eased it, played with it, teased it. Presently the Spad lifted again, and this time it kept going up until the tip of the ship soared over a tree top. The prop ground evenly, the motors throbbed with steady precision.

Eleven other planes followed the one Babyface flew. On their wings there was a mixture of colors, not unlike a rainbow. Babyface hadn't particularly noticed the design before, but now that he was flying one of the suicide ships, the ghastly effect gripped him. The wings were colored red, white and blue, and on the tips of them there was a black skull and cross bones, indicating that it was marked for death.

All of the suicide ships were old. They had figured in the war since the very beginning of the Yank air corps, and they were nicked and scarred from many battles. Crude little patches were woven into the wings, the motors could hold up so long and no longer. They were ships that had seen Fokkers burned down, had spat whirling Vickers' lead, and now, like the pilots who drove them, they were doomed!

The ground below unreeled beneath the bobbing wings of Major Garrett's ship in insane patterns. He kept climbing, climbing, and they were drawing farther and farther from the fighting Spads and Fokkers behind. They were flying into Bocheland to find a grave. Trees now, whirling beneath them, green, furry things of nature, some of them stripped like skeletons, and all of them puny and insignificant from this altitude. Patches of torn ground came next, and after that a dense forest.

Jed Garrett had been across the lines too many times not to know his way. Without aid of compass, he could sense his way from drome to drome. The nearest was the "K" club drome. It was the home of one of the most daring Boche air circuses in existence.

Roaring wings of twelve Yank planes, drumming through the heavens, like a dozen black birds, their slim shadows passing on the ground. Props spinning, wires flapping in the aged crates, patched canvas clinging to the frame of the vessels of the clouds. Eleven grim, white-faced young men going to die. And die willingly!

Babyface spotted the first drome. He spotted it in his sights, just over the nose of his ship. He became a little tense, and his stomach seemed to turn over. He hated this job of sending a pilot to hell. .. hated it with all his heart.

Motors droning, wings bobbing and props whirling, closer and closer they came to the K drome. Babyface moved uneasily. He closed his eyes for a moment, took off his goggles and wiped the sweat from his forehead. Then he adjusted his goggles again. He peered through the sights. His hand was trembling now, as he lifted it over the side of his ship.

He pointed to the farthest ship on the left flank. He saw the pilot stand up, salute and wave back. Babyface stood up. Hot tears rushed into his eyes until he could not see. He waved at the Yank.

In the next moment there was a screaming of wings, a Spad whirling downward like a comet. The wings ripped from the ship, but the plane kept dropping, dropping like a stone. It had been the farthest plane on the left flank, the pilot who had stood up and saluted. Dropping now, the first of the suicide squadron to go.

The roar of the bursting explosion reached Babyface's ears. He looked down, his thin lips creased in a smile. He saw the "K" drome splatter into the air. He saw Boches running. He saw bodies, twisted and mangled, and in all that, he saw a fragment of a plane's wing. A fragment that had on it a mixture of red, white and blue, like the colors in the rainbow, red, white and blue and a skull!

"Good work, kid," Babyface called to the dead Yank.

Then he signaled the others. The squadron swung around, heading deeper back into Bocheland. Throbbing motors, bobbing wings, grim-faced youths.

Over the lone drome of battery "B" now. It had been but a minute of flying. Babyface's lips were in an even line. He signaled the farthest ship on the left flank. The pilot in this was one of the old timers who had said he was no longer any good in the war. He didn't stand up and salute, he just waved with a toss of his hand; hurled out his helmet and goggles, and from where Babyface sat, it looked as though he were laughing! Laughing like a maniac—rocking back and forth in his cockpit.

Then the ship turned off, nosed down at a terrific speed. It landed squarely in the center of the drome. Pieces came shooting into the sky.

Babyface signaled for the squadron to turn off. There were only nine planes behind him now. They followed the Spad that Jed Garrett flew like disciplined soldiers, like submarines following a tender ship. They did not waver, did not turn off, yet they had seen two of their buddies plunge to their death. Awful sights, those, the whirling, turning of the dive the upheaval of the explosion.

Throbbing motors, pressing ever onward, flying, winging over German lines Babyface was slouched down in his seat now; his helmet was off, only his goggles remained. His hand was unsteady on the stick.

"Wish I had a drink, Click," he snapped, "God, but I wish I had a drink! Seein' these guys pop off this way, seeing 'em wave and dive for hell. ." He aired his collar, even though the shrill wind was ripping through the patched wings, and it was cold up here.

"If they only had a fighting chance," he went on, mumbling and cursing.

Through the sights now he spotted the three huge hangars of the "Q" detachment. He looked down, slightly sick at the thought of what was to come. Then his eyes narrowed. He saw men on the field running. Saw Archies explode their puff ball shots at the flying squadron of death.

The warning of the squadron's coming had been signaled ahead. This time the men were ready. Anti-aircrafts were pointed upward, two Fokkers were running off the tarmac below.

Quickly Babyface signaled a center plane out. The pilot was laughing, but his face looked green. He stood up in the cockpit, blew kisses to his buddies, in mocking tribute, then sat down again, ducked his head and started to dive.

Roaring and whirling, his canvas ripping to shreds, the Spad shot downward at the center drome. It dropped like a huge stone that has fallen from a blimp, straight and true. But when it was within five hundred yards of the destination anti-aircraft guns caught it. The plane shattered into a million pieces that rained down on the earth below.

The kisses the kid had blown, Babyface thought frantically, they had been fine. But his death scored the sheet with exactly nothing gained. He waved away another ship, and saw the pilot turn off without waving or standing up. His face looked as though he were sobbing, choking and sobbing, because although he had volunteered, he didn't want to die. His ship went shooting down.

But the guns chopped off his ship at a thousand feet. It exploded into a thin nothingness. The first ship to dive was still hurtling downward. The ground guns were cracking at it.

Babyface held his breath. Then he saw the ship zoom into the center drome, saw things splatter, and shoot skyward, saw ground guns ruined, and men slain.

Jed Garrett motioned the squadron in another direction. He counted the remaining planes grimly. Six. It had taken three to get "Q" drome.

Brrrrrt. . . . Brrrrrrt. . . .

He wheeled around. In his excitement to blow up the dromes, he had forgotten the two Fokkers which had taken off from the tarmac. He stared back now to see one of the Spads hit, to see it explode. The flying pieces ripped into the nose of one of the Fokkers, and zoomed into the cargo of one of the other Spads. That too exploded!

Two Spads, in pieces, falling to the ground! One Fokker, ripped apart by the explosion in the air, tumbling toward the earth, a horrible yellow ball of fire! The Boche pilot was struggling to get from the flaming cockpit.

Only four dynamited Spads now, five with Jed's plane. And one Fokker. The Fokker was making crazy motions in the sky. It was weaving back and forth. Some of the debris of the explosion had evidently flown back and hit it, also.

Babyface motioned the four planes onward, then he turned his Spad and winged madly back toward the Fokker. If he could take it by surprise, before the Boche could shoot at him, the menace would be removed.

But—one single shot from the enemy plane would explode Babyface's ship into a thousand pieces. Click whined at the daring movement; whined as if in warning. Jed's smooth, yet battered and tired old Spad hurtled through the sky. The canvas was ripping and tearing, the prop whirling, whirling. Babyface huddled down in his seat. His face was a bloodless white mask. His hands were frozen to the controls. His blood was surging wildly through his veins.

He was just getting into firing range, just reaching for the polished handles of the Vickers' gun when his eyes almost popped. The Boche pilot had straightened his Fokker around. He saw Babyface coming at him, and his gloved hand went up to grip the Spandaus gun.

There was a split second of eternity. Jed Garrett's action came through sheer instinct; it was the expert movement of a man who had flown stunt planes years before the war started. Experience. Hairbreadth movement, timed decision, and breath-taking courage. It saved his life. The Fokker ground out its steel stream of hell. The Spad had reared on its tail, was nosed straight toward heaven. Canvas ripped and gave, and flapped in the wind. Wires snapped with the tension. Steam, slip-stream and oil rushed back into the cockpit. Precarious balance. Click holding with his four paws, the pilot leaning forward.

Brrrrrt.....

The Fokker was nosing up at him now. Babyface jerked sidewise on the Stick, rolled the ship, so that it was a crazy, tumbling target. If just one bullet hit his dynamite—he'd be in bits, scattered over the ground!

He straightened out, then twisted the groaning ship in another turn. In a moment he was flying almost upside down. He stared up, saw the Fokker diving for him. Babyface Jed Garrett's bloodless lips let go an oath, his gloved hand jerked back on the Vickers.

Brrrrrt .... brrrrrt .... brrrrrt. .

The Fokker burst into flames. A siren wail screamed from it as it began tumbling toward the earth.

Babyface wheeled his wrecked old Spad out of the way, his dynamite loaded ship barely missing the fiery Boche coffin. Jed straightened out, sucked his breath-in huskily. He was breathing hard. His heart was still in his mouth. It had been close that time—too close!

He stared over the side of the cockpit and saw the flame encased ship still tumbling toward the earth. Then he looked forward, saw the four ships of the squadron far ahead of him. He throttled down to catch up. His torn wings ripped in the wind, his prop kept whirling around and around. He had to reach them, designate their targets of death, send those four pilots to their doom!

The Spad was laboring under the strain' that had been put to it; Jed Garrett was still breathing hard. But he kept thinking of the huge vans that were moving toward the Front, the thousands of men who would partic-ipate in tonight's big push. Babyface had to carry out this preliminary work to the best of his ability, so that that "push" would be a success!

CHAPTER FIVE

The Man Without Hands

T WAS NIGHT. Babyface Jed Garrett had finished the gruesome job of sending the dynamite planes to their death marks, and he was sitting in his little office. While he smoked a cigarette, the smoke swirling out through his nostrils, he was waiting and listening; every now and then he sipped at the cognac. The little tube was still clicking out Morse Code. It had been clicking all day, and now it was just a dull repetition of dot and dash and dot again in the major's ears. He lapsed into moments when his mind refused to link together the dots and dashes to spell out words; moments when he cared about nothing.

The shack was dark, and the adjutant was over at the canteen getting himself drunk. A helluva lot he had to get drunk about! When the big push started, he would be left here at the drome. Babyface sipped again at the cognac. He didn't like adjutants, he decided. A clock on the wall was ticking. It indicated eleven o'clock. There remained one hour and one minute before the drive began. Ticking. Tube tapping out the code. Vans rumbling toward the Front. Soldiers spilling into the trenches. Kids writing notes to their mothers—goodbye notes. Push. Big push. Ticking clock. Tapping tube.

He glanced at his fingernails, bit off part of one and spit it out. He rubbed his cigarette on the desk until the glowing end was dark. He reached his hand down and patted the faithful police dog at his feet.

"*One hour remains,*" the tube tapped out, "*defence has been established on the North. . All dromes will have every available plane ready to send into the sky. . . every available plane.*"

God, the sky would be dense, Babyface thought. What a picture it would be in the night! Red and green running lights. Bombs bursting, red, yellow and blue. Kids screaming for mercy. Machine guns chattering up and down the lines. Searchlights sweeping over the shell torn, barbed wire fields. The lines of men moving grimly forward, bayonets glistening in the moonlight. Glistening like the flashing white teeth of the human machine which would sweep into action tonight!

The adjutant entered the shack. He was teetering. Babyface looked up. He disliked the man's thin little mustache, his pale face.

"What do you want, Perkins?"

"What'cha sittin' here in the dark for?" Perkins asked. He snapped on a light.

"I want to be alone," Babyface said acidly.

"Oh, shure, sir. How'd the guys in the suicide squadron take it, anyway?"

"Fine."

"Of course, they weren't very important to—"

Babyface suddenly leaped from his chair, grabbed the man's tunic front, and shouted into his face.

"Listen you little skunk, they had guts! You don't know what guts is, do you? It's something that red-blooded men have. Something that you haven't got! You come in here drunk, blabbering about them not being any good. Do you think you're any good to the army? Do you think I want to talk about something that has been eating into my conscience like a ravishing scourge? Now get the hell out of here!"

The adjutant, white and shaking, turned and started for the door.

Babyface was a bundle of nerves. He hardly knew what he was doing. Before his eyes, like a red mirage, was the picture of the first kid that had gone down—the kid who had stood up in his plane and saluted. He had been young; it hadn't been very sweet to leave the earth at his age. Yet he had plunged to death, and afterward, men like Perkins—

"Perkins!" Babyface shouted hoarsely.

The lieutenant wheeled about. His eyes were flickering. He felt that his major had done him an injustice.

"Perkins, you can fly, can't you?"

The man quavered. "Why—ye-ye-yes sir. Before I got this office job I got to be in one spasm of fire. Boy, that was—"

"One spasm of fire," Babyface sneered. "One spasm, eh? Well, I'm getting a new adjutant. A kid that just came up from the school. He won't like staying on the ground, but I'm tired of seeing you around. You'll take the air tonight."

Perkins gulped. "I—I will take the air?"

"That's what I said!"

"But, sir," he was sober now, "my hand, it—"

"You'll fly, Perkins. No excuses!"

"Ye-ye-yes sir."

"Now haul your stinkin' little carcass out of here!"

"Ye-ye-yes sir."

Babyface turned off the light and sat back down at his desk. He was still trembling from his sudden outburst. War did that to you, he thought. War and screaming Spandaus lead. You got so you didn't know which end was up. He had hardly slept for three days, charting movements, having a conference every few hours with G.H.Q.; making decisions concerning the air part of the push. He needed a shave badly. His throat was dry, and he felt dirty. Terribly dirty. He thought that he stunk. But he didn't gave a damn. There wasn't time for anything in war. Anything but throwing a little stale slop down your throat and flying and fighting. Nothing but shooting down Fokkers, or battling gruesome figures who wore black robes. Mr. Death invaded what few hours sleep he was able to snatch.

But what he hated most was sending high school kids out to die; sending them out in canvas coffins of hell. Green babies to fight experienced German aces. He had never felt as badly as he did tonight, and it was the first time he actually wished that someone would pop him off and end it—or that the war would come to an end.

He paced up and down in the dark CO. shack of the 27th. The clock ticking . . . ticking. Fifty minutes until the big push now.

The Morse Code was saying:

"Keep the men quiet, keep the trenches dark. The attack will be a surprise in most parts of Bocheland. . . A quick, decisive sweep may end the war. . . Do not return rifle or machine gun fire on the Front. . ."

Suddenly Babyface straightened, cocked his ears to the tube. His face grew white there in the dark, and he lit a cigarette. He heard his name tapped out. .

"Attention Major Jed Garrett. . . We are sending an aviator to see you.
. . He has important information which he will divulge only to you. . . He
is hysterical, has just been rescued from No Man's Land where he had been
crawling through mud to get back to Allied lines. He escaped from the lab-
oratory of Mr. Death His name is William Carter. . . He was found to be
without hands, and he had caked clay to the stumps of his wrists to keep
from bleeding to death. . .. He has been treated, should arrive at the 27th
soon. . . Report the information he gives you to G.H.Q. as soon as you get
it. . . That is all, Garrett. . ."

The tube swung on, sending instructions and news to other parts of
the Front It kept going, a never ending series of tapping. And the clock
kept ticking.

Babyface shuddered, drew deeply on the cigarette. A man without
hands—escaped from Mr. Death's laboratory! Was Mr. Death concoct-
ing something by which he hoped to stave off the drive? It hard seemed
possible. Yet Babyface knew of the murder monk's cunning genius, and
he was suddenly afraid now that Death had an ace in the hole. That
there would be a twist, a turn in the last minute to ruin the splendid
months, weeks and days of preparation for this costly drive!

He took a gulp of the cognac, then left the shack. Click trotted at his
heels,

He was just in time to see a group of men headed for the shack. He
waited. Bill Carter was brought to him. The pilot's face was sunken,
smeared with dirt that was mixed with the crimson of his own blood.
His eyes, deep in their sockets, stared out like a madman's. His clothing
was in rags, clinging to which was all the dirt of No Man's Land, it
seemed. But his wrists were most horrible. Just stumps with white
bandages around them.

"Could I have a cigarette, sir," Bill Carter asked.

A match was struck there in the dark, and the little yellow flame
flared up, brought light into the wan face of the Yank who had suffered
the agonies of hell, and yet had kept his mouth shut.

Bill puffed on the cigarette, and a little smile twisted on his worn
face. "He didn't think I'd get away," he said in a low, husky voice, "but I
did." He laughed as though he thought it were very funny.

"Come into the office," Babyface said, softly.

Bill went into the shack and Babyface followed him. He turned down the lights and helped Bill to a chair. Babyface took the cigarette from his lips, then replaced it when the man without hands wanted another puff. At last Jed took his place behind the desk.

Bill Carter looked at him; there was wild gleaming in his eyes.

"Mr. Death says you can't stop him this time, sir. I told him you would. If you don't—every effort we have made for this drive will be dashed. A million men will die!"

"A million men," Babyface echoed.

"Yes sir. He has invented a powder substance, part of which is made from the bones of human beings. It is deadly. One speck of it on a man's face, or clothing, or any part of him, will kill him. It seems incredible, but having spent this day with Mr. Death, nothing he does can be entirely incredible. Am I right, sir?"

"Have you found out whether this invention is completed?"

"Yes sir. By twelve-thirty tonight, he will have enough for the whole Allied Front. He is taking a balloon which can rise far above the altitude of a plane—thereby assuring its safety—and will release a ton of this powder substance from compartments that will be beneath the balloon!"

Babyface looked at the clock. It was twenty-five minutes to twelve.

"I'll have to fly like hell," he said, half to himself. "Twelve, the push starts; twelve-thirty his stuff will be ready. It will take the balloon some time to rise—"

"You will stop him?" Bill Carter blurted suddenly, "won't you, sir?" There was hope and faith in his voice.

Babyface looked down at the man's stump wrists. His eyes were brittle.

"I'll do everything I can, Carter. I hope to God I can come back and tell you that I have killed Mr. Death!"

Bill Carter's eyes were bright. "I hope you can, too, sir."

Babyface rose to his feet, patted the pilot's back. "You've done fine work, Carter."

He turned, got his leather jacket and slipped it on. He strapped an automatic about his waist, then, catching his helmet and goggles in hand, he started for the door. Click followed him, while Carter watched with warm, appreciative eyes.

Babyface met a captain as he was crossing to the tarmac.

"Take charge, Tex," he said. "Go in and hear Carter's story, then telephone G.H.Q. and tell them that I have already gone after Mr. Death. I haven't time to hang around and talk to them about it. Tell them, above all, to have faith in me, and to let nothing detain the push. In fact, Tex, if the push comes at a quarter of twelve—five minutes from now, it will be better yet!"

"Yes sah!" Tex drawled.

Babyface left him and went quickly to a plane. He gave the mechanic instructions, then climbed in. Click backed, took a running jump and landed up in the cockpit. Babyface strapped the dog in.

Contact! The trim Spad slid forward, glided gently into the air. Babyface swung back and forth in the cockpit, eased the stick back a little. Then he was flying steadily, evenly.

Upon the success of his mission depended the success of the big Allied push!

CHAPTER SIX

Death Sets a Trap

BABYFACE had been to the tree enshrouded laboratory of the murder monk too many times before, to falter in his course for it now. Though he was heading in the direction of the most feared and despised monster of the war, Babyface Garrett knew no fear. He crossed his fingers and prayed that he would be able to prevent Mr. Death from carrying out; his plans. More than that, he hoped he would be able to kill him.

Wings bobbing over the dark fields of Bocheland, prop spinning, motor throbbing in a low buzzing hum, Babyface sat in the cockpit, motionless. Beside him was his dog—Click.

His eyes were on the instrument panels of the Spad. Now he leaned out over the cockpit, adjusted his goggles and stared down. He discerned the low, flat form of the laboratory. Beside it he saw a long, sloping roof of another building! At least it looked like a building from the sky. Babyface cut his motor, slid against the wind, then began coasting toward a nearby clearing where he could land.

The wheels of the ship scraped the leaves from a tall tree, then slanted quickly across the field. Babyface taxied a few feet, stopped, and jumped from the ship. He released Click and the dog jumped down. Jed looked at his radium-dialed wrist watch.

12:01

He stood very straight, his face lifted to the starry sky. A cool breeze touches his cheeks. Jed's lips moved, and he mumbled something—it was a plea to the god of war. The big push was on! And yet back here, how ghastly quiet everything was! How natural, and untouched. Tree and grass and wild, rambling weeds. The ground shook every now and then with the distant rumble of the guns, but there was tranquility here, and there was peace. Peace would be closer, the war nearer to an end, if the Allied push were a success. Those greedy gods of the red thunder planet must give him strength to stop Mr. Death; to save the lives of the millions who were engaged in the greatest conflict of the World War!

Babyface started forward, and his boots swished in the soft dirt. He took off his goggles and helmet and attached them to his belt. He unlimbered his automatic. Click trotted faithfully at his heels. The walk to the laboratory was some four hundred yards from where he had landed. Babyface approached warily, carefully. Too many times before had he struck at Mr. Death's home to find a trap set for him.

He drew to the edge of the thicket and stared at the long, sloping roof. He saw now that it was merely a camouflage, covering an underground basement. It must be there, Jed thought, that Mr. Death was manufacturing his powder of rotting death. A heavy, stifling odor rose from the little roof. Faint lights gleamed from beneath its edge. The stiff, squarish black laboratory itself stood just the other end of the basement murder-factory. A slim shadow of light escaped from its curtained window. Boche sentries stood stationed around both the laboratory and the adjoining basement. There were approximately four; at least that was all that Jed could see from where he stood.

Suddenly there was a great commotion. Germans rushed up a stairway from the basement, shouting. Babyface retreated, swung into the branch of a tree. Click hovered back in the shadows. Then he saw what the noise was about. A large black ball was descending from the heavens.

It was a balloon, the largest balloon that Babyface had ever seen. A heavy net seemed to cover the gas-filled ball. The Huns were erecting special ladders now, while others were staking the balloon to the ground. In place of the usual observers' basket there was a long, oval compartment. Babyface knew immediately the reason for this. The balloon had to rise above plane altitude, and in doing so, the occupants of the little car would have to be protected from the freezing atmosphere; the thin, unbreathable air. The car was no doubt equipped with oxygen tanks, with enough artificial air to last for several hours.

The busy activity around the balloon, lasted for fifteen or twenty minutes while Babyface shifted uncomfortably on his limb and watched. At last the Boche soldiers were sent back to their regular dromes, a half mile the other side of the laboratory. At this time, other men came from the basement carrying large white boxes. A floodlight was turned on them, and Jed could see that they wore special, rubber-like suits. They attached these boxes beneath the car, while the men inside drew them up on cables.

When they had finished, the door of the laboratory swung open and a figure in long black robes came out. His bony face was illuminated in the floodlight, and Jed could see the glittering eyes and the slit-mouth. Mr. Death inspected the balloon's car quickly, then waved the figures in rubbery suits away. Two German officers climbed into the car. The men in the white suits began jerking up the balloon's stakes.

Babyface Garrett was impatient, yet he knew enough to remain motionless. Mr. Death was still on the ground and the balloon would-n't start without him. Jed saw Click at the trunk of the tree. The dog's hair was bristling, his nostrils had caught the scent of the murder monk!

Suddenly Mr. Death started up the steps into the car of the balloon. Babyface had to risk everything to stop him! He dropped coolly from the limb of his tree, aimed the automatic.

Just then the floodlight swung quickly in his direction, caught him full. Blinded, Babyface fired. He heard running feet. There were wild shouts. Boches were grabbing him. His gun was snatched away. Click was barking, snarling, leaping at the Germans.

Something thudded on Babyface's head and he slumped into the arms of one of the Boches. But he fought to retain his consciousness. He was being dragged across the ground now, dumped into the stair-way leading down to the basement. His body rolled down the steps, and he lay in a crumpled heap at the bottom. Blood was trickling down across his cheek.

Babyface moved. Something slammed against his chest. That some-thing howled; it was Click. The dog's head was bleeding, his eyes watery. Jed Garrett looked up in time to see Mr. Death coming down the steps.

Garrett climbed slowly to his feet while Death gripped his heavy Luger. He shoved it into Jed's stomach. The monk's bony face was twisted into a snarl as he spoke in a clipped voice.

"I knew when my men were stupid enough to let Carter escape that he'd get back to you and that you would be idiot enough to come over here and try and stop me. We were waiting for you, Garrett!"

"And I walked into another trap, eh?"

"That's right. Now that you're here, know this: nothing will prevent my flight in the balloon. The Allied army will choke to death on my poison powder!" He waved his robed arm in the direction of several large vats, a boiling tub of liquid, and hideous, huge siphons. "We have manufactured enough to do us nicely— thanks to the corpses of your dead comrades!"

"You mean you've plundered the graves?" Babyface snapped.

"Just that, my American friend. This is an instance when the dead will kill the living."

"What do you intend to do with me?"

"Kill you, of course. Don't think I'm going to take you with me—to let you watch your friends die. Something might happen if I did that. I'm going to kill you here. A very pleasant death in comparison to what I would give you if time were not more precious."

Babyface Garrett's dark eyes flickered. He stared into the gruesome countenance of the fiendish inventor.

"Yes, and that is—"

"Perhaps you have noticed a pot over there. A heavy liquid of my own concoction is boiling in it. I used this to take the flesh from the corpses. It strips a man clean, leaving only a white skeleton. You see, my friend, a white skeleton—the bones—were all that I needed. I think I would like to have you that way. I will put your pretty skeleton up in my laboratory to look upon, and," his voice lowered, "to spit upon when I'm so inclined, American!"

Jed Garrett's skin quivered, his heart beat faster. Sweat was standing out on his face. Click was at his feet, trying to get up, shaking his furry head.

"Your dog will accompany you," Mr. Death concluded, "that will be two mongrels in the same pot!"

Jed suddenly leaped back, smashed his hands down at the Luger. The gun exploded into the dirt floor of the basement. But in a fleet second, Mr. Death jerked it back and aimed again.

Babyface dove in, this time swinging his whole weight down on the gun wrist. The Luger dropped from Mr. Death's hands, and Babyface scooped it up.

A shot rang out.

Babyface staggered and dropped, the Luger slipping from his fingers. A bullet had creased his head. But before Jed fell to the floor, his hazy vision took in the figure of a German officer at the top of the steps. The officer had a square, ugly chin, and a short-cropped hair cut. His black eyes were glittering.

"I guess I got him that time, Mr. Death," he said, "Hunkle—" he patted his own chest with the barrel of his Luger, "he never misses."

Mr. Death paid no attention to the boast. "Come help me, Herr Hunkle," he said. "Get a rope from the corner over there and swing it over the bar above the pot of boiling liquid. I will attach the other end around the American's waist, and we will lower him slowly."

They worked quickly over Babyface.

"Time is rapidly passing," Hunkle said.

Mr. Death grunted, lifting Jed Garrett in his arms. "Are they ready to start the balloon?" he asked.

"We have but a few men left, sir," Hunkle said. "It is all they can do to hold it to the ground."

Babyface regained consciousness as they raised his prone body over the pot. He stared down at the bubbling substance and shuddered. His body went numb with the sight; his heart was in his mouth.

"You lower him then," Death said. "I will get into the balloon and take off. The Allied push is already on—time is too valuable to waste it further on one man. You drop him into the liquid, Hunkle. Drop him slowly, for I see his eyes are open, and I want him to suffer!"

"I will see that he suffers!" Hunkle snapped, laughing.

Mr. Death turned. With his robes sweeping behind him, he rushed from the basement. His black figure disappeared up the steps. Jed Garrett saw the glistening face of the Boche officer before him.

"It will be very painless," Hunkle said, "you will know nothing once you are entirely submerged. It was my duty to duck corpses in and out of this all afternoon.

It will be a pleasure to duck a living man into it!"

Babyface kicked his feet. The rope was just around his chest, looped tinder his arm pits. To slip from it, however, would mean dropping into the boiling liquid! He saw Click near the stairs. The dog was on his feet now.

Hunkle lowered the line a little so that Babyface was just a foot over the pot.

"I will do it slowly," the German leered. "First your feet, so that you may look down and see the bare skeletons that will be left."

Babyface was rocking his body back and forth, trying to swing. The Hun lowered him another two inches, and laughed. Babyface was swinging a little—just a little. His arms were free and he dug into his pockets. A knife slipped into his hands.

Another inch lower he went. His feet were just above the liquid. Hunkle was sweating. His square face was set eagerly. His eyes were glittering.

Babyface moved his body back and forth frantically. Suddenly, as Hunkle lowered enough for his feet to dip into the liquid, he reached up; swung over the bar to which the rope was attached. He balanced precariously over the boiling pot.

Hunkle stared, dropped the line as though it were red hot. He jerked out his Luger. His finger tightened on the trigger,

Tac . . tac . . tac . .

Whirling, screaming bullets tore after the figure perched on the cross bar. But Babyface had plunged forward—had dived over the pot and was landing squarely on the huge Boche before the bullets were even out of the gun.

He rode Hunkle to the floor, snatched the Luger from the gasping German. Without mercy, Babyface Garrett reversed the weapon in his hand. He slashed down, shattered the Hun's skull. Fury rode his soul. He lifted the prone figure, threw him into the pot.

Then he turned and raced out of the basement. The figures in the white suits were just outside. With sinking heart, Babyface saw the balloon lifting into the air. A line was dragging after it.

The men in white scrambled after him. Babyface jerked the trigger of the Luger. He saw Click who had followed him out of the basement, charge one of the men. Jed raced after the trailing rope from the balloon. He saw it jerk upward.

With a frantic effort he leaped into the air, felt the rope in his hands. He was slipping. The cord burned. He clung to it, lifting, lifting from the ground. In a moment he was dangling, holding on for his life, and swinging over a tree.

Click was on the ground barking out his lungs. But the dog would know enough to return to Allied territory—and to the 27th, as he had in the past when Babyface had been forced to leave him.

Jed Garrett looked up at the distant car hanging below the balloon, and at the white boxes lower than the car—the boxes that contained the deadly powder. He was still lifting higher and higher.

His hands burned. His legs kicked thin air. They were two hundred feet up, and ascending rapidly. Babyface stared vainly at the solid ground far below; and then at the car which harbored Mr. Death and his two associates. It seemed now that it would be impossible to get up into the car. And it was certain death if he did not.

Babyface Garrett swung on the rope, buckled some of it around his wrist. He tried desperately to fashion himself a boatswain seat, but he didn't know enough about such a knot, and the rope kept slipping.

The ground was six hundred feet below him now, and he was dangling like a rag doll at the end of a string.

CHAPTER SEVEN
Ceiling Zero

AT A THOUSAND FEET, he gave up trying to make the boatswain's seat, and started climbing up the rope. The job was not easy. He slipped almost as much as he climbed, and whenever he looked down on the disappearing earth beneath him, a cold shudder ran up and down his spine. It was a cold night, the wind was swinging the rope back and forth as he clung to it there, like a big, shivering ape hanging over a rocky ravine of certain death.

The balloon was lifting up too rapidly. If it kept up at this rate it would be above the atmosphere in which it was possible to breathe, long before Babyface could reach the top of the rope—if reach it he could.

The wind was pushing him around now, as though he were a human toy that had been put there to be played with. He felt his jacket ripping in the stiff breeze, his hair blowing wildly. He dared not loosen one hand to put on his helmet and goggles, although that would make the whole thing so much easier for him.

Why he had clung to the rope he did not know. Perhaps it was because he realized it was his last chance. If he had dashed back for his plane he might have had to stop to battle Fokkers. But even if he hadn't, it would take him time to get the ship started, and he would lose sight of the balloon. This had been his only chance—a wild, desperate one, to stop Mr. Death from releasing the contents of those white boxes that now hung beneath the car.

He climbed higher, buckling the rope over his elbow and shoulders, and winding his legs around it the higher he got. He stopped once and sucked in a breath of the icy air. To the West, he saw a blotch of red.

Bombs were bursting, planes were combing the skies, men on the ground were advancing with bayonets, machine-guns were chattering. Every force of the Allies was in action in the push.

But Major Jed Garrett clung dearly to a rope high over it all; clung there and kept trying to climb. There were no windows in the bottom of the balloon, and for that reason he was fortunate; if Mr. Death knew that he was here he would simply cut the rope.

Minutes passed—minutes of untold agony as he climbed. He looked down at the dangling end of the rope beneath him, and he realized, suddenly, that he was three quarters up the line. The balloon was but a matter of feet away. He didn't know what he would do when he reached it or how he would get inside. He only knew that that was what he had to do—get inside! Destroy the robed fiend who would destroy the Allied forces!

More moments fled by, with the balloon shooting ever onward toward the ceiling of the sky. Zero ceiling, and death to the Yank on the rope if they reached it before he got into the car where artificial air was pumped from tanks. The wind kept rocking him back and forth. Inch by inch, the palms of his hands blistering and bleeding now, he kept climbing.

He sucked in his breath as he climbed within three feet of the white boxes. He saw the trap doors on the bottoms of them; trap doors that could be sprung from levers inside the balloon's car. He clambered over the top of one of them, and holding tightly with one hand, clutched his leather helmet. Lying flat on his belly, he squeezed the helmet over his head, then the goggles. He felt better. The wind didn't sting his eyes or blind him now.

It struck him then, that he was lying on the white boxes of doom. The full realization of that came to him. He stuck his head into the wind. It was blowing toward Allied territory. That meant that he didn't dare release the trap doors now. Besides, if he did this, the powder would kill him before he could get any of the other boxes opened; that would ruin the whole thing—leave the other boxes for Mr. Death's satanic game.

The ground was thousands of feet below. Jed stared down, and suddenly he could see nothing. A filmy vapor swept into the air. They were cutting through a cloud! That meant they were higher than Babyface had realized. Soon they would be too high to permit him to breathe!

He stared, up at the black car. The door was on the side, and it would probably be bolted. The iron rungs of a ladder extended a little beneath the door, and he could cling to that, but it would do him no good. His eyes, safely beneath the panes of his goggles, searched the side of the car. There was a window to the right of the door. The glass in it was thick, undoubtedly bullet proof.

Babyface racked his mind for a moment. There was a possibility that the window would slide back. If it were a sliding window instead of one that locked down like the window in a house, there was a chance that he could wet his finger and slide it back. Mr. Death and his two officers would never in the world dream anyone would be coming in through the window this high in the sky! If they were taking care of the controls, were turned the other way—

Quickly, Babyface scrambled to the farthermost edge of the white box. He reached out. The iron rungs of the ladder were beyond his reach. He cursed quietly. He had to make it. He took in the distance— it was three feet. Did he dare to buck the wind and leap for it? To miss meant—His eyes swept the cloud misted air below. His teeth chattered in the cold.

He grasped the edge of the black car, stood up on the white box. The wind was howling around him, his jacket was blowing. He leaned dangerously over the side of the box. He sucked in his breath and mumbled a prayer.

His body tightened, became rigid. His muscles ached in anticipation of what he was going to try and do. Suddenly, he leaped!

One hand caught the bottom rung of the ladder. The wind tried to pull him off. Babyface swung his other hand up and climbed to the third rung of the ladder. He was clinging to the side of the black balloon car now and breathing hard.

Pressing his body close to the car, he reached slowly for the window. He grasped the window ledge, locked his feet on the rung below and stared inside the lighted room. He saw Mr. Death walking up and down, rubbing his bony hands, his black robes sweeping behind him. The other officers were fast at the controls.

It was now or never. Babyface wet his hand, jammed it against the window and pushed. Nothing happened!

His breath was coming harder now. He wet his hand again so that it was sticky. The balloon rose suddenly out of the cloud it had pierced. The sky was glittering with stars that seemed near—too near. The moon looked like a yellow monster riding through the heavens. The air was thin and dry, and it was freezing cold!

Once more Babyface Garrett jammed his hand against the window. He shouted an inarticulate cry of joy. The window shoved back an inch. He jammed his fingers in, pushed it all the way back. Mr. Death heard the wind and turned toward the window.

Babyface scrambled through it madly, landed with a thud on the floor inside the balloon!

He shoved the window shut, faced the horrible monk of murder. One of the Boche officers turned and stared at Babyface, as though he were seeing a ghost.

Mr. Death, his black robe clinging to his straight, steel-plated body, did not move.

"It's me all right," Babyface breathed in a low, pulsating tone, "I've come back!"

He plunged at the monk.

CHAPTER EIGHT
You Can't Beat a Yank!

JED KNEW where Mr. Death carried his Luger. Death had picked the gun up after the brief struggle in the basement; he kept it in his right sleeve. It was the right sleeve that the fighting Yank major dove for. He was desperate now, for he knew he had three men to defeat—three men, and his last battle would be won!

Mr. Death snarled, back-stepped, and slashed down his fists atop Babyface's wounded head. Death's bony fingers gripped the back of Jed's neck; the monk lifted. Babyface clutched the Luger. It was in his hand, even as Death lifted him over his back and hurled him to the deck of the car.

Babyface landed in a corner, his head throbbing with pain, his eyes blinded because of the broken glass in his goggles, but he was still holding the Luger. It exploded. The bullet resounded hollowly from the steel plate that covered Mr. Death's breast. The monk charged at Babyface.

Jed fired again. A bullet creased Death's bony white head and the monk spun around, his robes sweeping the deck. He shouted, cursed, held his bleeding head. One of the German officers was holding his Luger now and he fired it at Garrett. The bullet scraped the deck an inch from his leg.

Babyface struggled to his feet. The car beneath the gas ball rocked back and forth. A swirling mass of white beat against the thick window. The altitude glass showed ceiling zero. The balloon kept rocking back and forth!

The German fired at Babyface again, but a second before he had pressed the trigger, Jed Garrett had twisted and then escaped the screaming bullet. He held Death's Luger tight, then squeezed the trigger. A bullet sank squarely between the Boche's eyes.

Mr. Death rushed at Babyface again. Jed tore away the shattered goggles he was wearing, slammed the butt of the gun against Death's head. The monk shook and backed a little. Then Babyface slammed the gun down again.

The second Hun officer who had been at the controls had turned around. He was staring now, as Babyface slashed at his arch enemy. Then suddenly a great light shone in the Hun's dark eyes. He rushed toward the levers that would release the white poison powder and send it blowing in the direction of the Allied lines!

Babyface saw him just in time. He left Death, fired at the German and missed. But in the next moment he was upon him, pulling him away from the dangerous levers. The Boche turned about, his teeth flashed white as he slammed out his fist. The blow smashed into Jed's face and he stumbled back.

He fell directly into Mr. Death's outstretched arms. Madly, he fought, squirming and writhing to break loose. Death lifted him again, high over his head. Babyface saw with burning eyes the Hun trying to jerk back the levers controlling the trap doors of the white boxes. The car of the balloon lurched and the Hun dropped back. But he started toward the lever again, grimly determined.

Babyface crashed to the floor. He saw the vision of black robes sweeping down upon him. He pressed the trigger of the Luger three times. Only three empty clicks answered him. He reversed the gun, shoved it up into Death's scarred face; in the same movement he swung his left arm in a crazy arc that slammed into the murder monk's ear.

During the momentary stunning effect that these blows had on Death, Babyface was able to squirm from beneath him. He saw the German officer reaching for the controls. Babyface dove after him; dove like a football player dives in a tackle. He clutched the officer's legs and sent him crashing down on his face.

Mr. Death was coming after Jed again, but he didn't turn toward him. He scrambled on, over the prone body of the officer, clutched the Hun's slippery head between his fingers and began smashing it—face down—on the deck of the car! He smashed it violently, mercilessly, until blood oozed between his fingers.

Mr. Death clutched at Babyface, tore him off the officer. But the big

Hun was either unconscious, or, like his brother officer—dead, since he did not move. Jed Garrett swung toward his ancient robed foe, with all the wrath that had been boiling in his heart.

"This is your last game, Death," he breathed.

"Your last—" Death rasped.

They clashed again, the power of Jed's body swung the monk over backwards. His bony head crashed to the deck. Jed scrambled over him, grabbed his head as he had the head of the Hun officer. He stared down into the wide blotch-eyes of the monk. Then, his heart racing like wildfire, his tongue hot with the taste of blood, he began crashing Mr. Death's head on the deck.

Death twisted, turned, cursed! But Babyface Garrett was relentless. He slammed, jolted, and knocked Mr. Death's head until he was senseless on the hard deck. Jed stood up then and stared about him curiously. Everything was deathly silent.

Snow or hail—some white substance flew against the thick window outside. The car kept swinging back and forth. Babyface wiped the blood from his hands, and sponged his aching head. He glanced at the instrument panels. The balloon was one thousand feet higher in the air than the standing world's record!

They were above the earth's ceiling! Unknown peril seemed to lurk outside that thick glass, clawing to get in! Babyface leaped to the controls of the balloon. He shoved down on a lever to release gas from the ball. He turned wheels and operated intricate instruments. He had never been in a balloon before and he could only guess at the right thing to do now.

He stepped away from the controls and waited for a moment. The balloon began descending like a plummet. It was dropping three times as fast as it had risen!

Babyface went back to the controls, turned wheels and toyed with the machinery. He could not stop the balloon's rapid descent. He stared out the window. A ghastly breath of the eternal seemed to seep in through the glass. The car kept rocking—rocking!

The two German officers were dead, but Mr. Death stirred. He opened his huge blotch-eyes and stared at Jed Garrett, now working at the controls. Slowly then, and quietly, he moved to get to his feet.

His back to the approaching monk, Babyface worked at the panel. He kept watching the globe which recorded the altitude. He heard the hissing sound of the oxygen tanks.

Mr. Death stood erect. He gathered the torn fragments of his black robe about him, stooped and picked up the empty Luger. He made no sound. He reversed the gun in his hand, and started toward Garrett!

The hissing of the air tank—the car rocking back and forth, jolting—the balloon dropping now through the cloud it had bored through on its way upward! Major Jed Garrett facing the controls, a lithe figure, his head caked with hard blood. Then, behind him, a ghastly figure in black; its face like that of a skeleton, a slit for a mouth, blotches for eyes—a gun butt raised in the bony hand!

Suddenly Mr. Death plunged—struck down. But the car lurched, and the blow went wild, scraped Garrett's head instead of hitting direct. Babyface swung about and Death backed away. Babyface dove for the Luger.

Mr. Death slashed down viciously, but Babyface evaded the blow, tackled Death's legs and sent him hurtling backward. The monk rolled over and scrambled to his feet. Jed charged him again, grabbed his wrist, and cracked it over his knee. The Luger fell to the deck with a thud.

Babyface backed while Death stood against the bulkhead, facing him.

"We're together again," the monk said in a brittle voice, "facing each other— without weapons."

Babyface rubbed the blood from his mouth and glanced at the dropping altitude glass.

"You thought I'd be a skeleton by now —didn't you?" he asked. "But your man Hunkle was stupid. He forgot to tie my hands."

"Without weapons," Mr. Death said, "the best man wins, Garrett!"

Jed laughed harshly. "The best man wins! Do you think that after all I've gone through to stop you from releasing that powder that you can possibly win? And anyway, Death, remember this. Carry this message into your filthy grave with you: you can't beat a Yank!"

"It would almost seem as if that were true," Mr. Death said.

Babyface stared at him. It was the greatest concession the monk of murder had ever made to any Allied soldier. It was, in a way, a tribute to the valiant fight that Jed had waged to get into this position.

"But it isn't quite true," Death went on presently, "because—"

He dove for the levers that would release the powder. Babyface plunged after him, and pulled him away. Now the two were locked in a death struggle on the floor. Mr. Death was savage—a vicious, fighting killer!

Suddenly there was a crash. The car splintered, and opened.

They had hit ground!

Babyface rolled out to the earth. The impact of the crash had buried the boxes of the deadly white powder in the mud. Everywhere on the horizon there were cracking guns, gleaming bayonets and bursting bombs. Screams shrilled into the night air, while machine guns splattered from every side.

They had come down in No Man's Land and the big push was still on!

Mr. Death leaped from the other side of the smashed car. Babyface saw his slithering figure in the dark. He chased after him, caught up. Mr. Death turned. His great blotch-eyes glittered against the red of the battle field.

Babyface rocked back, then shoving his entire body behind the punch, drove his right fist into the side of Mr. Death's head—the side where he had been hit with the gun. The Monk sprawled forward fighting, mumbling, and cursing.

Machine guns chattering ... Kids on barbed wire screaming ... Yank and British and French soldiers walking forward—ever forward, holding their bayonets . . . Multi-colored bombs crashing everywhere . . . The big push going on and on—a parade of death—the price of the bloody earth!

Babyface slugged his fist into the side of Mr. Death's head again. The monk in the black robes slipped and fell. Jed shoved his face, down in the mud, held it there until there was no more movement.

Then he caught the robe-garbed arms of Mr. Death and began dragging the monk through the mud, over the shell holes.... dragging him through No Man's Land. Blood was burning on Major Babyface Garrett's lips. He strode through lines of Allied soldiers who were advancing across the field; strode on, still dragging Mr. Death.

Chattering machine guns . . . Big push . . . Bombs . . . Babyface Garrett suddenly laughed—a song burst from his lips. The Allies were winning their battle. Babyface had won a battle, too—his battle against the hideous and cunning Mr. Death. He had won and he was returning home with his human trophy!

Death, Guts, and Glory

There is no force that exceeds a brave man's love for his comrades; nor any hate fiercer than that of Mr. Death! This conflict is old, but its strength is new; the love of blood is ripe and that of justice, too. Fly if you dare with the screeching wings of Death. The devil may not be beaten, but a good man can always try!

Death, Guts, and Glory

FILLED with the fumes of the freshly dead, the long underground tunnel was silently foreboding. Mystic blue shadows, like the souls of gloomy ghosts, flickered through the darkness to reveal the shimmering steel bars of a cage, and the huge hairy hands of an ape clutched about those bars. Then, shattering the quiet of the tomb-like tunnel, came a low, throaty cry. The hairy hands shook at the cage bars in a frenzied fury. The clattering of the steel was like the bones of skeletons crashing through glass.

But suddenly there was silence again. The glittering little eyes of the beast, sorely red in their sockets, stared out through the misty gloom. Giant fangs were bared as it snarled again. Air was sucked up through the flat and ugly black nostrils of the animal. It beat its chest, pounded maddeningly upon the walls.

Other than that, there was no sound in the tunnel to reveal that anyone worked in the little room, eighty feet down from the cage; the little room in which there flickered only a blue light. The earth walls sweated and smelled and the tunnel was hot. The air was close and thin. It stuck in your throat.

The ape jerked again at the bars and a sly smile crept across its face. The gleaming, animal eyes settled on the cheap lock that held him prisoner. The ape did not know that. But a child's curiosity was guiding its powerful hands. They closed over this interesting toy. In pure puzzlement they tugged powerfully.

Something snapped. The ape's face became a mask of elated surprise. The cage door swung open. The beast sucked in the choking air, pounded a wild tattoo upon its chest. The lust for blood seeped into its nostrils. Reaching its long arms to the ground as it walked, it came from the cage, went down the tunnel, sniffing and growling, pawing through the semi-darkness.

At last it arrived at the door through which gleamed the blue light. Here the ape hesitated, peered in, as a tiger might. It clawed for a moment at its flat nose. Then, swinging the arms again to the ground, it entered the room. It stood for a moment, watching.

There was a long, flat shelf upon which were siphons and bottles. Bowls of queer chemical powders lined one side. His back to the ape, and working over the shelf, stood a tall, gaunt figure in black robes. The robes were those of a renegade monk, and they were torn and bloody. Beneath those robes, on the chest and back of the man wearing them, lay steel plates.

Mister Death, the cunning and brutal Master of War Murder, who, since escaping from a blown-up monastery, had enlisted his horrible genius to the Boche forces, was at work in his new underground laboratory. Not two weeks ago he had escaped an Allied prison camp where he had been put by Major Jed Garrett, a Yank who challenged each new death scheme devised by Mister Death. But the man who wore the tattered and filthy robes was sure that this time his chemical concoction was one that Garrett could not defeat. He worked quietly, and he was so intent that he did not hear the ape behind him.

The huge, hairy beast stalked forward. His hairy arms reached out, clutched the robes of Mister Death. Suddenly the Boche monk spun about. The ape fell back, gibbering and screaming inarticulate cries.

Mister Death's face had been torn away in the explosion. All that remained were the huge black blotches wherein burned his powerful, hypnotic eyes. His mouth was a lipless slit, and his nose a scar of a stump in the middle of his face. What were left of his ears clung close to his bony white head. He spoke now, crisply and sharply.

"Koko!"

The ape snarled, and swinging its long arms, started forward. Mister

Death folded his bony arms across his chest and centered his gaze into the beady little eyes of the animal. He spoke coolly.

"Koko—back! Get back."

The ape hesitated. Mister Death's eyes, large and burning, shot into the eyes of the beast. The animal became stunned. It stood in the middle of the floor like a dumb thing, its arms swinging helplessly at its sides. "Go to the corner and sit down, Koko." The ape turned around, crawled to a corner and stunned, it lay there. It was still dazed, was like a child.

Death worked for a few minutes without a sound, the ape watching him. Presently there were footsteps in the tunnel, and Mister Death looked up as a squat Boche captain entered the room, saluting.

"Herr Death—Captain Ackland, reporting for duty!"

Mister Death again folded his bony arms, and his wide blotch eyes surveyed the man. Ackland was dark, and muscular, not unlike an ape himself. His uniform did not fit him well and he looked generally sloppy. Obviously apprehensive of Mister Death, he appeared to be a fairly good natured sort, though hardly the type of a man that could be trusted out of sight.

"I was very happy when the major told me I could be of service to you, Herr Death," he said, rubbing his pouchy hands and attempting a poor smile. "I consider one is fortunate who can be of aid to a great genius like yourself. It frightens me to think of what the Fatherland would have done without you. I am honored in your presence."

"You are a little wordy," Death said sourly.

"It is because I am amazed that one so humble as myself should be permitted to present himself before you, Herr Death. I—"

"Never mind," Death said, his slit mouth moving slightly, his blotch eyes shifting. "What do you know about apes?"

Koko rose to his feet now and moved quietly in the back part of the room. Captain Ackland saw it for the first time, and his hand went automatically to his throat. He soothed himself with a short smile, but his eyes watched the beast carefully. At last he looked back at Mister Death.

"In Germany, sir," he said respectfully, "it was once my business to travel in the streets with an ape and an organ. I must beg to say, however, that my ape was not the size of that one, nor—shall I say—so vicious looking."

Mister Death surveyed the sloppy officer critically. "I will teach you how to control the animal," he said. "That is a simple matter. The point is, do you understand monkeys? With my assistance, do you think you could pose as an entertainer?"

"Yes, Herr Death. I am sure that I could. It is my happy ability to speak both English and Italian. I do not think I should have any trouble working as a spy."

Mister Death turned about, his black robes sweeping the ground. He looked at the bowl on his shelf, stirred a stick in it. He was pensively quiet for a moment, until he faced Ackland.

"For lack of someone better, I shall use you. If you blunder, it will cost you your miserable life. I have here a liquid which is like gasoline, but far more powerful. You can spill it or rub it on any surface while it is cold, and let it dry. As soon as the surface on which you have spilled it is heated, however—either through rays of the sun or artificial heat— it explodes. It is like touching a match to gasoline, except that much milder heat will cause the explosion, and that the explosion will be much more disastrous."

"Your genius is astounding!" gasped Ackland.

Mister Death's bony face was without expression, his blotch eyes alone gleamed with the evil that lay within his cunning brain.

"The planes taken from a drome for the dawn patrol are cold," he continued. "By the time the racing motors have heated the outside of the hood, the ships are high in the sky."

"I follow you perfectly," said Ackland, not too enthusiastically. "I am to slip into the dromes and spill some of the liquid on each of the planes."

Mister Death shook his hideous head. "No. It will be a habit of the character you are to portray, to go with your ape each morning on the tarmac and wave good-bye to the pilots. The drome would be guarded. But while you are among the planes on the tarmac, you can spill the liquid. No one will know what it is."

"I see said Ackland, glancing at Koko with some doubt. The ape was standing, swinging its long arms back and forth. The small eyes burned in their blood-red sockets.

"Through this method," Death continued, "you should be able to destroy many ships before your trick is discovered. You will delay this by going from drome to drome instead of staying more than two or three days at one. By the time they have all checked with each other— you can escape."

Ackland bowed curtly. "You are the master, Herr Death, and I am your servant to obey."

Mister Death wrapped his black robes tighter about his stiff body.

"You will go first to the 25th American drome," he said. "It is my hope that one of the first planes you spill the liquid upon will be that of Major Jed Garrett."

The captain, garbed in the sloppy uniform, hauled up his trousers. He aired his collar, and you could see the sweat oozing out of his forehead.

"I have heard that Herr Garrett is exceedingly clever," he said.

Mister Death stared through him, but he did not answer.

Major Jed Garrett, known to his comrades as "Babyface," because of his youthful countenance, adjusted his helmet, tucked in the strap on his neck. Click, the huge police dog who traveled with him wherever he went, stood now at his feet. The pair had flown together in an air circus before the war, and special orders permitted them to remain together in the service. More than once the dog had aided in saving Babyface's life.

"Well, Click," Babyface said, "we're off on the dawn patrol."

The dog whined.

"Great morning," Babyface went on, pulling up his boots. "And the kids are excited that their major is going to fly with them." He glanced sharply at the dog. "Being a CO. here at the 25th would never keep me out of the sky." He laughed, and getting up, started for the door. Click trotted after him.

When he arrived on the tarmac he saw that the planes were just being wheeled out. On the edge of the field a group of pilots huddled about a squat figure in peasant rags. An ape was chained to the peasant's wrist, and the pair were clowning.

Click rushed at the gathering, barking out his lungs. Babyface rushed after him, grabbed him by his red, white and blue collar and pulled him back. The police dog strained at the collar, tried to break away.

"Click, behave!" Babyface snapped.

The ape suddenly began straining at the chain that held him to the squat, sloppy looking peasant. The little man had to have the aid of some of the pilots to hold the animal back.

"Koko," he kept repeating sharply.

Babyface saw that he would have to put Click quickly into the plane to keep the dog from rushing the giant monkey. He lifted the squirming, barking dog and took him to the ship where he lifted him in and strapped him to his place in the specially designed cockpit. Click still tried to break loose.

Major Garrett climbed up into his plane. The mechanic spun the prop, and in a moment the motor roared. It was a signal to the others, and the pilots who had crowded about the peasant went immediately to their ships. Babyface saw the man with the ape going about, waving them goodbye. He had a funny little rusted can which had once been a garden sprinkler. He sprinkled a little liquid on each plane.

"For good luck, my laddies," he exclaimed.

The ape was still staring at Click, and the dog kept barking shrilly at the hairy beast. The peasant looked as though he wished to put some of his "good luck" liquid on Babyface's plane, but he dared not come within thirty feet of the ship, because of Click and the uncontrollable rage of the ape when he was near the dog.

Presently Babyface lifted his gloved hand out over the side of his plane, and taxied forward. The wheels rolled swiftly over the smooth ground of the tarmac, then lifted into the air.

One after another the other ships rolled across the tarmac and lifted to the sky. In a few moments the entire seven ships were flying in perfect formation, motors droning the grim song of the sky lanes. It was a clear morning and Babyface looked toward Bocheland with happy anticipation.

They had been in the air approximately ten minutes and were flying over No Man's Land when the ship on the right flank suddenly spurted with an explosion. It was not an explosion of sufficient damage to blow up the ship, but the whole motor covering burst with flame.

The pilot leaned out over the side, and Babyface waved him down. It was apparent that something had gone wrong with the engine, he thought. The kid flying the Spad began dropping, but his young eyes took in the lines of trenches, the cross fire, and he wavered for a moment, back and forth in his cockpit. The flames soared and whipped back with the wind. They reached the fuselage, of a sudden, and the ship burst in mid air!

Major Babyface closed his eyes and looked away. But he had no sooner done this when the ship on the left spurted with the same dull explosion, and the motor panels licked with red flame. He stared as the pilot zoomed down, his wings screaming in the wind. Then he saw the Spad explode and shatter.

In the next second, two other planes broke out in flames. The frightened pilots nosed immediately for the ground. They were across No Man's Land by now and there was a short clearing where a landing might be made. The Spads seemed to be racing to reach earth before the inevitable fuselage explosion. Their canvas wailed a shrill siren into the morning air.

They did not reach earth. The ships crashed into tiny bits and showered the ground like a rain of human flesh and bone.

Major Babyface Garrett gritted his teeth tight. He was not surprised when he saw the remaining Spads go through the same procedure.

Alone in the sky now, when a few seconds ago he had been in the company of six other Spads, Babyface was at loss. He could not believe what his eyes had seen!

Filled with insane rage, he drove like a comet through the air, his mind still turning for the answer. Suddenly it came to him. If it had not been for the obvious fact that the man who was apparently a peasant entertainer, had not been able to approach his ship, he may not have been able to figure it out. Indeed, there would have been no one left to figure it out. G.H.Q. would think that the whole squadron had been downed by Boches, unless some eye witness made a report of the spectacle, and even then, the man with the ape could not be proven guilty.

It was Click's fury at sight of the ape, and the ape's natural instinct to tear at the dog that shattered the clever death scheme and gave Babyface the solution.

The sprinkler had been filled with a liquid—.

The roaring motor of a Fokker throbbed over him. Babyface looked up, saw the black panther plane of Mister Death hurtling through the sky toward him! The murder monk had been watching the death spectacle, and now that Babyface was left he intended to kill him.

In that split second Babyface realized that the idea of the man with the ape had came from the cunning mind of Mister Death.

He wheeled his plane in the direction of the speeding metal Fokker. He saw the robed figure sitting in the cockpit, long, talon-like hands gripped on the sides of the ship.

"Rotten devil!" Babyface spat.

Click tensed himself and whined, as Babyface's expertly trained hands gripped both the stick and the handles of the Vickers. In the next moment, tracers, spurting orange fire in the morning sky, belched from the muzzles of the gun.

Brrrrrrrrt .... Brrrrrt . .

Mister Death's oncoming Fokker was not slowed by the chewing chunks of steel. The bullets sliced into the metal of the ship scraped along the sides. Death's hand reached for his Spandaus handles.

Brrrrrrrt. . . Brrrrrt. .

The bullets sailed through Babyface's right wing. Tore away part of the canvas which flapped in the wind. Garrett dove beneath Death's ship as it hurtled over him. He twisted the stick and cut back up for altitude.

Mister Death saw the tactical movement and turned about before Babyface could gain sufficient altitude to be on equal terms with him. Snarling, Death drove down toward the wrecked right wind of the Spad. He gripped the Spandaus handles.

Brrrt. Brrrt. .. Brrrt..

Jed Garrett's ship groaned under the abuse. He hauled back on the stick, tried to pull his ship up into the sky.

Mister Death brought his metal Fokker about, cut down again, plunging almost atop Babyface's tail assembly. The screaming Spandaus lead tumbled through the body of the Spad, tore holes in the canvas as a vicious animal tears a rag.

Babyface, his heart pounding like a trip hammer, and his pulse beating wildly, brought his protesting ship about in the wind. Mister Death was forced to dive to avoid collision. Babyface took immediate advantage. He catapulted his crate after the Fokker in the manner of a tiger charging a deer.

Brrrrrrrt.... Brrrrt... Brrrrt..

Belching, coughing, sputtering, the thin streams of Vicker's lead tore into the sides of the black ship. Mister Death jerked at his controls. Lifted his ship right in front of the Spad's nose. Instead of turning off, Babyface plunged after him. Death was forced to spin away, but he was not in time; the two ships touched.

Babyface's wing was almost completely torn away and the ship was crippled. Mister Death's fuselage was leaking from the terrific bombardment He was easing the ship toward the earth, but at the same time sailing like a drunken and speeding torpedo back to his own drome.

Jed could not follow. He would have a difficult enough time trying to force his wrecked ship to make a landing that wouldn't kill him. He zigzagged toward the ground like a kite, and at last, reaching a short clearing, pressed suddenly down. The wheels crunched into the earth, rolled a few feet, then stopped. The plane was still upright, but Babyface knew it would never fly again. He released Click, and the two of them hopped to the ground.

Babyface took off his helmet and shook out the sweat. Click barked. A drone of planes sounded overhead.

Jed looked up to see another Yank patrol coming back from Bocheland. He hopped atop his ship, began waving frantically. Click ran around in circles and barked.

Presently one of the planes turned off and commenced coming down to make a landing.

"Once we get back," Babyface told Click savagely, "you can do anything you want to that ape."

It was night. Major Jed Garrett gulped down a shot of brandy, then rose to his feet as he heard a scuffling in the outside office. Two lieutenants dragged in a squat, sloppy looking man, garbed in peasant clothing. "Let me go, let me go!" he shouted. The lieutenants released him, and the peasant stood in the center of the floor, hotly indignant.

"Where's the ape?" Babyface said to the sloppily dressed man.

"He is gone."

"We saw a black plane lift out of the woods nearby," one of the lieu-tenants reported. "I guess it was Mister Death's plane. We rushed to the clearing where it had taken off and when we arrived we found this man there. He seemed very frightened."

"Was he armed?"

"No sir."

"Very well, gentlemen. You may go. I'll speak to this prisoner alone."

They saluted and departed. Click stood back in the shadows of the C.O.'s office, growling. Babyface, remembering the helpless pilots who had died in the air before his very eyes, leaned on the desk and stared at the squat man.

"So your little scheme goes to hell in a hurry, doesn't it? Because you couldn't get close enough to my plane to spill some of your hell juice on it."

"I do not know what you are saying. I wished only to give the pilots good luck."

"Good luck!" Babyface laughed bitterly. "In a pig's eye, you dirty rot-ten spy!"

"I am not a spy, I—"

Babyface stepped forward, his tight fist moved eight short inches in a blow that crashed brutally across Ackland's face. The spy fell back, Babyface was tight lipped.

"You come across with the goods, my German friend, or I'm going to pound the living hell out of you!"

"I know nothing!"

Babyface charged him, caught his ragged coat and holding it with one hand, bashed his fist squarely into the Hun's nose. Blood spurted. Babyface punched his rock-like fist across Ackland's lips. The German cringed back.

"Talk, damn you," Babyface said, "or I'm going to let my dog go to work on you."

Click snarled, baring his white teeth.

Captain Ackland stared at the hound, wiped blood from his face, then began babbling.

"All right—all right. Why shouldn't I talk? Mister Death came over when he realized the scheme was a flop. But did he save me? God—no! He saved that damned ape! He wouldn't let me ride in the ship!"

"He's evidently got further use for the ape," Babyface said acidly, "and no more use for you, you yellow swine."

"He left me here to be caught," Ackland babbled on.

"Go on," Babyface prodded, 'let's hear all about it. What kind of fluid is Death using now? Where does he keep it?"

The sloppy little German captain broke down and told all he knew. Major Jed Garrett sat on his desk, smoking a cigarette and listening. When Ackland had finished, Babyface grabbed him by the collar and dragged him out of the shack.

The two officers who had been waiting, ran up. Babyface's countenance was a mask of hatred. His buddies had died, and this, he told himself, was the first revenge for their deaths.

"Slap him into the cell below the canteen," he said. "I've held my own court martial on him. Tell G.H.Q. he has confessed."

"Will you save me? Make me a prisoner of war?" Ackland begged, gibbering in his fear.

"You'll be shot at dawn," Babyface told him crisply. "And I'd hate like hell to be in your boots when those six pals of mine up there get their hands on you— they died without a ghost of a chance. You've had your chance!"

Ackland sobbed as they dragged him away.

Babyface returned to the office, got into his jacket and helmet and left again. He walked quickly across the field to the drome where he ordered a mechanic to make ready a machine for him. In a few minutes it was ready to go. He helped Click up into it, then climbed into the cockpit after the dog.

Contact was established. Babyface warmed the motors, waited impatiently for the moment that he could take off. His face was white, and bloodless, his eyes like marbles. He was going after—Mister Death!

Babyface glanced over the side as he raced over No Man's Land. He saw the red flares of torches, and the small yellow specks of gun fire. "A helluva war, isn't it, Click?" Babyface said. It was his favorite phrase.

Babyface knew the way to Mister Death's new headquarters. He had learned from the frightened Ackland where he might land, and though it was dangerously close, he risked it. The Spad skimmed down over the tree tops and huddled like a hen into a spot barely large enough for a decent landing.

Rage seethed within Garrett. He unleashed the dog and the two of them made their way through the forest. This time he knew exactly what he was going to do.

Ackland had furnished Babyface with a clear description of the underground tunnel and the room that was at the end of it, Babyface arrived at the mouth of the tunnel. Two sentries stood at guard. Babyface lifted his automatic and without qualm or fear that his shots would be heard, sent a bullet into each of the men's heads.

He ran across the ground, entered the tunnel. He quickly descended the steps and Click followed warily behind him. Babyface stood at the end of the long corridor of earth and stared toward the room from which the blue light flickered. Presently he heard an insane growl, and a clattering of steel.

He turned to see Koko the ape pounding at the door of his cage. Click snarled, and the police dog's fur bristled stiffly. The ape crashed through the cage. Babyface lifted his automatic, but at that moment Click leaped for the beast's neck, and Babyface could not fire in fear of hitting his dog.

Attracted by the noise, Mister Death, his black robes tight about his stiff, gaunt body, appeared at the door of the room at the end of the tunnel. The renegade monk drew a huge Luger from his sleeve.

Babyface fired in his direction, then raced toward the room. Death fired twice, and the shots blazed yellow in the dark of the tunnel. Death retreated back into the room, Babyface after him.

In the tunnel, Koko and Click were waging a terrific struggle. The ape threw the dog from him, and screaming in rage, plunged after Click. Click, on his back, snarled and snapped. His teeth sank into the hard hide of the ape. Koko beat his hairy fists into the dog's head. He bent to sink his gleaming fangs into Click's back.

Meanwhile—Babyface entered the room in which he knew Mister Death kept his liquid hell. He saw the robed figure facing him, his Luger level. They exchanged shots. Babyface's hand spurted with blood. He dropped his gun.

Mister Death, his robes sweeping about him, his ghastly face a horrible mask, and his blotch eyes glittering, charged at him. Babyface leaped out of the way, rushed over to the shelf and with a sweep of his hand, swept down the glass tubes and siphons.

Mister Death snapped two more shots at Babyface, then his Luger clicked empty. He came after Babyface, his hands reached. Jed hoisted himself on the shelf, lifted his booted foot and pounded it into the steel plate that covered Death's robed chest.

The monk spun back and Babyface catapulted from the shelf after him. He clutched a hold about his neck, began pressing. Death rolled, slammed Babyface's head down. Babyface jerked from under, staggered to his feet.

He reached back on the shelf, picked up a bottle of the liquid. As Mister Death rushed toward him, he crashed it over his head. He saw the monk go down, his bony white skull spurting with blood. He watched as Death groveled on the ground.

Jed turned again to the shelf; he ripped it apart and discovered a supply of the liquid that Death had made. He tore part of his trousers off, made it a fuse, and jamming one end into the liquid, lit a match to the other end. It would not burn. Babyface dipped the cloth into the liquid, then lit it. It flared up.

Babyface turned to make his escape, then was held stock still by the sight that met his eyes. Click stood at the door, his furry coat matted with the blood he had given to fight the powerful Koko. But despite the ragged, ghastly condition of the dog, its tail was wagging in victory. Sprawled in the doorway was the lifeless form of the ape. The dog's grin was almost human. It said, in effect, "I won, master, I won!"

Babyface raced over and kneeled beside his dog. In that moment, a black figure rushed by and Garrett knew that the hated Death had recovered consciousness. Flames were engulfing the room now, and Click whined loud in protest. The dog was weak, but able to move under his own power. He followed Babyface in pursuit of Mr. Death. Racing madly, Jed caught up with the robed figure. He dove at the legs of the black monk and both went crashing to the floor of the tunnel.

"Fool!" Death screamed. "That tank line is piped to our nearest drome. It will explode at the other end of the tunnel and we will be trapped!"

Babyface laughed madly. "Then we both die, don't we!"

"You are insane!" Mister Death shrieked, hurling his bony arms at Babyface.

Explosion followed his words. The open mouth of the tunnel burst into flames. The fire from the room that had been lighted was crawling from that end of the tunnel. Babyface and Mister Death were hemmed in between the two roaring hells of fire!

Babyface climbed to his feet, and Mr. Death also stood up. Both were without weapons. They could only speak their hate.

"This is the end of both of us, Herr Death," Babyface lipped grimly.

"Does it give you pleasure to sacrifice your life so that I may die?"' Death rasped.

"Damn well right it does," Babyface hurled at him. "Your invention of that fire liquid will eat away your bones, Death, My bones too. But the point is that you and your schemes to kill off the Allies are over. When those six Yanks died this morning I swore that would be the end of you!"

The flames from both ends of the tunnel were coming to the center at a rapid speed. The yellow arms of the twin fires reached greedily. The heat was suffocating. Sweat drenched Babyface; he tore open his collar, then leaned back against the wall, laughing the grim laughter of death. He felt he was going to die, and it was strange that he was happy. Happy to see Mister Death so terrorized in his own trap.

The fire kept coming. Mister Death hauled his bloody black robes about his body, rocked back and forth on his heels. His blotch eyes rolled crazily. He wanted to live to avenge the Allies who had caused the explosion which had wrecked his face and body. Other than that, Babyface saw now that he was not particularly afraid of death. It was his burning desire to kill off Allies, his horrible hatred that made him wish to continue living.

Crackling, creeping, scorching, the fire licked out, came within feet of the trapped men. And Babyface only leaned against the wall, tearing his jacket from him, sweating and laughing.

"You are an idiot!" Death rasped above the roar of the flames. "But a brave one, major."

"I'm not brave. There isn't a Yank alive who wouldn't give his life to kill a fiend like you!"

But all the same, Babyface was suddenly not so keen about dying. Never again to fly. Life lost.

Suddenly the huge tanks at the end of the tunnel where the room had been, exploded. The whole tunnel shook. Earth flew everywhere, shooting high into the sky. Flame followed it, shooting out into the night air. Babyface looked up suddenly to see that the entire roof of the tunnel had been blown off. Stars glittered above them. Earth was beginning to pound back down upon them.

Mister Death scrambled up over the side of the tunnel and climbed to firm ground. Babyface followed him, with Click right behind. Another explosion rocked the earth!

The whole earth seemed to be afire now. Babyface tried to follow Mister Death, but he lost him in the rush. He caught up Click and ran back to where they had hidden the Spad. Hurriedly, he established contact. The motors roared. Babyface managed a difficult take off.

His ship rose above the ground and into the sky. He looked down over the cockpit, saw the flaming ground. The fire was running along the pipe line to a nearby German drome.

Somewhere down there was Mister Death. Although Babyface had destroyed the hell fluid, he had failed to kill the monk. His attempt had been a sincere one and he could not blame himself. But he somehow had a feeling that the robed figure whose face was a hideous mask of bone was only laughing hoarsely at his escape.

Death in the Fleet

High in the sky, and in the deep, dark waters of the sea—moves the relentless scourge of Mister Death! There can be no reprieve from a sin that will not die—that haunts the hours of living men wherever they may be. But Courage, too, is a deathless thing—that does not die with mortal men. Jed Garrett flies high with the banner of Courage and settles the score of Death in the Fleet!

Death in
the Fleet

THE black night set icy hands upon Lieutenant Griner, as he stood in the tiny conning tower of the American submarine; his white-topped officer's cap tilted on the side of his head, his uniformed figure rigid. Ahead, the quartermaster hovered above the steering lever; beside him was Jones, his executive officer.

The red and green running lights of the sub were turned off. Not even so much as a shadow of the sturdy little pigboat glinted on the moonless water as they glided surely and swiftly into the zone of death. All seemed clutched in foreboding silence—except for the swish of the sea beneath them, and the pump-pump-pump of the huge Diesel engines below.

Lieutenant Griner was the skipper. And because the responsibility of the mission which he was about to carry out lay directly upon his shoulders, he was nervous and restless. He wished to light a cigarette. Wished to walk up and down. But he could do neither. It was imperative that the submarine remain totally dark; and the conning tower was too small to afford pacing.

Griner's face was deathly white; his eyes glowed in their sockets like coals afire. He ran his tongue over his dry, parched lips. His face was hot. He was feverish with excitement.

"See anything yet, Jones?"

"No sir."

"It's going to be tough," Griner said. "Damn tough, old man. You don't look to come out of this alive, do you?"

Jones, tall and slim, smiled a ghostly smile through the night. "I wrote my mother and father before we shoved off, sir," he said.

Griner grunted. His breath was short, wheezing. It is not pleasant to feel that you are going to die. But it was the dynamite-loaded pigboat's mission to ram into the side of a German battleship. In war charts, in calculations of winnings and losings, one sub and her crew was a good trade for a battleship and her crew. The battleship carried between eight hundred and a thousand men. The sub carried only twenty-seven sailors, including the four officers.

It was a silent and unspectacular glory for which they were headed. If they were successful in ramming the battleship, before the German war vessel was aware of their presence, the Allies would rejoice the victory. But Lieutenant Griner, his comrades from Annapolis, and his loyal crew of sailors, would be dead.

"They're late with those orders," Griner growled. "I suppose we'll just have to cruise in this direction until we get them."

"I'm afraid so," Jones replied. "Spies are getting the longitude and latitude of the battleship's latest position now. They'll radio us in code."

The pumping and throbbing of the Diesels engines still mingled with the silken swish of water. The black hulk of the pigboat moved on across the dark sea. Griner wiped sweat from his face. He felt like a man waiting to go to the chair. He thought, vainly of his home in the States, of his lost boyhood, of his parents, of the girl he intended to marry. He wondered how much he would be missed.

Presently a figure emerged from the C.O.C, tube. "Radio message, Captain Griner."

Griner turned, nervous as a cat. He ripped the message from the radioman's hand. Stooping in the enclosed tower he lit a match and read aloud, so that Jones and the quartermaster might hear. The radioman and an officer below deck had already decoded it:

CODE — PRIORITY — CODE Objective Enemy Vessel five miles off port bow. Bear direct NW course 320. At two miles distance from battle-ship submerge and proceed underwater.

—CinC United States Battle Force.

Griner crumpled the message in his hand. Somehow he did not feel so badly —now that the course was charted for him—now that death was inescapable. He turned to the quartermaster and gave him instructions. Then he glanced back at Jones.

"Well, fella, we have one satisfaction—trading 27 of us for around 800 of them!"

Jones' face flickered in that same ghostly smile. "Too bad we can't be alive to see that 'wagon' go up into pieces!"

"Yeah. The dynamite is secure in all four of the torpedo tubes, isn't it?"

"Yes sir," Jones said.

They were silent again, moodily silent. The pigboat seemed to move faster. Phosporous bubbled on the water. The moon slipped from behind a cloud; its silver rays silhouetted the small submarine against the ghastly blackness of the night.

Suddenly Griner heard the roar of an airplane engine in the sky. He looked up but could see nothing. The plane's motor throbbed closer and closer.

"Secure hatches!" the skipper bellowed. "Man all stations for diving! This may be an air attack!"

"Aye, sir," Jones snapped. "But it only sounds like a single plane."

The words were scarcely out of his mouth when he pressed a button. The clattering bells for general quarters began ringing through the hollow iron craft. Sailors bolted the torpedo tube and battery hatches, then ducked below. Jones climbed down through the C.O.C. tube. The quartermaster turned.

And then—before they could possibly dive—the plane was upon them. It swooped down. The pilot, garbed in flapping black robes, stared over the side of the cockpit. His eyes were glittering blotches, his face the shape of a skull. He dropped something on the pigboat's deck. Then his plane lifted, and soared away.

Captain Griner watched. He was dumbfounded. At last he climbed down from the conning tower and inspected what the Boche had dropped on deck. He found a body. Lighting a match, he read from the note attached to it:

This is an American whom it was my misfortune to have to kill in the duties of war. But now that he is dead I wish for him the honor of decent burial. Thus I deliver him to you.

Your friend and enemy,

"A German Flying Ace."

Griner had not seen the face of the pilot in the black Fokker, and now he shook out his match and put the note in his pocket.

"Damn nice," he muttered.

But he looked down at the corpse and the thought came to him of the burial. It was a mockery. A corpse delivered for burial when Griner himself—and his whole crew—were on their way to death! He reached down and lifted the body.

"Well, I'll take you below, and at least you can go to hell with the rest of us, buddy."

He hauled the cold corpse into the conning tower and ordered a sailor to take it below.

"Drape the body in an American flag," he said. "That's about all we can do, I'm afraid."

The sailor obeyed. Griner presently closed up the conning tower and climbed below. In the center of the control room, a square compartment, glistening with steel and wheels and levers, he found the major part of his crew. They were at their stations for diving. Death was in their eyes. Their faces were drawn and agonized. Griner thought again—grimly, how dearly the bravest of men will cling to life.

The corpse was laid in a red, white and blue flag near the radio shack. Griner sat down at the periscope. He gripped the bars in his hand. Junior-Lieutenant Jones stood back—that ghastly smile still twisted on his face.

Griner shoved back his officer's cap and pressed his eye to the sights. He snapped his orders. He was hot, more feverish than ever. He gripped the bars with sweaty hands. His forehead was drenched in perspiration.

The doomed sailors worked quickly and efficiently, as the huge Diesel engines snapped off and silence rode the tiny sub. A breath of cold, clammy air swept through the compartments. The batteries snapped on, but they made no sound. The nose of the pigboat slanted downward, and the waters swallowed the ship as it plunged beneath the surface—like a gray tomb sinking to a frozen grave.

The bulkheads dripped moisture, and it seemed as if they would cave in with the pressure from the outside. Griner kept gripping the bars of the periscope. He was trembling now as the sailors watched him, their lips clamped tight, their eyes wide with the gleam of deathless sacrifice. They wore only dungaree trousers and undershirts—short-sleeved cotton undershirts which stuck to their bodies.

"Ease her, for Cripes sake ease her," Griner barked. He was calm now. A man is calm when there is an important job for him to do. He kept watching through the sights.

The sub rocked back and forth like a cradle, rocked with the sway and current of the ocean. Fish darted about the outside, goggling at the strange iron thing which had invaded their domain. The atmosphere within the bulkheads was tense, electric. Only the skipper's snapped commands broke the silence.

The body of the American wrapped in the flag lay still, ignored.

"Got her sighted!" Griner snapped.

"Where?" Jones asked.

"Dead ahead. She's a cinch target. Sure those dynamited tubes are fixed?"

"Positive, sir."

The sailors stared at one another. It meant they had only a few minutes left to live. They sweated in their torture. One, a kid, shrieked; he fell to the deck, trembling and shaking.

"God Almighty, I don't want to die! Turn back! I want to fight! I don't want to die like a dog without a chance!"

No one paid any attention to him. Griner pulled down the voice tube to the battery room.

"Ahead full. Give her all we've got, Ryan."

A hollow voice echoed back through: "Aye, aye, captain."

Griner still clutched the tube in his trembling fingers. "And Ryan—"

"Yes sir?"

"Goodbye, old man. You've been a good engineer officer."

"Thank you, sir."

He hung up and faced Jones. His glance signified more than words. The skipper looked at his men.

"Well, fellows, in another five minutes we'll be blasted to hell. But we'll go with almost a thousand Boches. In that thought, we—"

Something strange happened. Captain Griner's sentence was never finished. The corpse draped in the American flag lurched. A loud ticking filled the strained silence of the room.

Then came the explosion. Griner yelled. The sub was blasted into a hundred pieces. In less than a minute there was nothing left of her but black oil on the surface of the ocean. Black oil—and a pair of officer's caps—those of Lieutenant Griner and Junior-Lieutenant Jones. They floated side by side, just as the two men had served side by side as shipmates.

On the distant horizon the immense German battleship sailed smoothly through the water, unharmed.

Mister Death paced up and down in the small shed he had constructed as his temporary headquarters on the waterfront, while two Boche majors stood watching him respectfully. The robed figure of doom was chuckling; his ominous laughter echoed from the wooden walls.

"That makes the third American ship upon which we have worked our corpse ruse," he said.

"So it does, Herr Death," spoke one of the officers. "That is very good work indeed."

"Considering that the last submarine was going to blow up one of our battleships," Death snapped, "it is admirable work."

"Quite so!" said the other major.

Mister Death paced some more. He was a tall, gaunt figure, whose black robes swished across the floor as he walked. He had once been a monk; but the explosion that blew up the monastery had all but completely wrecked him. Surgeons had basted steel plates on his chest and back, and he had emerged, still wearing his robes, to become the most hated and most feared monster of the skies.

His face was a horrible blotch of scars, completely without expression. Only one man had prevented Mister Death from wiping out the Allies and winning the war for the Fatherland—Major Jed Garrett, of the Yank flying force—whose sole mission in the war was to kill Mister Death.

Death turned about. "I have increased the power of my explosives now, so that I think we can successfully place bodies aboard the larger ships."

"The doctor has four new bodies hollowed out and ready for the time explosives," the first major said. "He is waiting so that he may sew the corpses up when you have placed the concoction inside."

Mister Death's huge blotch-eyes glittered. "Good. We will try minesweeps and destroyers with these four corpses. I will go now and arrange the timing."

"Just how does this explosive you have invented work?"

Death turned his ghastly face toward the major angrily. "I discuss only the physical effects of the things I invent. Not their formula. I will tell you, however, that it is on the order of a time bomb, more simple than my other inventions. Of course, the explosive is much more powerful than a bomb, since it consists mainly of nitro-glycerine."

"It is the method you have of placing these explosives aboard enemy ships that is clever," the Boche said flatteringly.

Death's slit-mouth curved down. "It is because the Americans are such fools about their dead. They attach sentiment to a corpse. They don't suspect the truth. And once a ship is blown up, no one is left alive to tell of the corpse having been delivered aboard. That makes the cause of the explosion unknown to the rest of the fleet."

He surveyed the two officers for a moment, then wrapping his bloody black robes tightly about him, swept out of the room.

Major Jed Garrett sat behind his desk at the 25th airdrome smoking a cigarette. His huge, brown police dog, Click, lay at his feet. A general from G.H.Q. sat across the office from Garrett. "I tell you Mr. Death is behind this thing. Our spies report he is no longer behind Boche lines. Connect that with the mysterious explosion of three of our ships—three ships which were not engaged in enemy battle, and were not in the vicinity of mines—and—" the general shrugged, stuck a cigar in his mouth and lighted it.

Major Garrett had been nicknamed "Babyface" because his countenance had not changed since he was seventeen. His reputation was that of a grim battling ace who had knocked Mister Death out of the sky repeatedly, thwarting his hideous plans. Still, his face was young, boyish. You might have thought him a green fledgling had you not known who he was. At this moment his blue eyes shone, and a lock of his brown hair hung over his forehead. He whisked it away.

"I think you've got a right lead for once, General," he said. A thin, deathless smile curved on his lips. He flicked cigarette ashes in a tray. Smoke billowed out through his nostrils.

"I am sure that I have!" ejaculated the general.

Babyface Garrett studied his superior officer coolly. "Sir, I know the fleet zone is out of my territory. But I want permission to go and get Mr. Death. I'm afraid if something isn't done there will be more than three ships listed as mysteriously exploded!"

"Permission granted," the general barked. "But bring him in alive, Garrett! Don't take his word for how he is effecting these explosions, nor any physical evidence you might see. Death's cunning mind is too full of ideas and schemes; secret plans that his aides will work out, even if he is dead. We must learn from him what they are, so that we will be prepared to meet them! Do you understand? Bring him in alive!"

Click's brown ears were standing up straight. The dog was panting.

"I understand," Babyface replied slowly. "I quite agree with you. Death is the brains. If we killed him his schemes would be executed anyway. I'll—I'll do my utmost to bring him in!"

The general stood up with a worried smile. He extended his hand and Jed Garrett shook it grimly.

"Good luck, Garrett!"

As the commanding officer left the office, Babyface turned and reached for his helmet and jacket. Click stood up, stretched. Jed departed from the room. He swung over the ground to the tarmac.

A few minutes later his plane was rolling across the ground. It lifted into the air. Click sat back in his special compartment, his fur whipped by the breeze.

The Spad's motor hummed evenly as Babyface pulled back on the stick and climbed for altitude. The Yank major's eyes were grim, behind the panes of his goggles. He watched the ground below him; glanced at the taut guy wires on his wings; fingered the cold steel of his Vickers' handles.

Above him floated white clouds of war. The sun shone down without mercy. Babyface's Spad hurtled through the air lanes, prop spinning grimly, as Garrett turned and spoke to his dog.

"It's Mister Death again, fella!"

Click only growled.

The war zone of the fleet is large, and for two days after arriving, Major Jed Garrett searched the skies in vain for any sign of Mister Death's black Fokker. Meanwhile he received the news by radio that four more Allied ships had been mysteriously blown up.

He paced the office of a Naval headquarters now, restless and worried. He was ashamed that since his assignment to the case four new ships had been blasted to hell. It seemed to pick up the trail of Mister Death, and for once, the murder monster had completely covered his trail. Men reported having seen the black Fokker, but no one ever knew where it went. The Allied spy forces in this zone were assigned to keep a look out. Captured Boches were grilled without mercy for information, but they had none to give.

Jed Garrett was both bewildered and confused. Hatred for Mister Death filled him as never before. Ships were being blown up all along the zone and he was helpless to do anything about it. He spent long hours in the sky, waiting for sight of the Fokker. But he never got it. It was his inability to find the murder monster and fight him that filled him with rage. His nerves were ragged, on end. The morale of the Allied fleets was at stake. No one knew how these explosions came about— these ghastly visits of Death that ate so many many lives.

There was a radioman in the office in which Babyface paced, and now the radioman became alert. Jed glanced at him, saw the expression in the man's eyes. He rushed over and pushed him away, putting on the ear phones. Click, who had been lying in a corner, sat up.

"News of Mister Death flashing from somewhere down the line," the radioman said.

"All right, I'll get it!"

Babyface leaned over the table, pad and pencil ready. He heard the clicking of the set:

Dash dot dot dot dash dot dash dot dot—dot dash dot dash. . . .

"The first word is 'black'!" Babyface said. It had been quickly spelled out in code.

The rest of the message came through rapidly. It said that a black Fokker was shooting past at terrific speed and that it should be in the sky opposite the office occupied by Babyface within a few minutes.

Babyface leaped to his feet, grabbed up his goggles. "This is what I've been waiting for! Phone the mechanic to warm my plane immediately!" He turned to the dog. "Come on, Click!"

He rushed from the office and ran all the way to the improvised shed in which his Spad waited. The mechanic had the motor roaring. Babyface hopped into the cockpit, while the mechanic helped Click up.

Surging forward at a terrific speed, Babyface lifted into the air. The engine hummed, the canvas on the wings fluttered in the wind, as higher and higher the roaring Spad climbed. Babyface was grim, feverish for battle. His skin tingled, and his blood raced hot. Too long had Mister Death evaded him! Too many ships had the murder monster wrecked!

His eyes searched the heavens for sign of the black Fokker. He saw it presently, catapulting through the sky at an almost unbelievable rate of speed. It was Death's special ship, forged of metal and geared to a speed that made ordinary Fokkers ridiculous.

Babyface gunned his Spad directly in the path of the oncoming Fokker. In a moment he could see Mister Death's black robes flapping wildly in the wind; could see the white, skull of a face behind the windshield in the cockpit.

Jed's gloved hand went up and gripped the handles of his Vickers.

Brrrrrrrt. , . . Brrrrt. . . .

The screaming yellow nails of hell coughed from the muzzles of his gun and ripped through the air like baby comets. The lead of those tracers clipped into the metal on the onrushing Fokker.

Mister Death, taken by surprise, nosed his ship upward, so that it climbed like a black hearse tugging to reach the top of a hill. Babyface Garrett laughed wildly. A smile of hatred was twisted on his lips. He wormed his Spad in beneath the belly of the Fokker.

"Help yourself to a bellyful of lead!" he spat.

Brrrrrrrt. . . . Brrrrt. . . Brrrt.

Click stood up, howling. The wind whined about the lithe body of the dog.

Babyface's tracers sliced the sky, tumbled like pellets of iron rain along the bottom of his enemy's metal Fokker.

Death, his slit-mouth tight, his blotch-eyes wide with their glare of horror, nosed his ship down—mercilessly aiming for Jed Garrett's right wing—knowing his metal ship could take it off without serious damage to the Fokker. He hauled back on his Spandaus guns.

Brrrrrrrt.... Brrrrrt. .. Brrrrrt..

Coffin pegs of murderous destruction slammed through the canvas of the Yank Spad. Yellow balls of glinting steel chewed at the wing. Babyface saw the Fokker roaring down upon him. With the trained hand of a pilot who barnstormed before the war; a pilot who knows his ship and how to handle it, he jerked away with only a split-second to spare.

Mister Death's ship went hurtling by as Babyface hauled his crate around into the wind. Laughter broke from his thin, tight lips.

"Try again, Death!" he screamed.

But Mister Death needed no invitation. His robes still napping madly, he jerked his Fokker up and around. Babyface banked out, but he heard the chattering Spandaus bark from the black Fokker.

Brrrrrrrrt.... Brrrrrrrrrrrt...

Leaden death gripped his undercarriage to shreds and left the skeleton of wooden framing to hold the Spad in the sky. Babyface wove back and forth in the cockpit, his eyes everywhere at once, his hand tight on the stick. He cut back. The black Fokker was shooting up past him.

Babyface again hauled on his Vickers. His hand was steady as he chopped for the one vital spot on the metal Fokker— the gas tank!

Brrrrrt.. Brrrrrt.. Brrrt..

Short, snarling spurts of devil's death shrieked from the muzzles of his gun. They slammed through the spot at which Babyface had aimed them. Death rocked in the cockpit, brought his Fokker around. He punched his Spandaus but when the tracers came slinging after Babyface, the Yank lifted his ship above them.

Mister Death's plane was losing gas. The tank was punched full of holes. He circled and Babyface winged after him. Suddenly realizing that his time in the sky would be short, because of his punctured tank, Death started whirling back down the line.

But the phenomenal speed of his Fokker had been impaired by Garrett's Vickers' bursts. He could only manage to keep out of the firing range of the pursuing Yank. Death looked back, his bony face contorted and ghastly.

"Perhaps we settle this time, Garrett," he muttered. "Perhaps it is best that you land at my base!"

He throttled the Fokker ahead, Babyface close upon him. He sucked in his breath, wiped perspiration from his face. Click moved uneasily. Now Babyface could find out where Death had been located during those maneuvers with the fleet. He would destroy it! Yet, he had no idea of what he would come into when he found the mad monk's base. A sense of grave foreboding came to him. Perhaps Mister Death would trap him!

But he followed, his torn wings and framing flapping insanely, his motor spinning, throbbing—pulling him like a streaking star through the sky.

After ten minutes, Mister Death could scarcely hold the Fokker in the sky. The motor sputtered and coughed, while the robed murder monster rocked back and forth in his cockpit, his eye on the shore line below. At last he turned, cut the motors and went gliding down toward a long shed with a galvanized tin roof.

Babyface Garrett zoomed his Spad in the wake of the metal ship. He saw Mister Death ease to a three-point landing on a strip of land facing the shed. The Fokker skimmed easily over the improvised tarmac. But it was so short and narrow that Babyface could not land without crashing into Death's ship. He hauled back on the stick, intending to lift and circle back. His eyes were on the ground. Mister Death climbed from the Fokker.

Something happened then. The torn canvas wings of the Spad were clattering against the framing and the ship had lifted no more than ten feet. The Spad was hurtling straight into the thin shed!

Quickly Jed pedaled the rudder and swung the plane out to the left. At that moment, losing altitude rapidly, the Spad broke from his grip and nosed for the water beyond the shed. With the ship out of his control, Jed could do nothing but sit tight. The Spad crashed into the water and floundered, while the motor drowned in the current.

Babyface released Click, then hurled himself away from the sinking ship. He swam toward the: shore and Click dog-paddled after him. Already Jed could see two German officers working on Mister Death's plane. The robed figure was speaking to them, pointing toward the water.

Crack ... Crack ... Crack ..

Reaching shore, Jed climbed up on the bank, dripping with water. He pulled out his automatic, aimed it.

Splut...

Babyface cursed softly and tossed away the weapon. Click hauled himself up on shore, shook his furry body, then, with a low growl, rushed forward at Mister Death. Bullets from a Luger chopped the ground on both sides of him. But the police dog, his fur bristling, didn't waver.

When only five feet from Death he sprang for the murder monster's neck.

Mister Death howled, jerked the dog away and threw him to the ground. The officers working on the plane rushed forward, their Lugers drawn. One of them clipped a bullet straight at Click. The dog whined and fell to his side.

Babyface was on his feet, coming forward. There was an insane light in his eyes; a deathless smile on his face. Unarmed, out-numbered, his dog lying with a bullet in him, the American major came grimly forward.

Mister Death laughed harshly. He turned his bony, hideous face to the closest Boche officer, grabbed away his gun.

"I'll take care of the American! You two return to the plane. I want those holes fixed, and the tank refueled within fifteen minutes!"

"Yes, Herr Death!"

They rushed back toward the plane while Mister Death drew his long black robes closer about him and straightened his shoulders. His white face contained a look of living horror; blotch-eyes were wide, livid. Kicking his booted foot into the wounded Click's side; he fingered the loaded Luger.

By now, Babyface Garrett was almost to him. There was no sign of fear in his face, no trembling of his body. He was pale and grim. His eyes were smoldering things, sunken in their burning sockets. "Bring him in alive!" he reflected bitterly.

"I've come for you," he said. "Have come to get you, Mister Death." There was a harsh ring in his voice. He was more like a devil at that moment than a man. He was speaking for the ships full of men—the seven war vessels and their crews which had been blown up.

"You have come only for your own destruction," the robed figure replied, his slit-mouth barely moving. "Don't move another step forward, Garrett!"

But Babyface, within eight feet now, did keep moving forward. His hands were at his sides, fingers were working in and out. His nostrils moved with each breath he took. His mouth was a tight line. Bring him in alive!

"You've engineered more murder, Mister Death—and this is the end. Nothing can stop me—not even your Luger!"

Mister Death, uncanny genius of warfare, was for the first time in his life bewildered. There was a wavering question in his mind. He had faced men under every condition. But he had never seen anyone walk into the jaws of hell without arms, facing certain death, and being so sure of himself as was Major Jed Garrett at this moment. He suspected trickery, yet he did not know what trickery there could possibly be. He decided to give Babyface another moment to live; he wished to play for time, so that he could better understand the cold, berserk rage now sweeping through the American's breast.

"You have learned of my game, Garrett?" he said. "Placing timed explosives of nitro-glycerine inside American corpses, then putting them on board ships—requesting that the corpses be given burial?"

For a moment Jed Garrett stopped. He stared into the blotch-eyes of his enemy. He laughed, but it was laughter from hell.

"No, Death," he said. "I didn't know how it was done. You were careful to see that no one was left alive to tell. But your manner of killing doesn't matter. What matters is that you are through!"

"You are an insane fool!" Mister Death spat, advancing a step, his robes sweeping the ground. "I hold the gun with the bullets that spell murder, and you—"

What happened then, happened so fast that even Mister Death was for an instant taken off guard. Jed Garrett careened forward; it was as though his body had been belched from the muzzle of a fourteen inch gun. There was a streak—a clashing of fists!

Mister Death drew back, pumped the trigger of the Luger. The bullets went a foot wide. Babyface clutched Death's gun-wrist with both hands. Bones crunched. The Luger fell to the ground.

Babyface Garrett stooped, scooped it up. He gripped the weapon in his right hand, and there was still a grim, deathless smile on his face as he raised it in his hand and aimed at Mister Death's head. He pulled the trigger!

A crimson gash streaked across the side of Death's bony, white head. The monster of murder shrieked with pain—clutched at his head. Blood oozed between his fingers and his legs buckled beneath him. His robes, like filthy black rags, fluttered over his crumpled figure as he fell to the ground.

Babyface bent over Click. He smoothed the dog's wound, patted his head. Click opened his eyes.

"Your plane is ready, sir, I—"

Jed Garrett looked up to see that one of the officers had returned from the plane. Babyface snapped a shot without moving from his crouched position, and the German's gun fell from his nerveless fingers. He fell to the ground with a thud.

Mister Death moved an arm and straightened his legs as Babyface stood erect.

"We're getting out of here," Jed muttered. Hastily, he picked up Click and carried him to the huge cockpit of Death's black Fokker. He noticed that a corpse was strapped to the body of the plane, then returned to where Mister Death lay wounded, and carried him to the Fokker. He jammed his unconscious body into the roomy cockpit and was about to cut away the corpse on the body of the ship, when he heard the other Boche officer calling men from the shed.

Death had devised an automatic starter and Jed had but to press his foot down on it. The prop spun, and the motor roared. He wheeled the black Fokker around, swung quickly down the narrow tarmac and lifted into the air.

In a moment Babyface checked with the compass and headed back in the direction of the front lines. He would return with Mister Death to the 25th airdrome. It mattered little about getting the captured murder monster medical aid. Babyface was human, but he cared not whether Death died or lived.

When the course was set and he was gunning the metal ship through the heavens at its terrific rate of speed, he bent and again petted Click. The dog was returned to consciousness. He looked up at Babyface with pleading eyes.

"It's all right, old fella, you did your best. And that was plenty!"

Mister Death moved on the floor of the plane, opened his blotch-eyes and stared upward. Blood was caking on his bony head. His eyes were on the ship's instrument clock. It registered fifteen minutes to four.

"You're taking your last ride," Babyface said grimly.

Death's slit-lips parted a little, revealing his toothless mouth. He nodded weakly.

Wind whipped about the metal of the black Fokker as the prop kept spinning, pulling the ship through the sky. Mister Death's arm moved to a gear locker and a door fell open. Babyface looked down to see the robed figure struggling with a white parachute.

"That won't do you any good," Jed said, "you're staying in this plane 'til we get to the 25th!"

Mister Death closed his eyes again, as though in pain. He lay very still. When he looked up again the instrument clock registered five minutes to four. Death slipped into the parachute while still lying on the floor of the plane. He sat up, his bony face horrible.

"I am going to get out," he said calmly.

Babyface laughed.

Mister Death's blotch-eyes were glued on the instrument clock. "Is that corpse still strapped on the body of the plane?"

Suddenly Babyface thought he understood. Apprehension filled him. "Yes," he replied.

"It is one of those bodies. One that has been hollowed out and contains the explosive. I was taking it out when I met you today. It is set for four o'clock."

Babyface's lips went tight. "You're lying for your life," he said.

Mister Death shrugged. "That is not true. I am giving you a chance for your life. If you wish to cut the body away it means that you must put the plane under mechanical control—by pushing a lever you will find on the port side of the dash board you can climb back there and cut it yourself. That would give me a chance to push you off and seize control."

Babyface knew that Death spoke the truth. His feverish eyes were straight on the clock. Four minutes to four ....

"My alternative," Death said, "is that I leap overboard now, and with the parachute, land in safety. Then you may cut away the body without fear of my doing anything. It is a fair bargain. If you refuse we both die!"

Two and a half minutes . . .

Babyface was restless. A moment ago he had been confident that he had won. Now—a last trump card, played by the murder fiend, had trapped him into eternity.

"I'll never release you," Babyface said. "Since I have to sacrifice my life that you die—I do it gladly!"

Two minutes to four ....

And then, suddenly, like a chess player who in the last desperate moment, sees a move, Babyface came in possession of the answer. He would knock Mister Death unconscious! But—wait! Death was wounded already. Another crack on the head might kill him. His orders were: bring him in alive!

Grim hate suddenly seized Babyface. For once he'd call Mister Death's bluff, see how brave he really was! He reached for the Luger. Death, treacherous and cunning, saw the move. Jed jammed the weapon next to Death's head.

"I'm going to blast out your brains!" he spat. He knew it was a lie. That because of orders he could not do it. Yet— in a few seconds that body would explode.

"No!" Death gurgled strangely.

Triumph leaped into Jed Garrett's eyes. "All right—then get back there and cut away the body. Do it now, or I'll—"

Mister Death's horrible blotch eyes came up, stared into Babyface's countenance. He read the chill of hatred there.

A minute and a quarter to four

"Go on, get back there! Cut it away!"

And then suddenly Mister Death, stretched prone over the body of the black plane and kicked back his foot. It hit Babyface squarely in the jaw and sent him reeling back.

Jed struck out, caught Death in the forehead. Mister Death's bloody face was twisted into a ghastly look of horror. He clutched Jed's neck. Babyface struck again, but Death, knowing another blow would down him, ducked away. A wild light shone in his huge blotch-eyes, he suddenly catapulted over the side.

Insane with rage that he had gotten away, Babyface stared over the side. He saw the parachute open.

Three quarters of a minute left . .

He jerked off the automatic control and swung the black Fokker around. Grimly, desperately, he droned low, over the floating 'chute. And then he snapped on the mechanical control again and leaped back to the ship's body.

He hauled out a knife and slashed at the secured corpse. He heard a ticking inside of it. The bomb! Sweat stood out on his face It was hard to cut it away, and he was afraid he would not get it off the ship soon enough. At last the lines were free!

Ten seconds.

He let the corpse dangle over, and holding to one line, he jumped back to the cockpit. He swung the plane back again over the parachute. Then he released the line he held.

With bated breath he watched. But he had watched only two seconds when a roar rent the air. The sky became red and hideous.

Jed could no longer see the parachute below. He did not know whether Mister Death had landed before the explosion, or if it had consumed him. But he was certain of one thing—if it had not killed him, it certainly had wounded him, permanently. He laughed hoarsely. God, what an escape it had been!

And he had solved the mystery of the exploded vessels.

He thought again of Mister Death; and he remembered suddenly the steel plates the monster wore on his back and chest. He suddenly, had a premonition that he had not killed the robed fiend; a feeling that no matter how crippled or deformed or hideous the bomb had rendered him, that someway—somehow he would return.

It was more than the cold air that made Babyface Garrett shiver.

About
the Author

Stephen Gould Fisher was born on August, 29 1913, in Marine City, Michigan and grew up in the Los Angeles area. His mother, an actress, was often out of town. She enrolled Fisher in Oneonta Military Academy. He hated it and ran away from the school when he was sixteen and enlisted in the navy. Fisher spent four years on a submarine, and during this time wrote more than two hundred stories about navy and submarine life, many of which were published in navy publications.

He wanted to be a fulltime writer, so when he was discharged from the navy Fisher returned to California. He had trouble selling his stories and, frustrated by his lack of success, he moved to New York City in 1934. For a few months, Fisher struggled to make ends meet. He was evicted and, on several occasions had to pawn his typewriter.

Gradually Fisher's stories began to sell, beginning with "Hell's Scoop" in the March 1934 issue of *Sure-Fire Detective Magazine.* His versatility was evident in the fact that he sold stories to every genre of pulp magazine.

During his years in Greenwich Village and other New York neighborhoods, Fisher became acquainted with other writers, including his close friend Frank Gruber, who profiled Fisher's life in *Pulp Jungle* (1967). Some of his other friends were Roger Torrey, Cornell Woolrich, and Carroll John Daly. They all belonged to the American Fiction

Guild, a society for pulp writers. During this time he also met and married Edythe (Edie) Syme, an editor at *Dime Detective.*

Fisher's big break in the pulps came when Frank Gruber convinced Fanny Ellsworth, the new editor of *Black Mask*, to buy Fisher's story "Murder at Eight." He would ultimately publish over five hundred pulp stories. He created several memorable series characters, including Kip Muldane, a Hawaiian private eye (*Black Mask*), Danny Garrett and Sheridan Doome (*The Shadow*), and Captain Babyface (*Dare-Devil Aces*). Most of his pulp stories appeared under his own name, but he also wrote some under his two pseudonyms, Grant Lane and Stephen Gould.

Like many of the pulp writers of his time, he aspired to sell stories to the "slicks," large-circulation magazines printed on slick paper that paid better than the pulps. Fisher's first sale was "About Bread on Water," to *Liberty* magazine in June 1937.

Fisher decided to move to Paris in 1939. Many artists and writers chose this route to take advantage of a lower cost of living while they polished their craft. It was during his six months in Paris that Fisher got his foot in the door in Hollywood. He sold the short story "If You Break My Heart," to Universal Pictures. It became the film *Nurse from Brooklyn* (1938). Likewise, "Shore Leave" was sold to Monogram and made into *Navy Secrets* (1939). Paramount Pictures then bought a story that became the film *Typhoon* (1940). The money he made from these stories enabled him to return to the United States.

By now Fisher had two infant sons and needed more money than he could earn writing stories for the pulps and the slicks. He knew a studio contract would get him what he needed, so he went to Hollywood late in 1939. Fisher found work as a writer at Paramount, but his option was not renewed and he returned to New York. Finally, in 1941, he and his family moved permanently to Los Angeles.

Over the next ten years he contracted to work with Paramount, Warner Bros., 20th Century-Fox, MGM, and Columbia. Fisher's salary increased from $400 to $1,500 a week as he established a reputation as a reliable writer of original screen stories and screenplays. As well as he was doing financially in Hollywood, Fisher never felt it was enough and continued writing for the pulps and the slicks. As the pulps disappeared in the forties and fifties though, his career took a downswing.

It was the growing popularity of television that gave him an opportunity to make a good living as a writer again. In the late 1950s Fisher started to write scripts for *The George Sanders Mystery Theatre* and *Michael Shayne, Detective.* His career in television was at its height during the 1970s when Fisher wrote for many different types of shows, including *Starsky and Hutch, Barnaby Jones,* and *Fantasy Island.*

Although for most of his career Fisher earned his living as a writer of short stories, screenplays, and television scripts, he also spent a lot of time writing novels. He met with mixed success, but Fisher's *I Wake Up Screaming* (1941) is a classic hard-boiled tale that was twice made into films.

He died in March 1980.

Made in the USA
Charleston, SC
01 November 2015